Hugh contemplated the situation across the room with growing anticipation.

His nightly brawl was going to come about rather easily tonight, it seemed. As he made his way through the crowd, Hugh kept his eyes on the girl, who was struggling with the biggest of the men facing her.

"Your pardon," Hugh said politely, making a slight bow. "Is aught amiss?"

The big man surveyed Hugh's muscular frame from head to foot, then replied, "Leave us be."

Hugh smiled. "Good sir, you mistake me." He pushed past them. "I addressed the lady." He looked into her frightened face inquiringly. "Mistress," he began, then stopped and held his breath. She was more beautiful than he had expected, more beautiful than any woman he had seen in a long time. Without thinking, Hugh reached up to pull the hood of her cloak away from her head, causing her wheat blond hair to spill free and removing the shadows that hid her eyes...sky blue eyes that gazed at him, filled with pleading.

"Please, sir," she whispered, "I pray you, help me."

With only those few words, falling from her pretty lips, what had begun as a game for Hugh became something deadly serious.

Dear Reader,

Sparks fly when a rogue knight who is running from his past rescues a strong-willed noblewoman who is running from her future in Susan Paul's *The Heiress Bride*. We hope you enjoy this lively medieval romance, which is the second book in the author's Bride Trilogy.

Love and loyalty clash in *Devil's Dare* by Laurie Grant, a fast-paced Western about a sweet-talking cowboy and a straitlaced preacher's daughter whom he mistakes for a soiled dove.

The Gambler's Heart is the third book in Gayle Wilson's Heart Trilogy. This passionate Regency features a war-scarred French gambler who acquires a wife as payment for a debt, and must learn to accept her love for him.

And our fourth selection for the month, Elizabeth Lane's *Lydia*, is the touching story of a former Union spy who moves to Colorado and falls in love with the brother of a man who died as a result of her actions.

Whatever your taste in reading, we hope that Harlequin Historicals will keep you coming back for more. Please keep a lookout for all four titles, available wherever Harlequin books are sold.

Sincerely,

Tracy Farrell
Senior Editor

Please address questions and book requests to:
Harlequin Reader Service
U.S.: 3010 Walden Ave., P.O. Box 1325, Buffalo, NY 14269
Canadian: P.O. Box 609, Fort Erie, Ont. L2A 5X3

SUSAN PAUL

The Heiress Bride

Harlequin Books

TORONTO • NEW YORK • LONDON
AMSTERDAM • PARIS • SYDNEY • HAMBURG
STOCKHOLM • ATHENS • TOKYO • MILAN
MADRID • WARSAW • BUDAPEST • AUCKLAND

ISBN 0-373-28901-4

THE HEIRESS BRIDE

Copyright © 1996 by Mary Liming.

Printed in U.S.A.

Books by Susan Paul

Harlequin Historicals

The Bride's Portion #266
The Heiress Bride #301

SUSAN PAUL

lives in Duarte, California, with her husband, two young daughters, two dogs and two cats. She started her first novel when she was in her early teens, but eventually put it aside, unfinished, in favor of more important interests...such as boys. Now happily married and—somewhat—settled down, she's returned to her love of the written word, and finds it much easier to finish the books she starts.

Chapter One

England, 1416

"Please, my lady, you must awaken."

The voice sounded so very far away, as though someone were calling to Rosaleen from outside her chamber window.

"My lady," it pleaded again, more urgently, and Rosaleen felt a light, gentle touch on her cheek. As weary and stiff as she felt, she struggled to awaken, only to be greeted by sharp pains shooting from her head to her toes. An unbidden moan escaped her lips.

"Rosaleen," another voice came, a deep, masculine, much hated voice, "either rouse yourself right quick or I'll do it for you."

The words brought Rosaleen to life as nothing else could. She opened her eyes a crack to see Sir Anselm's dark face close to her own. She was lying on her stomach in deference to the bruises and welts he had placed on her back only a few hours earlier, and when he reached out to take a fistful of her hair and lift her face off the feather mattress, Rosaleen cried out from the pain.

"Good," Sir Anselm said with a chuckle, shaking her head a bit before releasing her. "She's awake and looks to be in a more obedient mood than she was this morn." With his fingertips, he pushed her head to one side, so that she was facing him, and met her weary gaze with his own amused one. "Are you not, Rosaleen? You will be a very obedient lady from now on. As meek and mild as a lamb."

Rosaleen stared at her uncle with as much hatred as she thought any being could ever feel. The memories of him stripping her clothes from her back, of the shocking feeling of that first strike on her bare flesh, all came back to her. "I'll not mar your face, Rosaleen," he'd murmured when she had finally given way and stumbled to her knees. "You shall be as lovely on your wedding day as you have ever been." It hadn't been too much longer before his blows had felled her completely, sending her into a blissful oblivion.

Until now.

She didn't answer him quickly enough, and his fingers bit into her hair again.

"Yes!" She gasped against the pain. "Yes!"

"Good girl." He released her once more.

Rosaleen didn't dare to move. "I hate you!" she whispered fiercely. "If my father were alive . . ."

"I know, Rosaleen, I know," he said wearily. "You needn't tell me again what your life would be like were either of your parents still alive. Truly, dearling, it is most ungrateful of you to persist with such talk." He crossed his massive arms over his chest. "I've spoiled you these past many years, 'tis clear, else you'd be more ready to show me your gratitude. This morn was regrettable, I grant, but you've no one to blame but yourself. You must learn to command that fierce temper of yours, my dear, for Simon of Denning will not find such as that acceptable in a wife, and you would like his taming much less than mine, I vow."

Rosaleen's hands curled into fists.

"Simon of Denning is an animal! I'll not wed with him."

"You will."

"Never!" she vowed. "You put me up for sale like a prize mare and he was naught but the highest bidder!"

"'Struth, dearling," Sir Anselm admitted, reaching down to squeeze the fine bones of Rosaleen's chin between two large fingers. "But as you were mine to sell, there was no wrong done. The king himself wouldn't dispute it." His eyes glowed with amusement. "And 'tis not my fault that God made you so very lovely and so very, very—" he laughed "—sellable. Sir Simon wants you, my beautiful girl, so much that he has willingly parted with all that was most valuable in your dowry in order to possess you. He shall have you, and I shall have Siere and all that goes with it. The title, the lands. Everything."

"Siere is *mine!*" she said furiously. "Sir Simon has no right...*you* have no right to take it from me!"

"I have every right, Rosaleen. Never, ever think otherwise again." He squeezed her chin harder, until tears welled in her eyes. "Now, you will do as I say, else I'll treat you to more of what I gave you this morn. Sir Simon will be here to claim his bride before the day is out, and you must needs eat and bathe and prepare yourself to receive him. When the priest arrives I'll fetch you. Until then you will behave yourself and think on how to best please your future husband and your loving uncle. Will you not, Rosaleen?"

Rosaleen closed her eyes. "Yes."

"Good." He rose. "I'll leave you with Jeanne so that you may prepare." He went to the door and opened it, pausing only long enough to look at the maid, who stood trembling in a corner. "Make certain she is in her best looks, Jeanne, else you will know your master's displeasure."

"Y-yes, my lord."

He closed the door, leaving them alone, and Rosaleen let out the long breath she had been holding. She tried to move, to push herself into a sitting position.

"Jeanne . . . please . . ."

Her maid was beside her in a moment, the girl's face pale as she put her hands beneath Rosaleen's shoulders to help her rise.

"Oh, my lady!" she cried, and burst into noisy tears just as Rosaleen finally sat up.

"Yes," Rosaleen replied absently. She felt dizzy, weak, and put one hand up to her damp forehead in an effort to still its spinning while using the other to hold up the remnants of her dress. The open places on her back burned like fire, and she could feel the skin there stiffening with dried blood. "Jeanne," she whispered, wishing that her sensitive maid would cease the wailing that only made her head pound all that much more, "I will need some salve, and some cloth to bind the wounds. I must put on clean clothing . . . something very plain and simple. And after that I will need you to help me. Jeanne—" she met the girl's frightened gaze "—I am going to escape before my uncle can come to get me." Reaching out, she gripped the maid's arm. "I *must* escape. Do you understand? Will you help me? I promise that you shall not be suspected or punished."

Wide-eyed, Jeanne shook her head. "Escape? But, my lady, how can you do so? Your uncle has placed guards at every door. You could not even step out of your own chamber without being caught. And...your back, my lady...you could not get very far with it so.''

Rosaleen could hardly disagree with that, her body ached so badly, but nothing could make her stay at Siere and play a part in her own ruin. "That," she stated firmly, "is my worry. All I need from you is a little help, and I shall do the rest. I swear that my uncle will never be able to suspect that you aided me, and even more so do I swear that he shall never have Siere. I would rather die than give it over to him, and I would rather kill myself with my own hands than marry Simon of Denning. Will you help me, Jeanne?''

"But where will you go, my lady? And how will you keep from being caught? You know full well that your uncle and Sir Simon will be after you before you can get very far. Oh, please, my lady," Jeanne pleaded, wringing her small hands, "do not do this! I could not bear to see you beaten again at the hands of Sir Anselm! The next time he might kill you!''

Determination steeled Rosaleen in spite of the fear that threatened to overtake her. "I have said that I would rather die than wed Simon of Denning," she replied sharply, "and so do I mean it! Somehow I will manage to keep from being caught.'' She struggled to her feet, holding together the bits of what was once one of her most beautiful surcots. Jeanne helped her, but still Rosaleen could not hold back a groan of pain. Her breath came quickly and seemed to catch in her side. "And as to where I shall go,'' she went on, forcing the few steps toward her mirrored table, "why, I shall go to King Henry. He must help me, for my father was a great favorite of his father's as well as being the Earl of Siere, and for that alone he must lend me aid.'' She collapsed into the chair set before the mirror. "I shall tell him what my uncle has done, that he has sought to wed me against my will and to steal my rightful inheritance, even my title, from me." She met her maid's doubtful gaze in the dim reflection of the polished steel mirror. "He'll help me, Jeanne," she insisted. "He will."

Jeanne didn't believe that this was so, for the world was a man's world, and King Henry was only a man.

Rosaleen understood the expression on Jeanne's face, but she refused to be swayed by it.

"He *will* help me, I know he will. But you must help me first, else my fate is sealed here and now."

Jeanne's voice trembled as badly as her slight body. "Yes, my lady," she whispered. "I will help you."

"Damn you, Hugh! Must you win at every game?" Peter Brenten scowled and picked up the dice before him. "It's ungodly, that's what it is. We should have you tried for sorcery. God only knows what a blessing it would be for all the honest gambling men in England."

The dark-haired man sitting across from him laughed, settling back in his chair and draining off a good part of his ale.

"Now, Peter, don't go saying things that aren't true." He wiped his mouth with the back of his hand. "You forget that you won against me only three days ago, at Newcombe."

"At Newcombe!" Peter repeated. "Bah! We wagered for a mere draft of ale. Why is it that I always win whenever the stakes are little, while you win whenever it pleases you?" He tossed the dice on the table, saw the outcome and swore loudly, drawing more laughter from his friends.

"You'll never learn, Pete, lad," Stewart of Byrne said with a laugh. "I was well taught back in Rouen not to wager with Hugh Caldwell. I'll never forget how he fleeced me till I was naked as a babe. He has the devil's own luck, don't you, Hugh?''

Hugh paused only long enough in counting the money Peter had passed him to flash his companions a charming smile. "Friends, friends," he said soothingly, "I deny such a charge. I have it on the very best authority that I am *always* innocent in such matters as these."

Stewart of Byrne laughed outright. "And what poor, misguided soul ever told you such a lie, man? 'Twas certainly no man who has ever met you across a table."

Grinning, Hugh pocketed his winnings in a leather pouch. "Nay, 'twas my mother," he admitted, gazing heavenward. "God bless her sweet soul."

"Mmm," Sir Gerald Walson intoned. "That may be as it is, Hugh, but your mother probably never had the pleasure of gambling with you. It's a damned good thing we'll be quit of one another on the morrow, else none of us but you would have a mite to call his own. Oh, hell. Hand me the dice, Peter. I'm ten kinds of fool but I'll try my luck once more on our last night together. What odds will you give me, Caldwell?"

"The same as always, Gerry," Hugh replied. "But first I want more ale. Gaming with you fellows is thirsty business, I vow. Here, girl!" he called into the smoky depths of the Red Fox Inn, but the serving maid who had hovered dutifully about them all night didn't appear. A commotion at the far end of the room kept her, and everyone else in the tavern, occupied.

"What's going on there?" Peter Brenten wondered aloud, straining to see better.

"It's…a woman, I think," Stewart of Byrne said, standing half out of his chair. "Mmm, covered down to her feet and arguing with the innkeeper. I wonder what she's about."

"A whore, mostlike," Sir Gerald put in, making an experimental toss with the dice. "Though she must be an ugly one if she's covered up."

Hugh contemplated the situation across the room with growing anticipation. His nightly brawl was going to come about easily, it seemed.

"I rather think she's trying to cover her beauty," he said thoughtfully. "Our portly innkeeper is drooling over the sight of her. I'm sure she's having none of that, though." He laughed. "That old man is the last thing I'd want to take to bed, and that's as sure as the new day dawning."

"I don't think the old man's going to get her," Stewart of Byrne said, sitting down again. "Her first customers for the night have just arrived. Three knights of the realm it seems, though she looks no happier with them than with the innkeeper."

"I'd welcome having a woman tonight," Peter Brenten said, his eyes wandering over the girl's slim, cloaked figure. "I wonder how quick she is. Mayhap I'll have a visit with her when she's finished with those fellows."

"Not with her, you won't," Hugh said, standing and placing a light hand on his sword. "It's the tavern wench for you, Pete, old lad. This one's mine."

All three of his friends looked at him and groaned as one.

Peter Brenten put his head in his hands. "God's toes, Hugh, not tonight."

"Tonight of all nights!" Stewart of Byrne said angrily. "Can we not have a little peace on our last eve together?"

"One would think you'd have had enough troublemaking at the inn we destroyed last night," Sir Gerald added, putting the dice aside with a look of regret. "And I'll have you know that I don't appreciate setting up against my fellow knights."

Hugh Caldwell's green eyes glittered mischievously. "Don't start feeling badly for what you are, Gerry. You're the only dubbed man I can tolerate next to my own brothers. And we did not destroy the White Bull last night," he insisted. "We only... rearranged it."

"Damn you, Hugh Caldwell!" Sir Gerald returned angrily, checking the readiness of his own sword. "What's gone wrong with you? We haven't had a night's peace since setting foot in Britain three weeks past. You were never so troublesome in France."

Hugh made no reply but kept his eyes on the girl, who was struggling with the biggest of the men facing her. Stewart had spoken true... the girl didn't want these particular customers, which only made the matter of taking her for himself that much simpler. What the big fighting men would think, well... Hugh's mouth relaxed into a confident smile.

The knight who held the girl didn't turn when Hugh tapped his shoulder. It took a strong hand on his arm to make him look around.

"Your pardon," Hugh said politely, making a slight bow. "Is aught amiss?"

The big man surveyed Hugh's muscular frame from head to foot, then replied in a surly tone, "None that I can't take care of myself." The two knights behind him laughed. "Leave us be."

Hugh smiled. "Good sir, you mistake me." He pushed past him. "I addressed the lady." He looked into her frightened face inquiringly. "Mistress," he began, then stopped and held his breath. She was more beautiful than he had expected, more beautiful than any woman he'd seen in a long time. Not since Lillis had he met with such perfection. Without thinking, Hugh reached up to pull the hood of her cloak away from her head, causing her wheat

blond hair to spill free and removing the shadows that hid
her eyes . . . sky blue eyes that gazed at him, pleadingly.

"Please, sir," she whispered, "I pray you, help me."

With only those few words falling from her pretty lips,
what had begun as a game for Hugh became something
deadly serious.

"God, she's a greater beauty than you thought, Cyril,"
one of the other knights said. "My turn comes after
yours."

The girl's eyes lit with fire. "I am not . . ." She didn't
seem to know how to finish. "I am *not* a . . . a . . ." Struggling against the knight who held her, she pleaded with
Hugh once more. "Please, good sir. I beg you."

"I told you to lose yourself, man," Cyril repeated in a
tone full of warning.

Ignoring him, Hugh gazed into the girl's distressed face
and tried to decide what it was about this situation that
disturbed him. There was something here that wasn't right.
She was far too beautiful to be a whore. And she was pale,
as if she were in pain, as if she might faint.

"She doesn't want you, Cyril, lad," Hugh said slowly,
"and a lady should always be given her choice, is this not
so?" He graced the girl with his most charming smile.
"What say you, mistress? Would you rather go with him
or with me? I'm clean, I promise, and I'll be gentle with
you. I swear it on my own soul."

"Be gone!" Cyril shouted angrily.

"You!" she cried.

Hugh looked at the big knight. "You have your answer, Cyril, from the lady's own lips. Now release her and
be on your way, like the good and godly knight you are,
else take your chances."

Cyril's eyes narrowed. "You, man, are going to die!"

Laughing, Hugh unsheathed his sword with an easy, fluid movement. "One day, yes," he admitted, "but not this night."

Cyril freed the girl, and Hugh pulled her against himself, hearing her groan of pain and feeling the stiffening of her body.

"Are you mad?" the other man demanded. "You are one against three! Do you seek death, then?"

The sounds of Cyril's fellow knights pulling out their swords was enough to bring silence to the crowded tavern.

"Oh, please, please, good sirs," the innkeeper begged to no avail, "don't...don't..."

"The day I willingly seek death, Sir Knight, is the day the sun stops rising," Hugh stated with bald confidence, his heavy sword dancing in the air as though it were a feather. "Especially at the hands of such a one as you, for, truth be told, I'd rather be devoured alive by swine." He smiled pleasantly.

Cyril gave an angry, animal sound and advanced on Hugh slowly.

"Then I'll make certain to toss your body into the wallow outside when I've finished with you," he promised. "Now set the girl aside, fool, unless you mean to use her as a shield."

The insult flew over Hugh's head; his heart was pounding too erratically for him to mind it. In another moment the hot pleasure of the fight would pour over him like some soothing drug. He would let himself be consumed by it, but before that happened he must send the girl to safety. He wasn't even certain that she was still conscious; she felt lifeless in his grip, but that wasn't his worry now. Later he would have no other care than her full awareness, and he would make certain that it was centered fully on himself, but now... now he wanted only to feel the sweet relief the coming fight would bring.

"Take her, Pete," he said, excitement shortening his breath. "Take her and keep her safe. When I've finished with good knight Cyril and his good knightly friends I'll come to claim her, and God only knows how I'll need her all in one piece." Lifting his sword almost to the level of his chin, he smiled. "Now, sirs," he murmured, "let us see who ends up in the wallow."

Chapter Two

A soft, melodic sound drifted into Rosaleen's dreams, beckoning her to wake. A lute, she thought dimly, her mind struggling to lift out of its sleepy stupor. Someone was playing a lute. And she was…where? In a room? Yes. Not her room at Castle Siere, but a room somewhere. Without opening her eyes she could sense light, the kind of light that meant day, and a gentle breeze caressed her shoulders and face. The bed she lay upon was firm and comfortable, the sheets were cool against her skin. Stretching, yawning, keeping her eyes closed, she snuggled into the mattress and tried to make sense of it all.

Her memories were blurred, at best. She had been so very weary and in so much pain. The wounds on her back had felt hot as fire and had stung as though soaked with lime. The battle to keep going had been fierce, indeed. And then she had caught sight of the inn. What had she done with her horse? she wondered. She couldn't recall whether she'd had enough sense to stable it or not, only that she had somehow dragged her aching body inside the smoky depths of the inn to request a room.

The memory made Rosaleen frown. Aye, she had requested a room, and the innkeeper had given her a great deal of trouble. What was it he had said? Something about having to share her night's profits with him? Whatever had the filthy creature meant? She hadn't been able to make him understand that she only wanted a room, and when she had tried to explain it once more she'd been accosted by three lecherous brutes, one of whom had gone so far as to lay hands on her.

Her memories after that became less clear. There had been a handsome stranger, with a handsome smile and handsome green eyes and handsome manners, who had come to her rescue, and then there had been only this. A comfortable bed, the taste of bitter medicine, a soothing of her pain, gentle hands caring for her... and dreams.

Dreams, she thought hazily. Only dreams, and yet they had seemed so real. She could recall them vividly, as if she were dreaming them all over again. She could almost feel his hands and lips on her again, moving over her body, and she could hear his voice, soft, whispering. It had both unsettled and soothed her, just as he had....

"You're smiling, sweeting. That means you're either dreaming of last night or you've finally come awake. Now, which is it, I wonder?"

Rosaleen's eyes flew open.

"Ah, you're awake. Good."

Warm breath touched her cheek. Rosaleen turned her head very slowly. There, smiling down at her, his face inches from her own, his arms like pillars on either side of her, was the handsome stranger.

The scream that came out of her mouth startled both of them. The stranger quickly stood up, and Rosaleen, ignoring the pain it caused, leapt out of the bed on the other side. A shock of cool air on her skin caused her to look down at herself, and the unexpected sight of her completely naked body made her scream again. She dived back into the bed and pulled the bed covers all the way up to her chin.

"God's bones, mistress!" said the stranger, laughing, his green eyes filled with amusement. "Must you make so much noise? You'll have our good hosts bursting in to see whether I'm murdering you."

"How d-dare you!" she sputtered, tightening her grip on the covers. "How d-d-d-dare you! Get out!" She pointed a shaking finger at the door. "Get *out!* Now!"

The man raised an eyebrow at her. "You would throw me out of my own room, mistress? After all I've suffered in it for your sake these past two days?"

"*Your* room!" Rosaleen was flooded with confusion. "God's teeth! What am I doing in your room? And where are my clothes? My things? At least send up a maid and go away so that I may make myself decent. Dear God in heaven!" She set a hand to her forehead. "How long have I been here? I don't even know where I am!"

"It appears you're feeling better, at least," he commented. "Your back doesn't pain you?"

"My back?" she repeated. Was the man deaf? Why was he still standing there when she had asked him to fetch a serving maid? "Yes, it's much better. Now go away and send the maid at once to attend me."

He sat on the bed beside her, causing Rosaleen to lean away and clutch the blankets even more tightly. "Whoever beat you like that ought to be strung up by his feet and repaid in kind, sweeting, and if I ever meet up with the bastard I promise you I'll do it. I'm half-tempted to alter my plans and go after the fiend anyhow, so help me I am. What in God's holy name did you ever do to deserve it?"

Making sure to keep herself covered, Rosaleen scrambled as far away from him as possible. The fact that he was sitting on a bed that contained a totally naked lady didn't seem to bother him in the least. Indeed, he looked perfectly at ease.

"Well?" he prompted.

"I..." Rosaleen faltered beneath his green-eyed perusal. Merciful heavens! He was certainly handsome enough. His long dark hair, tied up neatly in a tail at the back of his head, had been lightened several shades by the strength of the sun. His face, squarely built and strongly featured, was the most perfectly masculine face she had ever seen. His lips, full and sensual, seemed drawn into a permanently mocking grin.

"Please get off the bed," she said.

He laced his fingers around one crossed knee. "Not until I have a few answers from you, sweet. I've not wasted nearly two full days biding my time at this wayside inn for mere pleasure. The sooner you answer my questions, the sooner we can both be quit of this place."

"Sir, if you will please just...go *away* for a few minutes so that I can...can..." She clenched her teeth. "If you've not yet noticed, *I am not dressed.*"

He grinned. "I'm not blind, mistress."

"Well, then?"

"Well?" he repeated.

What in God's name was the matter with him? Was the man an idiot? "Well then," she returned patiently, "would you please go away and send the maid to me?"

"As soon as you answer my questions, I'll answer yours," he offered, unlacing his fingers and reclining across the bed near her feet, keeping himself propped up on one elbow. "We'll begin with something easy. Your name."

"My name?"

"Yes, sweeting, your name. What is it?"

"It's..." None of your concern, she nearly told him, then thought better of it. She didn't have a great deal of time to waste bantering with this fool. She had already lost an entire day, a day during which her uncle would have been looking everywhere for her. If he hadn't yet come this direction, he soon would, and Rosaleen had to make certain she was on her way to London before that happened. "Rosaleen," she finished.

"Rosaleen," he repeated approvingly. "Very nice. You're certainly as pretty as any rose I've ever seen. What's the rest of it?"

Rosaleen bit her lip, wondering how much information she could safely part with. This man had saved her from an unpleasant situation and had clearly made certain that she'd been taken care of while she'd lain sleeping, but how far would his chivalry extend once he knew she was the heiress to one of the most powerful and richest titles in England? If he were to discover the truth, might he not try to force her back to her uncle with the hope of a reward?

"Just Rosaleen," she whispered.

"Just Rosaleen?" His eyebrows rose mockingly. "I find that hard to believe, sweeting. Even the lowliest of serfs has more of a name than that. Come, tell me the rest of it. I'll do you no harm."

Rosaleen shook her head. "I cannot tell you," she said, "and I would rather not lie. I do not know you or anything about you."

She expected him to press her, but instead a look of understanding passed his features, and he smiled. "I'd rather you not lie to me, either, sweet. Honesty is a virtue I prize more highly than others." He nodded his head in tribute. "Rosaleen will suffice. Now, lovely Rosaleen, where have you come from, and who beat you, and why did he do it?"

Resigned to the fact that he'd not be satisfied until he had his questions answered, Rosaleen replied, factually, "I come from a small village north of here. I was beaten by my uncle for refusing to marry the man he had chosen for me. And before you bother to ask, I am on my way to London. Now, may I please be allowed to dress?"

"In a moment," Hugh said thoughtfully, settling his long body more comfortably on the bed, oblivious to the fact that Rosaleen drew herself into an even tighter ball.

He was quiet for a time, considering her words.

She had been beaten by her uncle for refusing to marry the man who'd been chosen for her. It was a common enough offense, and by law her guardian had every right to do exactly as he had, but that didn't matter to Hugh. When he had carried her up to his room two nights before, he had been sickened to discover the condition she was in. The wounds on her back had opened and bled through her clothes, soaking them so thoroughly that he'd had to cut them off and throw them away.

The memory made Hugh frown. The bastard who'd beaten her was an animal, and hunting down such animals was one of Hugh's very favorite sports. But she clearly wasn't going to be forthcoming with enough information to lead him on that hunt, a fact that only made Hugh that much more curious.

She wasn't a whore, of that he was certain, but if she was a lady, possessed of any kind of gentle birth, she couldn't be anything grander than the daughter of some vaguely landed lord. The plain clothing she'd worn had given testament to that, and she'd already admitted as much, having said that she came from a small village.

He could almost envision what had happened. Her destitute uncle, desperate to better his standing, had decided to use his beautiful niece to his advantage by marrying her off to someone wealthier and better landed. Rosaleen had balked, her guardian had promptly tried to beat her into submission, and she had escaped and ended up at this inn. And with him.

"On your way to London, you say? What do you imagine awaits you there? You don't think to petition the king for aid, I hope." Hugh chuckled at her surprised expression. "The king would never grant you an audience, sweet, despite your admirable charms, and he would certainly never take your part over your uncle's. Or did you think to find some other kind of refuge there?"

Rosaleen understood very well what he meant, and the suggestion that she would seek any man's protection in return for her favors angered her.

"I have relatives in London," she said, speaking the truth. Through her father, who had been the head of his family as well as the Earl of Siere, she had innumerable and very important relatives at court. The thought of not being received by the king, or at least by one of his regents, was laughable, though she wasn't about to tell this strange man that.

Her answer brought him a look of relief. "Relatives," he murmured. "Good. Much better than the other roads left you. Though with your beauty you'd no doubt end up in court, anyway." As a leman, he left unsaid.

"I'm so glad you approve," she replied dryly. "Now if you don't mind, Sir . . . Sir . . . what *is* your name?"

Hugh rose from the bed with fluid grace. "It's Hugh. Hugh Caldwell." He lifted a pile of clothes off a chair and returned to place them on the bed. "At your service, my lady," he added mockingly, with a slight bow.

Rosaleen gazed up at his towering, muscular figure. "I perceive that I owe you a debt of thanks, Sir Hugh, and I—"

"*Not* Sir Hugh," he stated tersely.

She looked at him with incomprehension. "But, you *are* a knight, are you not?"

"God forbid!" he said with feeling. "I am nothing more than what you see. Just Hugh Caldwell." He strode to the open window and gazed out of it. "And you may dress now, if it pleases you."

Rosaleen glanced at the clothes he'd left beside her.

"But these—"

"Aren't your clothes," he finished, still gazing out the window. "I know that. Your clothes were soaked with blood, thanks to your guardian's treatment of you and to your own foolishness in venturing out in your condition. They were ruined, and I had to throw them away. Those belonged to the innkeeper's daughter. I bought them." He glanced at her and shrugged. "They'll be a little large on you, but they'll do." He turned his gaze skyward again. "There's a girdle to secure them with."

Silence reigned in the room for a full minute, until Rosaleen finally cleared her throat to gain his attention. He spared her another short glance from where he looked out the window.

"What?"

"I wish to dress," she said as lightly as she could, hoping he would understand.

"And so you may."

"Alone," she clarified. "Or with the help of the maid, if you don't mind."

He smiled. "I don't mind at all, sweeting, save there is no maid and I'll not leave this room. You have about three minutes to get yourself dressed without me watching, so I advise you use them well."

"But . . . at least send up the woman who helped me to undress in the first place!"

This time he actually laughed. *"I'm* the one who un-
dressed you, sweet. If you desire my assistance, I'll be
more than glad to help. If you don't, you'd best do as I
advised earlier."

Being possessed of an amazingly quick mind, Rosaleen
grabbed the clothes and began to dress in a hurry. She
wasn't entirely successful, for she was not used to being
dressed without help, and her back still pained her with the
misery of slowly healing wounds. The underclothes provided, she discovered with dismay, were made of rough
wool and not of the soft, supple silk she always wore.
When she pulled the surcot over her head, her arms somehow got tangled in the cloth, and, muttering an angry
oath, she found herself unable to get them free.

Hearing her, Hugh Caldwell turned away from the window, took in her half-clad figure with a shake of his head
and strode to where she sat struggling helplessly. Grasping the light blue surcot, which matched the color of her
eyes, he tugged it over her head and down her body, freeing her arms, then he snatched up the girdle to fasten it
around her waist. "Your guardian was able to afford a
maid to lend you aid in dressing, it seems," he commented rather pointedly. "You clearly aren't used to doing it yourself." He knelt to fasten the overlarge leather
boots on her feet.

"My maid was a girl who came from the village," Rosaleen said truthfully, though guiltily. Jeanne had lived in
the village, but Castle Siere had more than eighty other
servants who had come from all parts of England.

Hugh nodded. "I see." He strode to the window again.
Once there, he leaned out, saw something he had evi-
dently been looking for and turned back into the room.

He fixed a leather strap around his left arm and sent a
sharp whistle out the window. With a great deal of flap-

ping, a compact, fierce-looking gyrfalcon settled on his wrist, and he drew her into the room.

"Sweet baby," he cooed to the magnificent creature. "Little darling. My beautiful Amazon."

Rosaleen sat on the bed, her hands in her lap, and watched with interest as Hugh Caldwell filled his mouth with water from a nearby cup, then bent his handsome head to let the bird drink the liquid as it dripped slowly from his lips. When the hunter had drunk her fill, Hugh Caldwell began to hum a little tune to her, over and over, the same simple tones in repetition, which kept the wild bird entranced so that he could set a hood over her head. Once the hood was fixed the bird was perfectly docile, and he proceeded to handle her deftly, tightening the jesses on her legs and setting her on the back of a chair to perch while he went about packing his things.

"She's beautiful," Rosaleen murmured appreciatively.

In the midst of stuffing his lute into a traveling bag, Hugh paused. His head shot up and he grinned at her. "You know about birds, then?"

"Oh, yes," she replied without thinking. "I've many fine birds of my own at—" she stopped herself just in time "—home."

"Do you? I used to have several myself, when I was a lad. Amazon's been with me this past year. She's quite young yet."

Rosaleen looked at the bird with open admiration. In her mews at Siere there were many fine hunting birds, and she was skilled in using them during hunts, but never had she seen a more promising gyrfalcon than the one Hugh Caldwell possessed. It occurred to her that there was more to him than met the eye. Perhaps he wasn't a knight, but no ordinary man could possibly possess such a creature, or afford one, either.

"She hasn't any bells," she commented, still watching as he continued to pack his things.

Hugh didn't stop this time as he tied the strings of his bag together. "No, she hasn't," he replied, straightening and lifting Amazon from her perch. "Well then, Rosaleen no-name," he said as he toted the bag up over one shoulder, "goodbye. It has been more pleasant than I could ever say, and I do hope you'll find your way to London with ease."

He started for the door, and Rosaleen shot up off the bed.

"What!" she shrieked.

He stopped just in front of the door.

"I said goodbye."

"I know what you said! What do you mean by it?"

His expression was openly bewildered. "I mean goodbye. I was not aware there was another meaning to the word."

"But you cannot mean to say that you're leaving!"

"I can't?"

"Well, no, of course not! I'm not ready to go. I haven't yet eaten to break my fast, and I don't know where my things are, though perhaps you've taken care of that already. They were on my mount, and you have taken care of my horse, have you not?"

"Ah, no, I haven't," Hugh replied. "I didn't even know you had a horse."

"Of course I had a horse!" she stated, wondering at how slow-witted he was. "How do you think I came to be here otherwise? Oh Lord!" she said with a groan. "I imagine he must have been stolen. I was in such a state when I arrived here that I didn't even think to stable him. Everything I had was on him. All my money, my change of clothing, everything!"

"Well, that's a stroke of bad luck, Rosaleen, and I'm sorry," Hugh said sincerely. "Listen, I've a good bit of money at the moment. I'd be happy to give you enough to help you get started...."

But Rosaleen wasn't listening to him. She cut him off with an imperious wave of her hand. "Never mind. It's too late to cry over what's been done, and it was my own fault, really, for not stabling the beast. You shall simply have to purchase another mount for me, and I shall have to make do with the clothes you've provided until we arrive in London."

Hugh blinked rapidly, certain he hadn't heard right. "We?" he repeated.

Rosaleen paced the room. "I shall need clean linen to cover my hair, and a brush, of course. If you would go now and ask the innkeeper's wife to bring me those two items along with some bread and cheese, I shall shortly be ready to leave." She stopped pacing and glanced at him. "You may make the arrangements for my mount while I'm eating."

When he simply stood there and stared at her, Rosaleen fluttered her hands as if to shoo him on his way. "Hurry, Hugh Caldwell. We've no time to waste. My uncle will be looking everywhere for me, so we must be on our way at once. How many days do you think it will take us to reach London?"

"Far fewer than you think, lady," Hugh replied stiffly. "I'm not taking you to London."

"But of course you are. You have to."

"What I have to do, sweet, is get myself on my way. I've surprised even myself by playing the gallant and watching over you these past two days, but don't think I've a mind to do any more. Now, I'm willing to leave you enough gold to get you to London, but that's all I'm willing to do. Take it or leave it."

"Your sense of humor is not only badly timed," Rosaleen chided, "it is sadly improper."

"And your understanding, mistress, is slower than a turtle's pace. What makes you think I'd take you to London?"

God's mercy! Rosaleen thought with irritation. The man was as dense as a tree. "How can you ask such a thing? Surely you know your duty as a gentleman!"

Shock possessed Hugh's features for a long, silent moment, and then, quite suddenly, he began to laugh. "My duty as a *what?* As a *gentleman?* God's bones, mistress, but it's been a long while since I've been so amused. I've already told you that I am no chivalrous knight, and if you could possibly think me gentle then you must have no care whatsoever for what passed between us last night in that bed behind you."

Rosaleen gasped out loud. "What!"

Hugh's laughter died into a very masculine grin, and he fixed her with a decidedly warm gaze. "Do you not remember, little one? Do you remember nothing at all? Or did you think perhaps you had only dreamed it? You were so sweet and warm, so responsive, that I would have wagered all I own that you'd not forget a single moment of what we shared."

"Oh!" Rosaleen cried. "Oh! You're lying! They *were* dreams!"

Hugh lowered his bag and set Amazon atop it to perch. Then he straightened and very slowly approached Rosaleen, who backed away from him. "They were not dreams, sweeting, and I should be most happy to renew your memory, if you like. Now, do you still think me gentle? Do you still wish to spend all those lonely nights on the road to London with me?''

Rosaleen rounded the other side of the bed, moving away from him as quickly as he followed. She wasn't frightened of him, she was furious. In fact, she wanted to kill him.

"You *swine!* You despicable knave! How dare you! How *could* you! I was a maiden, you wretched beast! I— I'll have you hanged for this!"

Hugh stopped and chuckled. "You truly don't remember, do you, sweet? I may be a knave and a swine, but I'm not so base that I'd take advantage of a half-conscious female. If you were a maiden last night then you are a maiden still."

"And I may be an ignorant girl, Hugh Caldwell, but I'm not a fool!" she cried. "You touched me!"

Hugh inclined his head. "'Struth, I did indeed touch you, lovely Rosaleen, and enjoyed every moment. But touch is all I did. You were restless and cried in your sleep. I only tried to comfort you. That's all. Most gentlemanly of me, do you not think?"

Rosaleen didn't believe him. The memories she had of his hands and mouth moving over her were dim, true, but they were there all the same. "You did m-more than t-touch me, you lecherous fiend!"

Hugh's grin was fully masculine. "A little more, yes, my lady. I considered it repayment for my kindness in taking care of you." He eyed her appreciatively. "Verily, sweeting, I have never been so pleased with any recompense in my life. Shall we get started for London, then?"

"You're an animal!" she shouted, pointing at the door. "Leave then, you wretched, unchivalrous rat! *Get out!* I wouldn't go one step in your company, you...you...

ravisher!'' Hugh laughed and turned toward the door. In a rage, Rosaleen followed. "And when I get to London, I'll have a warrant put out for you, signed by the king's own hand, you . . . you . . . defiler! I swear by God's holy name, I shall!"

"Good lack, woman! If this is the kind of abuse you heaped upon your uncle's head, it isn't a wonder he beat you so!" He stopped at a small table near the door and dug his coin bag out of his tunic. "Here," he said, placing several coins down. "I shouldn't be so merciful to such a shrew, but this ought to be enough to—"

"How dare you!" she screeched from right behind him, so that when Hugh turned he bumped into her. "First you abuse me, you . . . you . . . seducer! And then you try to pay me off like the veriest whore, you . . . you . . ."

"God's bones, I did not ravish you!" Hugh insisted, barely ducking in time when she picked up the coins and threw them at his head. "Calm yourself, Rosaleen! I only meant to help you, not hand you an insult."

"The only way you can help me is to get out of my sight!"

"All right, all right! I'm going!" He picked up Amazon and reshouldered his bag. "First you say I can't go, and then you throw me out. What a wild creature you are, Rosaleen no-name. Your gratitude for my care these past two days is overwhelming, indeed."

"Oh!" she gasped, taking a swing at him. "How dare you, you . . . you . . . great randy goat! If you think to wait until I thank you for deflowering me, then you'll be waiting until Satan's breath blows cold!"

"I did *not,*" he said with growing anger, "deflower you! If you don't quiet yourself, my sweet, I'm going to take you back to that bed and show you exactly what I did do!"

"Get out!" she shouted. "And when you get downstairs I wish you to send up one of the friends who stood with you the other night. Surely one of them will be chivalrous enough to help a lady in plight."

"You are quite right, my lady. Any one of my friends would have been pleased to play the good chivalrous fellow for you, more fool they, but they are gone, having left yesterday morn, as I, myself, should have done and now wish to God that I had!" He drew in a breath, then said more calmly, "I fear you shall have to seek London on your own, as you did before you ever came to this place."

Rosaleen froze, staring at him in surprise, as though he had struck her, and then she did the inexplicable. Her face crumpled and her eyes filled with tears.

"But I can't."

Hugh looked away, thoroughly aggravated. "You were planning on going alone before," he said gruffly. "If you'd let me leave you a little money you could still do it." It was a damned lie, and he knew it. A woman on the open road, alone, was as defenseless to every rogue and knave who came her way as a newborn mouse might be against Amazon.

She shook her head and spoke more to herself than to him. "I learned very well two nights ago that I will need protection. I *must* get to London. I must." She turned and walked back to the bed, wringing her hands. Sitting on the mattress, she bowed her head and was quiet.

Hugh cleared his throat. "Well, you'll be fine. Goodbye, Rosaleen. Good luck."

She said nothing, only kept her head bowed. Her fingers laced and unlaced in a worried rhythm.

"I said goodbye, Rosaleen. Godspeed."

"Yes, yes," she mumbled tearfully. "Goodbye."

He opened the door and walked out, shaking his head to rid it of the memory of her sitting so unhappily on the edge of the same bed where he had spent some exceedingly enjoyable hours with her. Well, he'd be damned if he'd feel guilty about that, he told himself as he made his way down the stairs to the main room. She had enjoyed herself quite as much as he had, though she didn't remember it yet. And he *had* considered it repayment for all the trouble he'd gone through. There wasn't anything wrong with that. She was a beautiful girl; any other man would have used her much differently had he had the chance.

The innkeeper was standing behind his serving board when Hugh walked in, and the little man smiled in greeting.

"Well, sir, are you on your way, then?"

"Yes, I'm on my way," Hugh replied. "The lady is feeling better this morn, and would like some food to break her fast with. She also wishes the use of a brush and needs clean linen to cover her hair. See that she has all she desires." He tossed the innkeeper a couple of gold coins and watched with disdain as the man pocketed the money with lusty greed.

"That I will, my lord," the man promised quickly. "The lady be well satisfied, I vow. Will there be anything else, my lord?"

Hugh gave the man a considering glance and wondered how far he could trust him. The innkeeper was willing enough now, when a fighting man was present, but how would Rosaleen fare once he'd ridden away? Aside from that, he hated the way the man spoke of her, as though Rosaleen were naught but a whore flaunting herself as something better.

He struggled for a long moment, telling himself sternly that he was going to regret this. If he only could have expelled the image of her sitting so defeated and miserable on the edge of that damned bed, he might have won.

"The *lady*," he said curtly, emphasizing the word, "will need a good mount. Is there anyone in this godforsaken village who owns a decent horse he'd be willing to sell?"

Chapter Three

"I am *not* taking you to London."

They'd been traveling together for only half a day, and already Hugh felt like strangling her.

"You needn't be so intemperate, sir," Rosaleen stated from where she rode beside him on a tiny brown mare that made his own magnificent black steed look like some mighty and fabled creature. "It certainly wasn't *my* idea that we go anywhere together. And if you think that escorting me to London will stop me from issuing a warrant for your arrest, you are sadly mistaken. I intend to go straight to the king regarding the matter of my ruin, and when he hangs you, I shall be at the very front of the crowd, cheering the executioner on."

Hugh gritted his teeth and wondered what sin he had ever committed to make him suffer this fate.

"Rosaleen, I am going to say this one more time, and if you ever again mention the matter I shall make you exceedingly sorry. Listen well, lady. You are still a maiden. I did not ruin you. And I am damned well *not* taking you to London!"

She perched as high as she could in her saddle, trying in vain to level herself with Hugh Caldwell.

"Then what good do you do me?" she demanded. "I've told you over and again that I must get to London as quickly as possible, yet you refuse to tell me how taking me to your brother will help me in getting there. Don't you understand anything? I must get to London!"

"I understand perfectly, Rosaleen," Hugh replied with what he felt was admirable calm, considering the measure of his vexation. "And I promise that my brother will be able to help you. He is a man of no small influence and can help you attain whatever goal you have. He could even get you an audience with King Henry, if you desired it."

With a sigh, Rosaleen settled back into her saddle and turned her eyes to the road. Hugh Caldwell was lying, there could be no mistake of that. What would such a man as he know about influence? His brother was probably a pig farmer, a big man in some unknown village who held a few dozen ignorant peasants in thrall. And as for Hugh Caldwell himself...well! She didn't care how handsome he was or how handy with a sword. He was as bad as a pig himself. Worse, even, for he hadn't the faintest idea of how to treat a lady.

"How far away is this so esteemed brother of yours?" she asked, thinking that she must start planning anew her route to London.

He sounded grim as he answered, "Two days' ride. No more than that."

"You live with your brother, then? In the same village?"

"No." He kept his eyes on the road ahead. "I've not been home in over ten years. In truth, I have no home."

"Really?" Rosaleen's womanly heart responded to the sad note of his reply. "That seems very strange. Ten years! Did something happen to keep you from returning to your family? A fight with your brother?"

He shook his head. "No fight, Rosaleen, and you may keep your curiosity to yourself. It's no concern of yours, just as you are no concern of mine. I'll take you to my brother and leave you in his care, and then I shall be on my way. If God is truly gracious, we'll never set eyes on one another again."

"Save on the day of your execution, of course," Rosaleen returned sweetly. "Will not your brother be surprised to see you after ten years?"

Hugh made a snorting sound. "You've no need to worry, Rosaleen. He'll not turn you away. You'll get to London."

"That's not what I meant. And I can very well get to London without any help from you, Hugh Caldwell, so you needn't think I'm worried about anything at all. I simply wondered whether your brother wouldn't be surprised to see you. And what of the rest of your family? What will they think to have you suddenly come riding into your village after having been gone so long? Why, if it's truly been ten years, you must have been little more than a child when you left."

Hugh laughed, but it wasn't a pleasant sound. "God's bones, what a chattering little creature you are, Rosaleen no-name. And if you're not worried about anything at all, then why do you keep looking about as though you expect someone to jump out at us any moment?"

"I'm not..." Rosaleen stopped herself. In truth, she *was* worried. They were traveling on a main road, out in the open for any and all to see. She had tried to impress upon Hugh Caldwell the need to ride more secretively, but the arrogant beast had insisted they would be fine...kept safe by himself, of course. It would serve him right if her uncle and all his men came riding down upon their heads.

"Why will you not answer my questions?" she asked, changing the subject. "How old were you when you left home? Ten and five years of age? Ten and six?"

"I'll not let anything happen to you, Rosaleen," he assured her, changing the subject, as well, "and I'll certainly not let anything happen to *me*, so you may rest easy."

"Well, God's mercy, Hugh Caldwell, I'm glad to hear it," Rosaleen replied with sarcastic relief. "I'd not want anything to happen to you, either, before I get a chance to see you hang."

Hugh sighed loudly. "You, my sweet, are a true example of the gentle flower of womanhood. Your sharp tongue causes me to wonder if your uncle wasn't beating the wrong person. It seems that the one who'd need the forcing would be the man picked to marry you, not the other way around."

Rosaleen gasped furiously. "Oh!"

"What a dread fate it would be," Hugh continued pleasantly, "waking each morn to be greeted by that sharp little tongue. On the other hand, of course, there is your soft body to make some recompense for your shrewish nature, as I know firsthand." He grinned at her lecherously.

"Why, you...you...you..."

Hugh clucked and shook his head. "No, I cannot think even that would make marriage to you a pleasant prospect. Are you certain this fellow your uncle chose *wanted* to wed you, Rosaleen? I find it very hard to believe."

"Oh, you wretch!" She knew very well that he was baiting her, purposefully trying to anger her. She knew, too, that she was behaving exactly like the shrew he called her. It wasn't like her to behave so badly, but then, she had never before found herself in the company of such a crude, infuriating man. "Yes, he wished to wed me, though you may choose not to believe it if you like. In truth, Hugh Caldwell, I don't care what you believe of me."

Hugh was disappointed with her tame answer. He had insulted her so beautifully that he'd been certain she would have flown into a good rage at the very least. Instead, she seemed to have understood his intent and had calmed herself and answered readily. She was smart, little Rosaleen no-name, and if there was one thing Hugh avoided as he would the plague, it was smart females. He'd have to keep his wits about him or he'd shortly find himself behaving decently, and the ten years he'd spent cultivating himself to do otherwise would be for naught. He'd already been too damned nice to her as it was. In truth, it might be said that he'd behaved chivalrously, a thought that actually made him shudder.

"I see," he said. "Then if your chosen mate was so hot to wed you, sweet, what was the trouble? Was he not to your liking? Or wasn't he good enough for such a fine lady?"

He'd meant the words as he meant everything he said, mockingly, but her reaction, the look on her face, made him regret speaking them.

Rosaleen shut her eyes and tried to push away the image of Simon of Denning. "No, he was just so..." How could she explain? How could she put Sir Simon's huge, terrifying hands...hands matted with the blackest of hair, hands that groped and squeezed and hurt...how could she put them into words? How could she relate his cruelty, his lust, his strength, which made her know only too well how easily he could crush her to his will when it pleased him to do so? God's mercy! She didn't want to think of him! She didn't want to remember what it felt like to be shoved up against a wall and held there by the weight of his hard body, fighting nausea when he vised her jaw between two strong fingers and forcibly opened her mouth so that he could thrust his tongue inside, or wincing at the pain of his strong fingers squeezing and pinching her breasts, or wanting so much to faint so she wouldn't have to feel the hardness of his sex as he rhythmically rocked it against her, speaking his crude, filthy words about what he was going to do to her when they were finally wed.

Twice he had actually found his pleasure with her that way, pushing himself against her, grunting like a hog eating its swill, until he finally shuddered with his release. Rosaleen had almost been relieved when he had, for at least he had let her go and, with the laughter of contentment, had patted her like a dog and jested of how he would have to suffer with the wetness she had wrought in his chausses.

He'd been so pleased on those two occasions, so pleased, while she had felt so sick and helpless.

"Rosaleen." Hugh Caldwell spoke to her. She felt a gentle touch on her cheek. "Rosaleen." His voice was strangely tender.

She opened her eyes.

The horses had stopped moving, and she and Hugh Caldwell were sitting on their mounts in the middle of the road, perfectly still. He was leaning down from his higher position, gazing at her with an expression of deep concern while his hand stroked her cheek. He was such a beautiful sight that she couldn't help but stare.

"What?" she asked dumbly. She couldn't remember what they'd been discussing.

He ran his thumb over her cheek. "Are you all right, little sweeting?"

"Yes," she whispered, still staring at him. She never wanted to stop, for when she looked at Hugh Caldwell she didn't think even vaguely about Simon of Denning.

Rosaleen's skin felt softer than silk beneath Hugh's callused hand, and he didn't want to stop touching her. The change she'd undergone when she'd thought of the man her uncle had betrothed her to had first stunned, then enraged him. It was clear that the man had hurt her badly, else her beautiful face never would have grown so stricken. He wanted to kill the bastard. He wanted to wipe that look of misery off Rosaleen's face. Permanently. All he could think of at the moment, however, was a temporary solution. And she would probably never know what a sacrifice it was.

Slowly he withdrew his hand and straightened in his saddle.

"I was ten and six when I left my home," he announced, nudging his steed, Saint, forward.

Rosaleen's little mare followed, as Hugh had expected she would, and in a moment her mistress had shaken her dismals and gazed up at him with interest, as he had also expected she would.

"Ten and six!" she repeated with amazement, all thoughts of Sir Simon thoroughly displaced. "Were you all alone? What made you leave?"

Hugh smiled. He hadn't known Rosaleen no-name very long, but already he could read her like a monk's new manuscript. He had never before spoken of the time he had left his home, yet here he was, about to reopen all his old wounds in order to distract a silly, sharp-tongued female. The idea almost made him laugh. The great Hugh Caldwell, famed for his hardness and lack of heart, behaving like any other damned fool for the sake of a mere female. He could scarce believe it, and desperately hoped none of his acquaintances would ever hear of it.

"I was alone," he began, "and more frightened than I was willing to admit, though of course I considered myself very brave, being as foolish as any sixteen-year-old is..."

Over the next few hours he told her of his life, those parts he could bear to tell, from the moment he had left home to all the adventures he'd had, including his sojourn in France, from whence he had just returned as a soldier for King Henry. Rosaleen listened raptly, laughing when the tale grew humorous and looking suspiciously teary when she thought it sad, and Hugh allowed himself to be amused at her interest in what his life had been.

Women! he thought silently. They were all the same, even this beautiful little shrew. They all seemed to think they knew what a man wanted and needed, but he'd never yet met the female who could even begin to understand the things that he barred so tightly from his heart.

"What will you do now, Hugh Caldwell?" Rosaleen asked. "Your brother will want you to stay with him in...where did you say you came from?"

"I didn't. And I'm not going to. We'll just keep our destination a little secret, shall we? That way neither of us will know what to expect."

The stiffness of his tone said more than his words did. For all that he was a big, muscular fighting man, it was plain to Rosaleen that he was as nervous about going home to face his family as a naughty little boy who'd done something bad might be, and the very thought softened her heart. Perhaps she didn't want to have him hanged, after all.

"Very well, Hugh Caldwell. It shall be a secret."

Hugh glanced at her suspiciously. "That meek tone suits you not, Rosaleen no-name. Much more of that and I'll be thinking you're not the same lady who called me every unthinkable name in King Henry's English this very morn."

She reddened. "And with good reason! Until I am proved otherwise, I shall continue to believe that you are exactly what I have proclaimed you."

"Why, Rosaleen," he uttered with feigned surprise, "should you like me to make proof of your innocence? There is nothing, I promise you, in all of God's earth that would please me more."

"You, sir, are a bastard," she replied, keeping her eyes forward and wondering if she shouldn't reconsider having him hanged.

"And your mouth, my lady, needs cleansing. How is it that your uncle ever allowed you to use such language?"

Rosaleen laughed bitterly. "It was from him that I learned it, my lord. Sometimes it was my only defense against him, though I was loath to so lower myself."

Again, Hugh felt a fierce need to kill the man who'd beaten her.

"Rosaleen," he said, "I'm going to do something I've not done in a long, long time."

"Oh? Behave decently, you mean?"

"No," he returned dryly. "I am going to beg your pardon for what I said a moment ago. About your language. It was amiss in me to judge you so hastily, and I'm sorry."

Rosaleen bit her lip to keep from laughing. It was evident that Hugh Caldwell was sorely unused to apologizing for anything at all. "Your apology is accepted, Hugh Caldwell, but only on the condition that you answer my question about what you mean to do once we reach your childhood home. Do you intend to stay there or no?"

"I'll only stay long enough to make certain you are taken care of, Rosaleen, and then I will leave. I am to become my own man," he added before she could ask why he wouldn't stay. "There was a fellow I fought beside in France, a baron named John Rowsenly, who possessed a fief called Briarstone, which he gambled away to me one night. I hadn't meant to keep it, as it was his family home, but he was killed at Agincourt, and I have determined that I shall go and make my life there as best I can."

He glanced at her and saw that she was gazing at him in disbelief.

"His people will be expecting me," he went on, "for I sent them a missive regarding their lord's death and assuring them that I would come and take care of them."

She kept staring, and he said, almost defensively, "I cannot let them sit unprotected any longer. Any band of wandering knaves might wreak havoc, seeing the place unmanned. Rowsenly was a fool to wager away his holdings, but his people don't deserve to be left alone because of it. I'm no great lord, but I can manage a small fief such as Briarstone without any trouble, I vow, and hold it safe against any intruders."

Rosaleen regarded the masculine profile he offered her, then let her gaze wander over his broad shoulders, his hard, lean body and long, muscular arms and legs. His hands were as big and hard as the rest of him, yet looked agile and skilled. He was a beautiful man, a fighting man, and she had seen enough of such men to know that he was good at his trade. He'd have no difficulty protecting his little fief, she decided, and he already spoke of Briarstone with a pride of ownership, though he'd not yet set eyes on the place. It must be a very small estate, indeed, for she had never before heard of it.

"Rowsenly left no heirs? No wife or children?" she asked.

"Not that I know of. He never spoke of any, and when I won the deed to the place he assured me it was mine and no one else's."

"The king has a say in such matters, Hugh Caldwell, though you may not be aware of it. He could declare Sir Rowsenly's lands forfeit to the throne and deed them to one of his favorites as a reward. It's his right as your liege, you know."

Her words brought a smile to Hugh's lips. She was a high-handed little thing, thinking him so ignorant as to need such instruction. He was tempted to play the idiot and let her spend the next hour making a fool of herself. God's mercy, it was going to be pleasant to see the look on her face when they finally rode through the gates of Castle Gyer and she realized just exactly who his brother was.

"I must needs take my chances on the king's leniency, then, will I not?" Hugh asked, keeping his smile to himself. In truth, he had already sought the king's approval for his taking of Briarstone, right after he had learned of John Rowsenly's death. King Henry had offered to make a knight of him more times than Hugh could count, and when Hugh had appeared before him after Agincourt he had offered to do so once again, insisting that it was only right that one of his best soldiers, as well as the brother of one of his most favored barons, be knighted. But Hugh had refused, and instead had asked for the king's favor regarding the matter of Briarstone. Henry had been only too happy to make him the master of the place, telling Hugh quite truthfully that it wasn't so grand a fief that he'd ever want to make a gift of it to anyone who'd done him a good service. Hugh had been relieved once Henry's approval had been given, for he hated seeking the favor of any man, even his king, and had vowed immediately afterward that he would never again lower himself in such a way.

"Aye, that you will, Hugh Caldwell," she answered, following the words with a *tsking* sound. "You're a stubborn devil, and that's as certain as the new moon rising. I think even Henry himself would have trouble standing against such a one as you."

"If he knows what's good for him, he'll not even give it a try," Hugh replied confidently.

"Hugh Caldwell! 'Tis your king you speak of!"

"Well, of course it is, Rosaleen. Who did you think I meant?"

"Oh, you *are* a devil," she said, pursing her lips in disapproval. "I'll wager your brother had his hands full when you were a boy."

Her words sent the oddest sensation tingling down Hugh's spine, and memory after memory waved in his mind. They were good memories, things he hadn't let himself think of for a long time. Unable to stop himself, he laughed, and unwittingly gifted her with a smile...a real, true, honest, rare smile, not one invented from the depths of his anger and bitterness.

"That he did, Rosaleen no-name. That he most certainly did."

Chapter Four

"I'll not take my clothes off just because you tell me to, Hugh Caldwell!"

Rosaleen backed away, looking wildly around for some heavy object to throw, but Hugh kept coming at her, slowly and surely.

"Don't be a fool, Rosaleen. I'm not going to ravish you. I only want to put some of this salve on your back, and then I'm going to put you to bed."

"Ha!" Rosaleen cried, bumping into a table as she moved around the small room. "You admit your evil intentions, you...you...lewd fiend!"

Hugh gritted his teeth and felt a headache coming on. He was tempted to throw the ointment the innkeeper's wife had given him that morn right out the window. If he hadn't known that Rosaleen was suffering badly after their day's long ride, he would have done just that, without the least hesitation, but she *was* suffering and he *was* going to put the salve on her. The girl was too damned stubborn to know what was good for her.

Drawing in a breath, he tried to speak more calmly. "Be reasonable. Your back pains you, and you're hungry, and you're so weary that you're about to fall on your face. Let me put a little of this on your back to give you ease, then

I'll go downstairs and fetch you something to eat while you get into the bed. How does that sound?''

Wonderful, Rosaleen thought, but that didn't mean she was going to disrobe in front of the likes of Hugh Caldwell.

"I'll put the salve on myself," she countered, "and you may have one of the serving maids bring me something to eat."

Hugh sighed, wondering if he'd ever met a more stubborn female in his life and realizing at once that he hadn't. If he'd ever met a woman more exasperating than Rosaleen no-name, he never would have forgotten her.

"I didn't bundle you into this inn in that heavy cloak for no reason at all, Rosaleen. If any of those men downstairs hear that I'm keeping a beautiful maiden in my room, I'll end up having to kill half of them just to keep your precious virtue intact. I can't take the chance of letting anyone see you, not even a maid. You understand that, do you not?''

A chill crept up Rosaleen's spine. She hadn't been able to make out much from the depths of the dark cloak Hugh Caldwell had made her wear into the inn, but she'd seen enough to know that the men patronizing the tavern were exactly the same sort who had accosted her two nights before.

"I understand," she replied meekly.

"Good. Now take off your clothes and let me put this ointment on."

Despite her weariness, Rosaleen hadn't lost any of her fight.

"I'll not, you lecher! You're only doing this to take advantage of me!"

That was it. Hugh had had enough.

"If I'd wanted to take advantage of you, sweet, I would have done so last night when you were begging me to give you pleasure!"

Rosaleen gasped. "I never...I *never* did such a thing! You filthy beast!"

"Rosaleen," he said in a low voice, advancing on her again, "I am tired, and I am hungry, and I want to go below stairs and have a welcome cup of ale, but most of all, my fine lady, I am past weary of being called every base name under God's sun. Unless you want me to undress you myself you will remove...your...clothes. *Now!*"

His roar seemed to shake the whole room, and Rosaleen knew that she had pushed him too far. She had only seen such a look of fury on one other man's face, and the last time she had defied her uncle he had taken a whip and beaten her. It was that memory that defeated her, and she bowed her head. With shaking fingers she began to unlace her surcot.

Damn, he was in a foul mood!

Hugh hefted his third tankard of ale and wondered what devils beset him so that he felt more sharply than ever the need to ease the bitterness that was his constant companion. If someone didn't give him a good reason to release his fury soon he would have to seek out a fight himself, and that was always a nuisance.

He set the tankard down and rubbed a hand over his weary eyes.

Damn her! *Damn* her! It was that wretched female's fault, every bit of it, and he only hoped she was as miserable as he was. God's teeth, he was beginning to hate women, the fickle, useless shrews. There was only one thing they were good for, and the particular female he was stuck with wasn't even any good for that.

Damn her...Rosaleen. He was miserable. He didn't want to think of her, didn't even want to think her name. He had lost his temper, he'd shouted at her, and the fight had gone out of her as though he'd actually struck her a blow. She'd started removing her clothing with trembling obedience, sickening Hugh with the realization of what he'd done and enraging him anew at the bastard who had abused her so badly. He'd made her stop when she'd gotten to her chemise, and then, feeling as great a bastard as her uncle, he'd carefully put the salve on without exposing her skin to his sight. She'd slid into the bed without a word after that, and when he had later taken her a tray of food, she had still refused to speak to him. He'd come downstairs feeling like nothing better than a great, hulking bully and had every intention of drinking himself into oblivion and then soothing his nerves with a good, vigorous fight.

His sharp eyes roamed the crowded tavern with acute skill, rapidly picking out the potential opponents to be had. Briefly, his eyes rested upon the full-figured serving girl who had earlier made him an offer he almost hadn't refused. She caught his gaze and winked at him, letting him know that the offer was still open, and Hugh eyed her prospectively. She wasn't a beauty by any stretch of the imagination, but she had a fine body. Her breasts were lovely, Hugh knew, for she had waylaid him in the shadows of the stairwell and displayed them quite prettily. They were made for a man to enjoy, just as the rest of her was, and Hugh was highly tempted.

Yes, indeed. Highly tempted.

And he needed something to take his mind off the morrow, for tomorrow he would finally see Hugo. After ten years...

Hugo.

He shut his eyes and felt himself plunging headlong into hell.

The next moment he shot off his stool and approached the biggest man in the room.

"Here, friend," he said, tapping the man's shoulder. "If your mother's as ugly as you are, then she must be the finest bitch in the king's own kennels."

The unknown man roared his outrage, the sound of which was solace to Hugh's ears. He clenched his fists and knew with contentment that for the space of the next half hour he would be able to banish every thought of Rosaleen, and home, from his mind.

The soft stroke of fingers upon her cheek wakened Rosaleen. It was dark in the room, but the light of the moon spilling through the shutters offered some visibility. Blinking, she tried to focus but couldn't make sense of what was before her eyes. It was broad and solid and flesh-colored, and lightly sprinkled with hair. She blinked again, and again.

"Tell me that isn't you, Hugh Caldwell," she whispered, "lying in my bed as naked as the day you were born."

His fingers continued to caress her, and she could hear the smile in his voice when he replied, obediently, "It's not me lying in your bed as naked as the day I was born."

Slowly, her eyes moved upward to look into his face. He was smiling pleasantly, as relaxed and happy as could be, and Rosaleen forced herself to remain calm.

"What, may I ask, are you doing here?"

"Preparing to sleep, sweeting, and touching you." His fingers ran lightly from her face down her throat and across the delicate bones of one shoulder. "Does this return memories, Rosaleen?"

It did, but the gentle touch of his hand made her tremble, and she was unable to speak.

She was as warm and soft beneath his fingers as Hugh
had remembered her to be, and the stricken look in her
eyes undid him.

"Yes," he murmured, drawing closer. "Memories like
this."

His mouth closed over hers, and Hugh lost no time in
pressing his tongue between her lips and into the welcoming warmth of her mouth. His arms enfolded her, careful
of her healing back, and he pulled her against his painfully aroused body. She lay stiff and frightened for a long
moment, and then, with a little cry, she gave way and set
her arms around his neck.

"Yes, Rosaleen," Hugh whispered, thrusting one leg
between her thighs and drawing a moan from her lips.
"Yes, love, like this. This is what we did with one another
last night, and more. So much more. You're remembering
now, aren't you, my sweet? You're remembering the ways
we pleasured one another."

Rosaleen shook her head and tried to draw away from
him. "No," she murmured, unable to escape the heat of
his hard body, of his mouth as it moved over her neck and
shoulders, of his hands as they eagerly roamed her skin,
pulling up her chemise and slipping beneath to caress her
bare buttocks. He grasped her there, gently, holding her
still as he rocked needily against her.

"No." She pushed at him once more. "It was dreams.
Dreams..."

"Not dreams, beautiful lady." Hugh took one of her
delicate hands and flattened it against his chest. "You
touched me, and I touched you. Everywhere, love. Everywhere. Like this. Oh yes, little love, like this." He kissed
her again, deeply, and pressed her hand over his hot skin.

"Remember, Rosaleen," he commanded. "Remember the pleasure we gave one another. I didn't take your maidenhead, but I gave you a sweet release, just as you gave me. You were so beautiful in my arms, so eager. I couldn't help myself, darling. I couldn't help myself."

It was too much for Rosaleen, too overwhelming.

"Please, stop," she begged. "Please, Hugh, don't."

She tugged frantically to make him release her hand, but Hugh was too lost in his passion to heed her. He dragged her hand down his body toward the place where he so desperately wanted her touch.

"Touch me, Rosaleen. Please, my beautiful sweet. Touch me with your soft little hands and take me to heaven, just as I shall take you."

This was wrong, Rosaleen thought wildly, struggling. Wrong, wrong, *wrong!*

"No, Hugh! Oh God, don't. *Don't!*"

He was so much stronger than she, and he was just drunk enough with both ale and passion to mistake her struggles and cries for pleasure. Gently but insistently, he wrapped Rosaleen's fingers around him, and for just a moment Rosaleen stilled with the amazing shock of what a man felt like.

Then, frightened, overwhelmed and horrified at her lack of courage, she burst into tears.

Nothing else had penetrated Hugh's passion-riddled brain until that moment, but her sudden tears worked on him like a bucketful of icy water. Shocked, he released her.

"Rosaleen! What—" He didn't know what to think. One moment they'd been making sweet love and the next she was sobbing her heart out. "Did I— God's feet, sweeting, did I hurt you? Your back? Did I...did I squeeze you too hard or..." He was at a loss, and Rosaleen only lay there, crying. He placed a tentative hand on her shoul-

der and she shoved it away. "Please, Rosaleen," he
pleaded. "Tell me what's wrong."

Rosaleen was in a fury such as she had never before
known. Even her uncle, at his worst, had never enraged her
so greatly. She stopped her tears just long enough to glare
at the man hovering worriedly above her.

"I'll tell you what's wrong, you lecherous beast! I've
been molested by the greatest bastard in King Henry's
kingdom! That's what's wrong!"

Hugh was so shocked that he sat up, but not fast enough
to avoid the stinging slap Rosaleen gave him as she shot out
of the bed.

"Molested!" he shouted indignantly. "You were as eager as I, wench! Don't try to deny it! And don't you *ever*
strike me again!"

"Strike you!" she screeched. "*Strike you!* By, God,
Hugh Caldwell, I'll do more than strike you! I'm no tavern whore to be tumbled whenever you please! I'm a lady,
you spawn of Satan! *A lady!*" She picked up a pillow and
began to hit him with it, hard and repeatedly, while she
continued raging.

"You—" *whack!* "—bastard! I'll—" *whack!* "—teach
you to—" *whack!* "—touch a lady in such a—" *whack!*
"—crude manner! You—" *whack!* "— beast!"

Hugh held his arms up to counter her blows.

"Dammit, Rosaleen! Cease this!" *Whack!* "I said
cease!" *whack!* "Cease or I'll—" *whack!* "—turn you
over my—" *whack!* "—knee!"

"I'd like to see you—" *whack!* "—do it, you rutting
boar!" *Whack!* "Better men than you—" *whack!*
"—have tried to tame me, you hound from hell—"
whack! "—but I'll bow my knee to no man—" *whack!*
"—save the king—" *whack!* "—you randy satyr!"

Something that sounded suspiciously like laughter drifted up to Rosaleen's ears, and two long, muscular arms reached up to grasp her, despite her efforts with the pillow. Hugh got a good hold on her, then tossed her to the bed, flinging the pillow away and pinning her beneath his body.

Rosaleen fought him, freeing one hand to hit his rock-hard chest. "Let me go, you lecherous goat! Let me go!"

Hugh was laughing so hard he could barely speak. "R-Rosaleen! D-don't!" He burst into another storm of laughter. "Stop it! S-stop, my l-lady!"

"Oh!" Rosaleen cried, outraged. "How dare you laugh at me, you foul ravisher! How dare you!" She drew up a fist and hit his solid chest again, hurting herself more than him. "I hate you!"

Hugh tried to stop laughing. He tried so very hard, yet he couldn't help himself. And Rosaleen didn't help. He had never seen anyone more perfectly beautiful and self-righteous in his life than she, outraged.

"I'm sorry," he managed to say, holding her tight even as she struggled against him. "No, 'tis the truth I speak, Rosaleen." He grinned into her furious face. "Last night you responded to me because you were drugged for your pain and hardly knew what you did. I assumed too much this night, thinking you would respond again just as readily. But I frightened you, did I not, my little innocent? You are but a maiden, and I have frightened you with my grown man's desire."

"You're disgusting!" she said angrily. "You crawled into my bed to ravish me apurpose, even when you knew I wanted no such thing! Have you no morals at all?"

"Few," he admitted honestly. "But I never would have taken your maidenhead, Rosaleen, I swear it. I wanted to share pleasure with you, sweeting, but I'd never do aught to hurt you.''

"You don't think that what you were just doing hurt me?" she asked incredulously. "You were ravishing me!"

"That's foolish," Hugh replied, rolling away. "You're too innocent to know what you speak of. If I'd been ravishing you, I wouldn't have stopped, and I'd even now be mounted on your lovely body, taking my pleasure of you." He stretched and yawned, then scratched his chest and settled beside her. "It's over. Forget about it and get some sleep. We've a long day ahead of us on the morrow."

"You can't mean to sleep here!" she cried with disbelief, tossing off the arm that tried to crawl around her waist.

Hugh yawned again before answering. "Of course I do. Where else is there?"

She sat up. "God's bones, man! You've the nerve of a devil!"

"Be quiet and go to sleep, Rosaleen."

"Sleep! If you think that I'll sleep in the same bed as you, Hugh Caldwell, then I pray you will think again!" Rosaleen started to get out of the bed but was stopped when a muscular arm wrapped around her waist and pulled her back onto the mattress and up against the hard body she had only minutes before been touching with her hands.

She opened her mouth to scream, but Hugh's other hand came up and firmly, though gently, closed over it.

"Rosaleen, my sweet," he said patiently, "we are only going to sleep. You have made yourself clear about not wanting to share any pleasures with me. I'd be a fool to force myself on such an unwilling shrew, especially when England is filled with warm and willing females who would be more than happy to lie with me. Now be quiet and go to sleep, else I'll tie you to the bed and place a gag in your mouth."

"You're naught but a brute!" she huffed when he released her. "And I wish you would stop touching me!"

Hugh was reminded of how he had intimidated her earlier and felt instant remorse. Pulling his hands away, he rolled to his back and heard Rosaleen shuffle over to the far edge of the bed.

"Yes, I am," he admitted, pushing away the desire to apologize to her yet again. He'd only known the wretched creature a few days and he'd already apologized to her more than he could remember apologizing to any other person. "And I hope you'll keep that in mind until I've got you safely lodged with my brother. I warned you before we set out that I'm no gentle knight, or any kind of gentleman. I dare what I please, Rosaleen, and I take what I want. Remember that."

A loud silence prevailed, until Rosaleen said, "I hope whoever you fought with earlier was able to match you. Mayhap you'll have some bruises to make you miserable for a while."

Hugh closed his eyes and smiled widely in the darkness. It would have been impossible for her not to have heard the fighting that had gone on downstairs two hours before, when he had taken on more than half the patrons in the tavern. They had pretty well destroyed the place, as usual, but Hugh had paid the innkeeper more than the trouble was worth. When it had all been over and he'd felt thoroughly relaxed, Hugh had bought drinks all around and had gotten pleasantly drunk with his newly found mates before finally coming upstairs to Rosaleen. He hadn't meant to touch her when he had first crawled into the bed, but she had looked so sweet lying there, like an angel, that he hadn't been able to resist.

"He was," Hugh admitted with easy contentment, "and I will."

"You are crazed, my lord," she said, yawning, "and I wish you the joy of your wounds."

"Good night, Rosaleen."

"Good night, you beast."

Chapter Five

It was late the next day before Hugh finally turned their horses off the main road. They rambled along a side road for a few minutes and then stopped. In front of them, still some distance away, stood an imposing, venerable monastery, that Rosaleen knew by reputation. In fact, though she had seldom been through this area of England before, she was well aware of where they were. It would have been impossible not to know, for this land belonged to Sir Alexander Baldwin, the Lord of Gyer, who was widely known as one of King Henry's richest and most powerful barons.

"Is this where we'll be spending the night, then, Hugh Caldwell?" she asked, turning to look at him.

He didn't answer, but sat stiffly atop his steed, staring at the monastery.

"Yes," he replied at last, his voice taut.

Rosaleen wondered at the change that had come over him during the past few hours. He had wakened in a good mood that morn; had, in truth, enjoyed himself greatly with teasing her over the fact that she had curled against him for warmth during the night. But during the last several miles he had grown quiet, and even short-tempered, answering her questions with sharp replies plainly meant to tell her that he wanted to be left alone, until Rosaleen had actually wished he would start teasing her again.

Earlier, when they had passed by the small barony of Wallewyn, he had become increasingly grim, and when Rosaleen had begged that they stop at that place and rest for a short time, he had practically growled at her.

"I'll not step foot in that damned place again," he'd said tightly. "Ever. We'll keep on."

Those had been the last words he'd spoken to her until this moment.

"It is early to stop yet. Should we not press on and spend the night in Gyer?"

He shook his head. "We'll spend the night here."

He looked so strange that Rosaleen felt a little afraid.

"Very well, Hugh Caldwell. We'll stay here."

He was silent again, gazing hauntedly ahead.

Rosaleen cleared her throat. "Will we be spending the night in the middle of the road, then? Or shall we go down?"

Hugh turned to look at her, and the fire in his eyes nearly burned her to a cinder. His hands were clenched so tightly around the reins of his steed that his knuckles showed white.

"We will go, my lady, but I want you to know that the only reason I even came within a day's ride of this place is because of you."

He spurred his horse forward and galloped toward the monastery, leaving a stunned Rosaleen to follow. Above them, Amazon, having been loosed to feed herself an hour earlier, circled and gave her fierce cry.

Hugh rode like a demon through the monastery's gates, causing the monks working in the surrounding fields to look at him wonderingly. Rosaleen followed more sedately, smiling and nodding politely at the bewildered men, hoping that they wouldn't turn them away because of Hugh Caldwell's rude behavior. When she made the gates herself she saw that he had gone straight through the courtyard and into the stables. She rode in after him and was grabbed and yanked out of her saddle before her eyes could adjust to the building's darkness.

Hugh set her firmly on her feet.

"Go and wait for me in the gardens. I'll take care of the horses and meet you there."

Well! thought Rosaleen. He treated her as though she were naught but baggage!

"I'll not be ordered about like a servant, Hugh Caldwell! And I'll not be tossed about like a sack of grain!"

Ignoring her, he took hold of the little mare and led her toward a stall. "Go wait in the gardens for me," he repeated. "They're just across the courtyard and through the half gate. You'll find them easily enough."

Rosaleen stood her ground, glaring at him. Hugh turned, saw her there and raised his eyebrows.

"Have you gone deaf, Rosaleen? I told you to go and wait for me in the gardens."

"I heard you!"

"Then get out of my sight, woman, and do as I say. Go on, now." He turned his attention back to the horses.

Rosaleen huffed loudly, then stormed out of the stables with as much dignity as she possessed. Ignoring the stares of the monks in the courtyard, she strode across it to the half gate, flung it open and slammed it behind her after she walked into the gardens.

"If he thinks that I came to the gardens because he bade me do so," she announced aloud, "then he's an even greater idiot than I first supposed!"

Making her way down one of several paths to a bench, she angrily plopped down upon it.

"I don't care if he *is* the handsomest man I've ever seen," she muttered. "He's rude and ill-mannered, and he probably thinks he's one of God's blessings to women!"

A cool breeze brushed her face, but Rosaleen's fury wasn't tempered by it.

"He'll be sorry when he discovers who I am." An angry, feline smile lit her face. "And I only hope I'm there to see it! By my troth, I'll make him grovel if it's the last thing I do. When he realizes who it is he's insulted, he'll be on his knees, begging my forgiveness!"

So caught up was she in her vengeful fantasies that she didn't hear the garden gate open again, or the sound of the careful footsteps that approached her.

"Wretched beast! Brother of a pig farmer! Thinking he can treat me, the daughter of an earl, without the least bit of common decency, as though I were naught but the lowliest whore! But he'll come to rue his behavior, I vow. He'll..."

"Careful, daughter, lest you say words you'll one day regret."

Hugh! Rosaleen thought, paralyzing with mortification. He had finished with the horses more quickly than she had imagined he would. Embarrassed beyond words to have been discovered talking to herself, Rosaleen flushed and slowly raised her eyes to look at him.

What she saw stole the breath from her.

"Hugh Caldwell!" she shrieked, shooting up off the bench.

He shook his head with confusion. "My lady?"

"How could you! Oh, how *could* you!" Rosaleen's hands flew up to press against her hot cheeks. "Merciful God in heaven! Are you insane?"

For one horrible moment Rosaleen thought she would be sick, so great was her shock. She was only grateful that she didn't faint.

He took a step toward her, holding out one hand.

"My good lady, whatever is the matter?" His voice was filled with concern. "Are you ill?"

She backed away from him in horror, as though he were diseased.

"Don't touch me, you...you infidel! You godless pervert! Stay away from me!"

He stopped and held his hands palm up. "Of course I'll not touch you, my dear," he said very soothingly. "You mustn't be afraid. I only wish to help you. All of us here—" he motioned back toward the courtyard "—only want to help you, good daughter."

She truly thought she would swoon. "Sick. Dear God, you are sick! Oh, Hugh, how can this be? What can I do to help you?"

His expression changed slightly, and he raised his eyebrows in the manner that was now so familiar to her.

"*What* did you call me?"

"And your hair!" she wailed. "Your beautiful hair! How could you cut it so dreadfully? Oh, Hugh!"

He frowned deeply. "I think perhaps you've made a mistake."

A sudden realization struck Rosaleen, and she stared at him anew, dumbfounded. "But it isn't possible! I left you in the stables only a few moments ago. You couldn't have cut your hair and changed your clothing so quickly. It's not possible!" Another idea occurred to her, and she felt sick all over again. "Oh my God, Hugh Caldwell! *I'm* the one who's gone mad! This is what's happened to me after spending time in company such as yours. I've lost my mind!"

His gentleness vanished and Rosaleen found herself grabbed up by his strong hands.

"You've called me that twice now!" he said angrily, shaking her. "Hugh Caldwell! What do you know of Hugh Caldwell? Tell me!"

Stunned, Rosaleen peered into his face, searching in vain for some difference. There was none, save his hair and clothes. He was Hugh Caldwell, or Hugh Caldwell's exact reflection.

"If you're not him," she squeaked beneath his stern gaze, "then I left him only a few moments ago in the stables."

He dropped her so fast she actually fell on her posterior, but Rosaleen scrambled up and raced after him as he strode out of the gardens and toward the stables. He flung the stable doors open so violently that they banged off the walls, startling every living creature in the building, including Hugh Caldwell, who quickly looked up from where he crouched, brushing Rosaleen's little mare.

His gaze locked with that of the man who stood in the doorway, and the brush fell out of his hand. He took one hesitant step, then two, toward Rosaleen and the man, and a tentative smile grew on his lips.

"Hugo," he said very softly. He took two more steps and held out his arms.

"You," the monk whispered, and with an animal sound launched himself at his brother. Hugh never even knew what hit him, Hugo's attack was so violent and sudden. A blow to his left cheek sent him sprawling into a nearby stall, and as soon as he landed Hugo leapt upon him, his fists pummeling him again and again.

Rosaleen was thoroughly stunned. She had never seen such a sight or imagined anything like it. A *monk*, of all people, brawling like a common knave! She didn't know what she should do, or what the precedent was for handling the situation. If it had been Hugh and some other common man, she would have dumped a bucketful of the horses' water on them, but she didn't know if throwing water on a monk was allowed by the Church, and she had too much consideration for her soul to endanger it by committing a sin in ignorance. Unable to think of anything more helpful, she simply ran around the fighting men, begging them to stop.

"No, no, Hugh!" she cried when he slugged the priest in the stomach, doubling him over before hitting him again to send him flying into a pile of hay. "He's a monk! A *monk,* Hugh! You mustn't hit him!"

"I know damned well what he is!" Hugh roared. "Stay out of the way, Rosaleen!"

He barely got the words out before Hugo slammed into him, sending the both of them sliding across the stable floor. This time Hugo ended up on top and quickly straddled his struggling brother, pinning him down.

"You rotten bastard!" he shouted. "I've been waiting ten years to do this to you, and I'll not be denied my pleasure!"

"Oh, oh, oh!" Rosaleen wailed. "Father, your language!"

"Be quiet!" both brothers shouted at her.

"Well!" Rosaleen stamped her foot.

"Do you have any idea how I felt that morn when I woke and found you gone?" Hugo demanded angrily. "Do you?" He shook him. "Sixteen years we were together, never apart, sharing everything, and yet you snuck off in the middle of the night without so much as a word to me! Not one damned word!" He lifted a fist and furiously slammed it into Hugh's face. "You'll never be able to imagine what that did to me! *Never!*"

"I'm sorry," Hugh mumbled, groaning, shaking his head to clear it. "I'm sorry, Hugo."

"Sorry!" Hugo repeated. "Ten years later and you say you're sorry!"

"I never meant to hurt you. I never meant that, Hugo, you know that's true. But I had to go."

"You didn't have to go," Hugo told him. "You could have stayed and worked through the pain, as I had to do all alone once you deserted me. We could have worked it out together. But instead you chose to run, and you're running still. Hugh *Caldwell!*" He spat the word out with disgust. "In all of ten years you never once came home."

"No, I didn't," Hugh agreed miserably. "But I did write, Hugo, so that no one would ever worry about me."

Hugo nodded grimly, shoving at Hugh's shoulders. "That's right. You wrote on occasion. And Lillis cried over every single missive, just as she cried her heart out for weeks after you ran away. She blamed herself, and nothing Alex or I or anyone else did or said could make her think otherwise. That's what you did to her with your selfishness, brother."

"Oh God," Hugh whispered, his voice filled with pain. "I didn't mean to hurt Lillis."

Hugo laughed bitterly. "You didn't mean to hurt me, and you didn't mean to hurt Lillis, and I'll assume you didn't mean to hurt Alex or Aunt Leta or anyone else, but you did, Hugh. You did." He moved off his brother at last and slowly stood. "Now, what are you doing here?" he asked coldly. "Why did you bother to come home?"

"Because of me," Rosaleen murmured, horrified at what she had made Hugh Caldwell return to.

Hugo turned to look at her as Hugh lifted himself from the ground.

"And who, my lady, are you?"

"Hugo," Hugh said, gingerly rubbing his bruised jaw, "please meet Rosaleen. I don't know her last name, so you'll have to live without that. Rosaleen, meet my brother, Father Hugo Baldwin. Rosaleen's in need of help, so I'm taking her to Alex. But I...wanted to see you first...so I thought we might spend the night here. If you want us to go, we will." When Hugo glanced at him sharply, Hugh added, "I understand, Hugo. It hasn't been so long that I don't know your thoughts anymore."

Hugo made no reply but turned his gaze once more to Rosaleen, surveying her first with the same anger he had directed at his brother, then with growing curiosity.

Rosaleen examined him in much the same way, just as angrily and curiously.

"Why, of course," she said. "You're twins. That's why I mistook you for Hugh." Unconsciously she inched toward Hugh until she stood beside him. Only then did she make a tiny bow. "Father Hugo," she greeted dutifully, and stiffly.

"My lady." He nodded at her. "If we have you to thank for bringing my brother home, then not only I, but my entire family, will be most grateful."

"You don't seem grateful to see your brother, my lord. Indeed, from your manner and speech I should think you'd rather string me up than thank me." The words came out of her with surprising tartness.

Instead of being angry, as he had every right to be, Rosaleen knew, the monk surprised her by lowering his eyes. Slipping his hands into the sleeves of his plain tunic, he looked suddenly meek and defenseless. "I think, then, my lady, that you know nothing about twins. You are wrong when you say that I am not glad to see my brother. His return is the answer to a prayer I have prayed every night since the night I saw him last."

"Hugo," Hugh pleaded, reaching out to his brother once more. Hugo quickly sidestepped him and started for the door.

"I shall see to your lodgings." His voice was stern again. "The evening meal will be served in two hours' time."

Their dinner passed more easily. Hugh and Hugo had silently agreed to at least be polite to each other, if not friendly. The three of them ate together in a small private chamber off the main dining area, so that they could converse without the restriction of the silence imposed upon the monks during their meals.

It was strange for Rosaleen to sit between two men who were exact copies, save for their hair and clothing. Even their voices sounded alike, so that she didn't think she would be able to tell them apart in the dark.

"You've turned into something of a firebrand, Hugh," Hugo commented. "We often get word of your adventures, even here at the monastery, though I generally hear of them from Alex whenever I visit at Gyer."

Pushing his soup aside, Hugh chuckled. "I've *turned* into something of a firebrand? You're one to speak, brother. Do you not remember all the mischief we got into when we were boys? Being a monk has affected your memory."

Hugo laughed in turn. "I remember, Hugh. The brothers here won't let me forget the time we loosed our dogs in the monastery's hen yard. Father Bartholomew still becomes angered over it whenever we have chicken at table. And Alex won't let me forget the time we kidnapped Lillis and brought her to Gyer as a prisoner. If he hadn't fallen in love with her I think we might still be suffering punishment for that particular deed."

"Trumpery!" Hugh replied, hefting a tankard of ale. "If we hadn't kidnapped Lillis, Gyer would have ended up at war with Wellewyn. We saved the lives of hundreds of people."

"You kidnapped your sister-in-law?" Rosaleen asked in disbelief.

"Well, she wasn't our sister-in-law at the time," Hugo explained somewhat shamefully. "She was the daughter of Gyer's enemy, Jaward of Wellewyn. Truthfully, however, we didn't know who she was when we first kidnapped her. We were playing highway thieves, you see, and were out to get any wayside traveler we could. If we hadn't ended up capturing the daughter of our brother's enemy, Alex probably would have strangled us."

"Your brother is Alexander of Gyer, then?" she asked quietly, keeping her eyes on Hugh, who wouldn't look at her.

Hugo gave her a strange look. "Of course he is. Did Hugh not tell you?"

Both Rosaleen and Hugh were silent.

"Ah," Hugo said with understanding. "He didn't tell you. Well, yes, Alex is our brother, just as Lillis is our sister. Did he tell you that?"

"Hugo!" Hugh growled.

"No, Father Baldwin, Hugh *Caldwell* has been very secretive regarding his true identity," she replied tartly.

"I've been more forthcoming than you, Rosaleen noname," Hugh returned.

"Hardly," Rosaleen scoffed. "I may not have given you my full name, Hugh Baldwin-Caldwell-whoever, but at least I didn't lie to you."

"I did not lie to you," Hugh insisted. "My name is Hugh Caldwell and has been for the past ten years."

"That's impossible!" Rosaleen argued just as angrily. "If your brother is Alexander Baldwin and your twin brother is Hugo Baldwin, then I can only assume that your true name is Hugh Baldwin, isn't that so, Father?" She looked to Hugo for aid but found that he had turned away.

Hugh, however, was looking at her so coldly that Rosaleen almost thought he might freeze her. "What I choose to call myself is my concern, my lady, just as your last name is yours. It makes no difference to you anyway, so leave the matter be."

"Oh!" Rosaleen huffed furiously, throwing her linen napkin on the table. "It does matter to me, Hugh Caldwell! You led me to believe that your brother was a pig farmer, not the richest baron in all of England!"

Both brothers gazed at her with shock, and silence reigned in the little room for several seconds. Then Hugo began to laugh.

"You did *what!*" he asked Hugh.

"What foolishness is this, Rosaleen?" Hugh demanded. "I never told you that my brother was a pig farmer!"

Rosaleen, realizing what she had said in her anger, flushed a bright, mortified red. Hugo was laughing so hard it was difficult for her to speak over him.

"Well...I just assumed...I mean...your *manners* Hugh, are so...so...and I just assumed that you were...well..."

Her fumbling words sent Hugo off again, and he laughed so hard that he nearly fell off his chair.

"Dammit, Hugo," Hugh said. "This isn't funny!"

"Your m-manners m-made her th-think that Alex is a p-p-pig farmer!" Hugo howled with delight, slapping a hand on the table. "That's th-the f-funniest thing I've ever h-heard! W-wait until I t-tell Alex!"

"You'll tell Alex no such thing! I'll not have it!" Hugh stated angrily. "And you, my lady—" he fixed Rosaleen with a heated glare "—should stop assuming that everyone else is like your uncle. Or does he even aspire to be a pig farmer? Mayhap I should think you were flattering me."

Rosaleen returned his glare with one of her own, and it was on the tip of her tongue to reveal her true identity to him. He would certainly be no less surprised to discover that she was the daughter of an earl than she had been at finding her ungallant companion to be a member of the highest nobility. Unfortunately, now knowing the truth about Hugh, she could trust him even less than she did before. If anyone in the Baldwin family should discover that she was Rosaleen Sarant, the heiress of Siere, they would certainly do what they felt was their duty and give her over to her uncle. Rosaleen had never been formally introduced to the Lord of Gyer, but they had been at court at the same time during several important royal occasions in the past. She would recognize him, she knew, but would he recognize her? She could only hope and pray that he wouldn't.

Both brothers waited for her to make a reply, and the longer she tried to think of what she must say, the more curious their expressions grew.

"Mayhap you should," she finally answered, then, reaching for a piece of bread, she quickly changed the subject. "Please tell me how it is that you came to be a monk, Father Hugo. You are very different from Hugh that way, are you not, even though you are twins?"

"Oh, my tale is tame and dull compared to most," Hugo replied with a grin. "I'd much rather hear more about you, Lady Rosaleen, and about why such a beautiful young lady must keep her identity a secret."

"As would I," Hugh agreed but, since he didn't at all like the manner in which his brother was looking at Rosaleen, regardless that Hugo had taken a vow of chastity, he added, "but I would also be interested to know why you've gone into holy orders. If anyone had ever told me when we were boys that either one of us would end up in the Church, I would have laughed until I was ill. I was just about done in, as it was, when I had news of you from friends." He popped a grape into his mouth and leaned back in his chair. "I couldn't believe it! When I think of all the things we did together, I wonder at how you ever got ordained. Why, if the Church only knew about all the women you and I used to—"

"Hugh!" Hugo chided. "That was long, long ago. I'm a man of God now and perfectly content to be so. Of course—" he looked at Rosaleen, somewhat embarrassed "—after my behavior this afternoon it may be hard for you to believe that, but it is true, nonetheless."

"Your behavior this afternoon was perfectly understandable," Rosaleen assured him, spearing a chunk of roasted lamb with her eating dagger. "Hugh deserved a good beating after leaving you as he did. In fact, you should probably beat him once more before we leave tomorrow day, just to make certain he's thoroughly punished."

"Thank you so much, sweeting," Hugh muttered.

"Of course," she continued, "he enjoys fighting, so it might be best to simply leave him be and let him suffer. But that is beside the point. Now, you must start right at the beginning, Father, and tell us everything. I greatly enjoy particulars."

What she didn't add was that, since it had been ten years since the brothers had last seen each other, Hugh would be hungry for the whole story of his twin's life during those years. Hugh was far too proud to ask for such information, of course, and Hugo was still too angry with his brother's abandonment to give it. None of that, however, was going to stop Rosaleen. She had been trained in the art of government since she was a child, and had learned her lessons well. The daughter of an earl needed to know such things as how to pleasantly bring conversation at table about, and how to direct its course. Men, she had learned very young, were much easier to manipulate in this manner than women, and Hugh and Hugo Baldwin were easier than most, since their desire to be reacquainted far outweighed their uneasiness.

"Very well, my lady, though I do warn you it is most dull."

Having made his disclaimer, Hugo launched into his tale. When he had finished, Rosaleen deftly brought Hugh to the point where he told a little of his own story. By the time their meal was over, Rosaleen was more than satisfied with the start the brothers had made in healing the breach in their relationship.

Rosaleen had long since left the table in favor of a comfortable chair beside the fire, leaving the two men to sit side by side, Hugh facing away from the table, his long legs stretched out in front of him, Hugo sitting at the table, his hands folded upon the tabletop.

Sipping a goblet of good red wine such as only the Church could provide, she watched the brothers as they talked, their heads turned toward each other, their manners relaxed. It was easy to see the deep bond they shared, though perhaps neither of them would realize it. They spoke in low tones, sometimes smiling and sometimes laughing, but always with a deep current of understanding that Rosaleen assumed twins must share, no matter how many years they'd been apart.

Watching them, Rosaleen felt a stab of jealousy. She had been beloved of her parents, but she had never had a sibling and had always felt the lack. Her mother had had a difficult time conceiving and bearing her; when Rosaleen was seven, her mother's second pregnancy had proved fatal. Her father had been a good and loving parent and had been the center of her life until his untimely death of the pox, yet Rosaleen had missed having a brother or sister. A brother, especially, would have been welcome, for he would have been the next Earl of Siere after her father's death. But there was no brother, and the responsibility of the earldom was in her hands alone. Thinking on it, she vowed anew that she would get herself to London, to the king and to freedom.

In the midst of their conversation, Hugh lifted one hand and gently stroked his brother's halo-shaven hair. Rosaleen couldn't hear what it was that he said in union with this action, for he was turned away from her, but she could see as well as hear his brother's immediate response.

Hugo shoved stiffly away from the table, stood and frowned down at his brother.

"I don't expect you to understand it. I don't expect you to understand anything about me or about what I feel or have felt in the past ten years. There was a time when I wondered how I would learn to live without you, and when I thought I would rather die than go through another day alone. But I have learned to live, without you and without anyone else, save my Lord. Don't ever ask me again how it is that I came into the Church, for I'll give you no answer. You gave up that right when you abandoned our family and me. Now if you'll excuse me, I must attend compline." He looked at Rosaleen, who was gazing at him with surprise. "I will bid you good-eve, my lady."

He strode to the door, opened it and was gone, leaving Hugh and Rosaleen sitting in silence.

Neither said a word, but eventually Rosaleen set her wine down and quietly walked to where Hugh sat with his head bowed. She stood behind him, lifted her hands and began to gently massage the stiff muscles in his neck. He responded like a cat, lifting his head and rolling it around, moving his shoulders meaningfully beneath her hands so that she would know better where he wished to be kneaded.

"I hope you're not thinking to comfort me, Rosaleen," he said after a moment. "I hate being comforted, especially by well-meaning females."

Rosaleen made a loud *tsking* sound. "I wouldn't be so foolish, Hugh Caldwell. Only people who possess hearts are capable of being comforted. I'd not waste my time."

He chuckled. "You're a good sort of female, Rosaleen, in your own way. Despite the sharp tongue and shrewish nature, I mean."

Rosaleen's fingers tightened on his neck until he squirmed and laughed.

"I do believe that's the closest I'll ever come to having a compliment from you, Hugh Caldwell. You may be certain I'll cherish it."

"Why, of course you will," he returned pleasantly. "I meant it as a compliment."

"Mmm." Rosaleen gave one final squeeze to his neck before she released him. "I do believe I will seek my bed, my lord. It's been so long since I've slept alone that I've nearly forgotten what it's like."

He reached out and grabbed her before she could skirt around him, and he drew her to stand between his open legs.

"I could sneak into your chamber and keep you warm tonight, Rosaleen." He squeezed her waist with his big hands and raised his eyebrows at her questioningly. "I kept you warm last night, did I not?"

Rosaleen smiled at him. "Most warm, my lord, but I would rather sleep with a cold-blooded snake than ever share a bed with you again."

"Now, be nice to me, Rosaleen," Hugh chided, pulling her closer even as she pushed against his shoulders, "else I'll go out into the gardens and bring you a snake, just as you wish. Have I not been good to you these past several days? Have I not taken care of you and kept you safe from harm? Am I not taking you to my brother and placing you in his care so that you'll be able to get to London, just as you desire?"

"And have I not had to put up with your rude behavior every step of the way during our journey?" Rosaleen countered, pushing harder when she felt the warmth of his groin through the cloth of her surcot. "And have we not already determined, sir, that you compensated yourself for your trouble with the use of my body while I was unaware?"

"And have I not had to face my family again for your sake," Hugh returned, sliding his hands until they rested lightly upon her hips, "and had to endure my brother's wrath today and the rest of my family's wrath tomorrow, simply because of you?"

"Ha!" Rosaleen said. "For that you should thank me, not count it against me. Your poor family! After the way you treated them I'd not be surprised if they took one look at you on the morrow and slammed their doors. And as for poor Hugo, why, abandoning him like that is the worst thing I have ever—"

"Rosaleen," Hugh murmured, "be quiet and kiss me."

His words surprised her, so that she stopped talking and gaped at him.

"K-kiss you?"

"Mmm-hmm. Kiss me, sweeting. You wanted to comfort me earlier, and I feel much in need of it now, when you have been so unkind. Come and kiss me, Rosaleen. Make me feel better after the terrible day I've had."

Without waiting for her answer, he closed his eyes and lifted his face to her, and his hands moved in gentle circles on her hips, encouraging her forward.

"But I..."

"I'm waiting," Hugh said patiently.

Rosaleen stared down at his ready face and closed eyes and couldn't think of anything else to say or do. "Very well, then."

She put her hands on his cheeks, held his face still and lowered her head to place a short peck on his lips. It was over almost before it began, and then she slipped out of his arms.

She was already at the door by the time his eyes flew open.

"*That* was a kiss?" he demanded. The sound of disappointment was heavy in his voice.

"Well, I certainly don't call it a slap," she replied, opening the door.

Hugh took a second look at her, then grinned. "Why, Rosaleen, you've turned red. What a foolish little creature you are. Come back here and let me give you a proper kiss."

She shook her head firmly. "Good night, Hugh Caldwell."

"Good night, Rosaleen no-name," he said after she had shut the door.

God's mercy, he thought, she was an entertaining female. He'd never met her like before, and he certainly had a wealth of women to compare her to. But none were like Rosaleen, his beautiful little no-name. She was budding passion and rampant ignorance mixed with the strongest will, aside from his own, that he'd ever come across.

The smile on his face faded as he thought of what the morrow would bring. Alex and Lillis and his other brothers and sister. It was the day he had dreaded, next to today, more than anything in the past ten years. What was Alex going to say to him? And Lillis? Perhaps Rosaleen was right. Perhaps they would take one look at him and slam the door in his face. He had envisioned such as that plenty of times before, and if they did do so he would never be able to blame them for it.

But at least, he thought, he had Rosaleen. Rosaleen would stand with him if his family refused him. She wouldn't desert him.

The realization came as a surprise, and he wondered at it. It had been an unconscious thought, yet it was true all the same. He had known Rosaleen for all of three days, yet he knew without a doubt that she would stand by him. He knew it as surely as he knew his own name, and it was something that, being the gambler he was, he would bet his entire fortune on.

Chapter Six

Rosaleen found the brothers together in the gardens early the next morning, talking and laughing as though angry words had never passed between them. Hugh was demonstrating Amazon's abilities, showing her off, and Hugo was appropriately impressed. Rosaleen watched with interest as Hugo tied Hugh's leather strap on his own wrist and proceeded to handle the bird with the same skill his brother did, and it occurred to her that the monk had missed his calling in life; he should have set aside holy orders and become a falconer. He would have made a fortune.

"Good morning, Father Hugo, Hugh," she greeted politely as she approached.

Both brothers turned and each graced her with an identical, somewhat overappreciative grin. Rosaleen was used to such open expressions from Hugh Caldwell, but it was rather unsettling to have a monk eyeing her with admiration.

"You're a beautiful sight this morn, Rosaleen," Hugh greeted. "You look as pretty as your namesake."

"Why, Hugh Caldwell, I do believe your manners are improving," Rosaleen remarked, lifting her skirt gracefully from the damp ground in what she knew was a pretty, feminine gesture. "Your brother's excellent behavior is having a good effect on you."

"Either that or his behavior is having a bad effect on me," Hugo jested, possessing Rosaleen's hand and kissing it. "You are lovely enough to tempt an abbot, Lady Rosaleen. I'm sorry that you must leave us today."

"Uh-uh-uh, Hugo," Hugh chided, pulling Rosaleen's hand from his brother's grasp and placing it on his own arm, where he kept it imprisoned. "None of that now, or I'll go calling for Father Bartholomew. You're married to the Church, if you'll remember."

"I remember perfectly well," Hugo replied easily. "And I may be a monk, but I'm not dead." He winked at Rosaleen and repossessed her hand with some difficulty. "Go and ready your horses, Hugh, while I entertain Lady Rosaleen. Come and stroll through the gardens with me, my lady. I'm sure you will enjoy them greatly."

"But I don't want to go get the horses ready," Hugh said, frowning as his brother led Rosaleen away. "Rosaleen? Would you not prefer that I show you the gardens? I know them as well as he does. I used to break in and steal fruit from the trees when I was a boy."

Except for Hugo waving one hand at him, as though telling him to stop bothering them, they ignored him.

"Well, if you need me, I'll just be getting the horses ready," he called after their retreating figures. He looked at Amazon, who sat patiently on his wrist. "Hugo's just being nice to her," he told the creature. "Isn't he, my darling?" He kissed the bird's beak. "And besides, she's naught but a troublesome female. You're the only lady I care about," he cooed to the listening bird. "She may be beautiful, but she's a damned nuisance. A damned, stiff-necked nuisance. And I'll be glad to get rid of her, won't I?" Making loving, clucking sounds at the bird, he made his way to the garden gate. "Then you and I will be able to get on with our lives," he said, placing his hand on the gate latch, "and we'll be as happy as we ever were. Just you and I, my beloved sweet."

He cast one last glance at his brother and Rosaleen, happily strolling among the rosebushes now. Hugo said something to make Rosaleen laugh, and she tilted her lovely face up to grace him with a smile so beautiful it made Hugh's heart lurch. Angrily, he threw the gate open, strode out into the courtyard and slammed the gate shut. He hoped sincerely that Hugo and Rosaleen heard it.

"God's mercy! The brothers will be needing a new gate if Hugh keeps that up," Rosaleen said, turning to gaze at the place where the gate was still quivering from Hugh's force. She looked back at Hugo. "He's uneasy to face the rest of his family today," she told him. "It is understandable, certainly."

Hugo chuckled and patted her hand. "You've no need to excuse Hugh to me, my dear. I have known him these many years, after all."

"Well, certainly you have," she said, fully embarrassed. "And I wasn't making excuses for him. Why, I should have to be crazed to make excuses for such a— a—" she faltered, glancing at Hugo, who was watching her with interest "—person," she finished, blushing.

Hugo grinned at her. "Rosaleen, you are a sweet delight. You mustn't hide your feelings for Hugh on my behalf. I understand him very well, and I can only admire your patience in dealing with him. There is only one other person I've known who has been able to bear him so well, and that person is myself, though you may think that untrue after what happened yesterday. But that is behind us now. I made my peace with God last eve, after I left you, and have asked my brother's forgiveness this morn." The smile on his face was so brilliant that Rosaleen thought he looked angelic. "Now, after all these years, I am finally at peace." He patted her hand again. "And I must thank you especially, Lady Rosaleen, for you have brought my brother home again and have been the instrument of God's peace. It would be difficult for me to tell you just how grateful I am."

"Oh," Rosaleen returned guiltily. "I wish you would not feel grateful to me, Father, for my relationship with your brother is not as you must think."

Hugo laughed. "You could probably never guess what it is that I imagine about your relationship with Hugh, my dear, but that is of no matter. We've little time, for my brother will soon be finished with your horses. I wish to speak to you, if I may, of what drove Hugh from our home ten years ago." He looked at her. "Should you like to hear it?"

"Indeed I should, Father, but I cannot think Hugh would want you to tell me. He seemed quite angry about the idea last eve."

"Yes, he did, didn't he?" Hugo agreed happily. "I'll not tell you the whole of it, then, only that which you'll need to know in order to understand him better."

"I hardly think it's necessary for me to be able to do *that,* Father. I'll not even be seeing the scoundrel again after today."

Hugo shrugged. "One never knows what might befall, and it's always best to be prepared, is it not?"

"Well, if *you* think it might be best, then of course I would be willing to listen. We must speak of *something,* and it might as well be your brother as anything else."

She was trying so hard to hide her obvious interest that it made Hugo laugh again. "Your long-suffering is admirable, Rosaleen, and I promise to make the tale as short as possible.

"In truth, there's not all that much to tell. You already know that Alexander of Gyer is our eldest brother. We always assumed, of course, that we were true Baldwins, like the rest of our siblings, and it was something of which we were very, very proud. Perhaps we could even have been said to be vain about it, and about being the sons of Sir Charles Baldwin.

"He was more than simply mortal to us, our father. Hugh and I worshiped him, and he, in turn, spoiled us terribly." He shook his head.

"I do not know why he did such a thing," Hugh said with a bitter smile. "I have thought and thought on the matter these past ten years and have never been able to reason it out. He treated us with such clear favor that, looking back, it seems like a madness. With Alex he was only ever in conflict, and Willem, our next eldest brother, he treated as a despised weakling. Our youngest brother, Justin, he simply tolerated, and Candis, our little sister, he ignored, blaming her for our mother's death, though the good Lord knows she hadn't a thing to do with it. But Hugh and me—Hugh and me he treated like little princes." He closed his eyes, squeezed them shut, as if he couldn't bear to see anything around him. "When I think of how we loved him and thought that he was everything that we ourselves ever wanted to be, it seems so foolish. So very, very foolish."

The pain in his voice made Rosaleen's heart ache, and she placed a gentle hand on his arm.

"Young boys are often foolish over their fathers," she murmured.

Hugo opened his eyes and looked at her with an expression that matched his voice.

"He died when we were but ten years of age, and what we felt at the loss of him . . . the agony . . . it was as nothing I could ever have imagined. We thought, in our childish ignorance, that he would live forever. His death only served to increase our godlike image of him, until we began to think of him as one of the saints of the Church." His expression grew chagrined. "We even used to pray to him, Hugh and I. Is that not foolish?"

Rosaleen shook her head. "No. You were ten years of age, Hugo Baldwin. You were a little boy who loved his father and who missed him when he was gone. It is understandable. It is to be expected."

"I suppose it is, though at times the memory fills me with shame." He drew in a breath and exhaled it slowly. "When we were ten and six years of age we discovered that Charles Baldwin had not been our father at all. We found out, to our great horror, that Jaward of Wellewyn, the man who had been Gyer's greatest enemy, was our natural father."

"What!" Rosaleen said at once, her voice filled with disbelief. "But how could that be? Your mother . . . ?"

"It was no simple case of adultery between our mother and Jaward of Wellewyn," he answered. "Charles Baldwin, the man we had worshiped so greatly, was the cause of it. He cruelly raped Jaward's wife, then made her shame widely known, causing the poor woman to take her own life. My mother and Jaward of Wellewyn, understandably distraught, searched for comfort in one another's arms. Hugh and I are the outcome of that search."

"Oh, Hugo! You must have been desolated!"

"Yes," he agreed softly. "It hurt badly. And it was much to accept all in one blow. It was my sister Lillis and my brother Alex who told us. You remember that we spoke of Lillis last eve? Of how we kidnapped her and brought her to Gyer?''

"Yes, of course. You did call her your sister last night, though I thought you meant sister-in-law. Why, how strange! Your brother and sister are married to one another. It almost seems like incest, does it not?''

"It does, but I assure you it's not. There is no blood relation between them. Alex is our half brother through our mother, while Lillis is our half sister through Jaward of Wellewyn. They were already married to one another when the truth was discovered, so I daresay it was just as great a blow for them as it was for us.''

"I can certainly imagine it was," Rosaleen agreed, "but for you and Hugh it must have been much more so.''

"Hugh and I were badly shaken for several days after Lillis and Alex told us the truth," he said. "We couldn't speak of it, not even to one another. It was too painful . . . too difficult for us to accept. The hardest part, for Hugh, especially, was that we suddenly found ourselves bastards, with no real name to call ourselves. What a bitter end to our pride that was! We who had lauded ourselves for being Baldwins, the nobly born sons of a nobleman, no longer legitimate. We were the bastard sons of Jaward Ryon, Lord of Wellewyn, a man we had been taught to hate from our cradle, a man whom Charles Baldwin had raised us to despise above any other being.''

"That's why Hugh goes by the name of Caldwell," Rosaleen murmured with sudden understanding, "and why he hates the nobility so.''

"Yes, that's why. Caldwell was our mother's maiden name, the only name he felt he had any claim to. Alex assured us that we were still his brothers and still Baldwins. He begged us to forget the circumstances of our birth and to accept our places in the family as we always had. In his mind nothing had changed, and I could see that and believe it and even came to accept it in time. I had never even met Jaward of Wellewyn, while Charles Baldwin, for all his faults, had loved me as truly as any father could. But Hugh couldn't accept that. He was obsessed with the fact that he had no blood claim to the Baldwin name, that in truth he was a Ryon and the descendant of a family he despised. I will tell you truly, my lady—'' Hugo gazed into Rosaleen's rapt face "—this thing tormented him, in the truest sense of what that word means.''

"And so he ran away,'' Rosaleen said, "rather than live with the pain. He ran away from his family and from you. And he has been running ever since.''

"Yes.'' He took hold of both her hands. "You can understand why I wanted you to know these things. Hugh is going home at last, and he must face the things that have haunted him. It is bound to be painful for him. If I could be with him I would, yet I cannot leave the monastery without permission. But you will be with him, Rosaleen, and you must stand by him and help him. If it had not been for you, he would never have come home at all. Surely you accept that?''

"Yes, certainly,'' Rosaleen said, adding sorrowfully, "I only wished to go to London, you know. I never planned that he should suffer so much because of me.''

"I wasn't trying to make you feel guilty, my dear,'' Hugo said kindly. "You've done a good and wonderful thing in bringing Hugh back to those who love and have worried over him. But if you will not stand beside him, he will have no one else. Please, will you help him?''

"I will,'' she vowed solemnly. "I promise you.''

A light sigh passed Hugo's lips. "Thank you, my lady. I am most grateful. Being a twin is a difficult burden, but today I shall feel easier knowing you'll be with Hugh.

Now, before he returns to lay claim to you, let us speak of your spiritual needs. Have you made your confessions recently, Rosaleen?''

"Uh, confessions?" Rosaleen repeated dumbly.

"Yes, my dear. Confessions. Have you sought absolution of late?"

She coughed uncomfortably, as though clearing her throat. "Not . . . not lately, Father," she admitted, thinking that Hugh's brother was the last person to whom she wanted to make a confession of any kind.

"Ah, wonderful!" Hugo declared with unfeigned glee, grasping her hand and dragging her in the direction of the sanctuary. "You cannot imagine how I'm longing to hear them, my dear!"

Chapter Seven

It hadn't really changed. Not much, anyway. On the other hand, nothing seemed truly familiar, either. Standing in the courtyard of Castle Gyer and staring up at the massive front doors to the great hall, Hugh felt as though he were walking through some kind of dream, as though everything surrounding him might at any moment waver and dissolve.

Only one thing anchored him to reality at present, and that was Rosaleen. She seemed more nervous and tense than he, and she was holding one of his hands, squeezing and patting it by turns. Whenever he began to feel overwhelmed by where he was and what lay before him, he would glance at Rosaleen and feel, of all things to feel at such a time, rather amused at the fierce expression on her face. She looked as if she were preparing for battle, as if she would protect him from whatever evils might come spewing forth from the doors that she was fairly close to glaring at with those beautiful eyes of hers.

Of course, Hugh told himself, he neither needed nor wanted her to mother or protect him. He hated being mothered and protected by well-meaning females. Hated it. Despised it. And he was only letting her get away with it because of the strangeness of the circumstances. Later, when Alex and Lillis had either welcomed them in or sent them on their way, he would make it clear to Rosaleen that she wasn't to behave in such a manner with him ever again. Anyway, he couldn't tell her to quit it now because he wasn't able to make his voice work, a fact that worried him somewhat, along with the trembling he appeared to have no control over, and which he desperately hoped Rosaleen wasn't feeling. That and the sweating, though how she could avoid knowing that he was sweating like fresh cheese left out in the sun when she was holding his hand the way she was seemed impossible to him.

"He's *not* Uncle Hugo."

Hugh's spine straightened, and Rosaleen stopped patting his hand midair.

"He *looks* like Uncle Hugo."

"But he's *not* Uncle Hugo."

Two tall, lanky boys walked from behind Rosaleen and Hugh to stand in front of them. They were dark-haired and possessed of stunning light blue eyes. They were somewhere around nine or ten years of age. They were twins.

"But he *looks* like Uncle Hugo," one of the boys repeated, gazing into Hugh's face without the least bit of wariness.

"But he's *not* Uncle Hugo," the other boy insisted. "Are you, sir?"

Hugh tried to speak, to say that, no, he was not their Uncle Hugo, he was their Uncle Hugh, but his voice still wouldn't work.

He shook his head instead.

Alexander Baldwin, the Lord of Gyer, was hard at work in his private chamber when he heard the commotion in the great hall. He had only just lifted his head from what he'd been reading when his youngest brother, Justin, walked into the room.

"You'd best come, Alex," Justin advised in the terse, serious manner that had defined him for all of his nineteen years.

Without a word Alexander got up and followed Justin out of the room and into the great hall, where he was greeted by the sight of his castlefolk crowding the many long windows, peering into the courtyard as though some great spectacle were taking place there.

"Make way for your lord," Justin demanded as he parted the crowd by the nearest window. "Make way, I said!"

Alexander pressed his way to the front and looked out.

He was silent for several long moments and he felt, somewhere behind his eyes, a strange pressure that he'd not felt in many and many a year. He blinked several times against both the feeling and what he was seeing, and then he gave way to both.

"Dearest God," he whispered. "Oh, my great and gracious God."

"I'll fetch Lillis," Justin said, but Alexander didn't hear him. He was already on his way, running, to the front doors of Castle Gyer.

Rosaleen had finally come to his rescue.

"This is your Uncle Hugh," she was explaining to the boys, patting Hugh's hand again in a comforting manner. "Your Uncle Hugh," she repeated to their astonished faces. "You know of him, do you not? He is your Uncle Hugo's twin, just as the two of you are twins."

The boys looked to Hugh for confirmation of this fact, but he seemed to have turned into an idiot. He stood and stared at his nephews helplessly, wondering what had happened to him. These were his nephews, for mercy's sake! If he couldn't make himself speak to them, how would he manage it when Alex and Lillis came?

And then the doors to Castle Gyer were flung open, and he had his answer.

He wasn't going to be able to manage it at all.

In all the years that he'd been away from his family, Hugh had never considered that they might age. Always, in his thoughts, they had stayed the way they had been on the day he had left them. It was something of a surprise, then, to see Alex, and to see that he had aged. His eldest brother's face had matured; a few gray hairs were sprinkled through his thick, dark hair. And he looked...smaller. His great, strong, eldest brother looked so much smaller than Hugh remembered, and then he realized with even greater amazement that Alex only looked smaller because he, Hugh, had grown bigger.

"Hugh," Alex was saying over and over, staring at him in disbelief. "Hugh. Hugh."

And he kept saying it as he moved forward, and then he began to cry it as he crushed Hugh in his powerful arms, and finally, after wetting him with his tears, Alex laughed it, joyously, disbelievingly and with relief.

"You came home," he whispered, pulling back from Hugh and taking hold of his shoulders. His eyes moved hungrily over his younger brother's face. "You came home, Hugh."

Hugh still couldn't speak. All he could do was stand there and stare into Alex's beloved face and nod.

Alex lifted one hand and gently touched Hugh's cheek. His fingers came back wet, which surprised Hugh so much that he lifted his own hand to touch his face and realized that he, too, was crying.

"Why, I'm crying like a babe," he announced with some awe, finding his voice at last. He thought to himself, belatedly, that the first words he'd said to his eldest brother after ten years' absence had been incredibly foolish.

Alexander laughed and hugged him again, long and tight, before loosing him. "We're both crying like babes," he said. "You have unmanned me in front of my people, Hugh, but I swear by all that is holy that seeing you again makes it well." He shook his head and laughed once more, victoriously this time. "You've come *home!* Hugh!"

Hugh laughed in return, and the brothers grinned at each other happily until Alexander finally noticed the young lady standing beside them. Hugh was holding one of her hands in a grip so tight that the poor girl looked as though she were about to go down on her knees.

"God's mercy, Hugh! Who is this lovely creature whose fingers you're crushing?" His face lit with a sudden thought and he said, before Hugh could answer, "Why, you've brought home a wife!"

"What!" Hugh released Rosaleen quickly. "No, Alex, this isn't my wife. This is—"

A great, joyful shriek rent the air, and then a blurred vision of white and crimson went flying past Rosaleen and leapt upon Hugh, nearly knocking him down.

"Lillis!" Hugh cried, hugging the creature who had attacked him. Holding her tight, he spun her around in a circle, causing her unbound white hair to flutter like some kind of silken banner.

Rubbing at the hand he'd nearly wrung off her wrist, Rosaleen watched Hugh with an odd mixture of relief and jealousy. His family was glad to have him home, so glad that the knowledge of it nearly brought her to tears. She was happy for him, truly. At the same time, however, she couldn't help but feel left out.

"God's feet," one of the twins muttered in a clearly unhappy voice, "I've never seen Mother or Father behave in such a way."

His brother shook his head with equal amazement. "It's not fitting," he declared.

"But they've not seen your Uncle Hugh in many years," Rosaleen explained in an effort to soothe them. "They're only welcoming him home, you see. It's perfectly fitting. Just imagine if you'd not been home in ten years' time. Your parents would be filled with joy to see you again, too."

"But we don't even know him!" the one nearest her argued.

The corners of Rosaleen's lips tilted into a smile. "From this day forward, however, you shall."

Hugh finally set his sister down, allowing his eldest brother to get their attention.

"And look what Hugh's brought home, my love," he said to his wife, turning her in Rosaleen's direction.

It was the first chance Rosaleen had to actually see the blur that had rushed by her moments before, and when her eyes finally rested upon the lady Lillis Baldwin, she drew her breath in.

The woman was stunning; white-haired and regal and beautiful as a queen. Rosaleen knew herself to be of good bearing, but this tall, lovely woman made her feel like a dwarf, and a plain one at that.

Lady Lillis's crystal blue eyes lit with fire as they took in Rosaleen, and then an ecstatic smile bloomed on her lips.

"Hugh!" she cried, moving toward Rosaleen with outstretched arms. "You've brought home a wife! Oh, my dear, welcome to Gyer!" She embraced Rosaleen warmly, and when she drew back, Rosaleen gazed up into the lady's happy, tear-streaked face, which was gazing with great joy down at her own shocked one.

"But I'm not..."

"Lillis," Hugh said firmly, moving between them and setting a hand lightly about Rosaleen's waist, "this is *not* my wife!" He laughed. "By the rood! I come home after ten years and you want to fetter me at once with a wife!" He drew Rosaleen forward. "This," he announced with what sounded amazingly to Rosaleen like pride, "is Rosaleen. And, in truth, you have her to thank for my coming home at all. Rosaleen is a damsel in need, and I have brought her to Alex for rescuing. She must needs get to London, and I thought he'd be the best one to get her there. I regret that I cannot tell you the rest of her name, for she has refused to give it to me. In spite of that, I affirm that she is an honorable lady."

Rosaleen politely offered the Lord and Lady of Gyer a slight bow and an unsure smile, and she watched, uncomfortably, as everyone present, save Hugh, gaped at her.

"Did you say *Rosaleen?*" Lillis asked in a shocked tone. "But, Hugh..."

"Welcome to our home, my lady," her husband said quickly. "We are more than pleased to have you with us."

"But, Alexander!" Lillis protested. "Her name is Rosaleen, and—" The words stopped when one of Alexander's muscular arms clamped tight about her waist.

"I beg you will pardon my wife," Alexander said with his most charming smile. "She has a cousin named Rosaleen, and I imagine the resemblance between the two of you has stunned her." Ignoring his wife's indignant look, he went on. "There is no question that I shall do all in my power to see you safely to London, my lady. It's the least I can do after you have brought my wandering brother home to Gyer. Indeed, I fear I shall never be able to fully repay you for this good deed but shall forever be, most gratefully, in your debt."

"I must say, Alex," Hugh said with a grin, "I much prefer your welcome to Hugo's."

Alexander laughed. "I wondered who'd given you those bruises on your face. I can well imagine how Hugo greeted you when he saw you."

"Oh, Hugh!" Lillis said unhappily. "You should have sent him some warning so that he could have prepared himself. These last few years have been very hard on him."

"So he told me," Hugh admitted grimly, rubbing his sore chin. "Most convincingly."

"Let's not speak of that," Alexander said. "You're home now. That's all that matters. I don't care what the past ten years have been like as long as you are here again, safe and whole. Come and meet my eldest sons, Hugh. You've yet to meet any of your nieces and nephews."

Alexander proudly drew his sons forward.

"Jaward, Charles, this is your Uncle Hugh. Hugh, this is Jaward, the eldest by five minutes, and this is Charles. They're as identical as you and Hugo are, so don't feel badly if you cannot tell them apart right away."

With his arm still about her, Rosaleen felt the fine tremor that shivered through Hugh as he faced his nephews.

"Hello," he greeted tentatively as first one, then the other of the twins, clasped his arm.

"Are you the one who won't be knighted?" Jaward, on the left, asked boldly.

"Jaward!" Alexander gave his son a stern look. "Mind your tongue! I'm sorry Hugh, but the boys have had their heads filled with tales of your adventures by the knights and soldiers who have sojourned here in the past many years. Every one of them seems to have heard of or known of you, and thus we've been entertained with accounts of your feats."

"We've not!" the twin on the right countered, crossing his arms over his thin chest. "It's Hugh Caldwell we've heard tell of, not Hugh Baldwin!"

"Charles!" Lillis gasped furiously. "Your Uncle Hugh is one and the same, and I'll not have you speak so rudely!"

Lillis's sons looked immediately contrite, and Hugh felt just as guilty for his own unfriendly behavior, but before any of them could apologize they were interrupted.

"My dearest, you mustn't be so hard on the boys! They're just babies still and don't know any better!"

Hugh knew who it was before he even set eyes on her.

"Edyth!" he said, looking past Lillis and Alexander to where his former teacher was bringing his remaining nieces and nephew out of Castle Gyer.

"Edyth!" he repeated as he strode to that small lady, picked her up off the ground and kissed her soundly. "How I have missed you!"

"Put me down, you foolish boy!" the elderly woman chided. Hugh did as she asked and Edyth looked up at him, touching his face and shoulders and chest with her hands. "Let me look at you, my dearest. Let me look at you. Why, you've become a man, Hugh Baldwin. A man full-grown, when I have always thought of you as a boy." Her smile widened. "Now, tell me that this old woman's face isn't that of a stranger to you."

He kissed her once on each of her cheeks. "You are as lovely and wonderful as when I last set eyes on you, my dearest Edyth! There is only one other lady whom I love as I love you, other than my beloved sister," he said, gracing Lillis with an affectionate grin, "and that is my Aunt Leta, who is now a married lady far gone from Gyer, or so I have heard tell. But, by God's own mercy, I am glad to see you again, Edyth of Lielyn!'' He hugged her against him, hard, until she laughed and pushed at him.

"Cease this foolishness, Hugh Baldwin! Come and let me show you your nieces and nephew." Turning toward the children, she led him first to an exquisitely beautiful little girl around eight years of age, whose white blond hair and clear blue eyes mirrored those of her mother.

"This is Eleanor," Edyth said, gently patting the child's head. "And this is Elizabeth." She indicated the five-year-old who stood next to her sister, another lovely child possessed of her father's darker looks. "And this," Edyth said, moving to the small boy who stood sucking on his two middle fingers and looking anxiously toward his parents, "is Rorian, whom we call Rory."

Hugh bent to the children's level. "Hello, Rory, and—" aware that the girl had been named after his own mother "—little Beth, and—" he picked the beautiful child up in his arms "—beautiful Eleanor." He kissed the child's cheek and showed her to an approving Rosaleen. "What do you think of my nieces and nephews?"

Amused at how quickly Hugh Caldwell latched onto his family after his long absence and deep fears, Rosaleen smiled. "They're lovely." She nodded at her hosts, who gazed pridefully at their offspring. "You have a fine family, Lord and Lady Gyer."

"But where are Willem and Justin and Candis?" Hugh asked, turning around in a circle as though he expected his other two brothers and sister to appear all of a sudden. "Never tell me they're away from Gyer!"

"I'm afraid that Willem and Candis are gone to London," Alexander admitted, "where our little sister is presently enchanting every man between the ages of twelve and eighty-five at court, or so I'm given to understand. But

Justin, or rather, I should say, *Sir* Justin, as he was knighted only three months past, is just inside and waiting for you to make a stately entrance for the benefit of those who are gaping out the windows at us.''

"Sir Justin, eh?" Hugh said, shaking his head. "Well, I'll be glad to see him in spite of that." He stopped speaking long enough to lift up his youngest niece, who was tugging at his chausses, until he held her secure in his other arm. With both nieces held high, he beamed with family pride. "Justin will be a grown man now. Is he as serious as when he was a boy?"

"More so!" Alexander assured him with a laugh, picking up his youngest son, who had toddled over to his Uncle Hugh in an attempt to be taken up with his sisters. "Now come inside and be made welcome, Hugh, Lady Rosaleen, before my people expire of curiosity."

"Yes, please come inside and be welcome," Lillis echoed, placing a light hand on Rosaleen's arm. "You must be weary from your journey, my lady, and in want of a warm bath and something clean to wear."

The thought of a bath...a warm, scented, delicious bath such as only a household the size of Castle Gyer could provide...was so welcome it nearly brought Rosaleen to tears. She had been used to bathing daily in her own home.

"Yes, my Lady Gyer," she said, "I should indeed like a bath. It has been several days, I fear, since I last enjoyed one."

Lillis smiled at her warmly.

"Then you shall have one without delay, and I shall send you something clean to wear from my sister Candis's wardrobe. She has not your height, but I'm certain I can find something to fit, and she has left behind some lovely clothes."

"I am grateful to you, Lady Gyer," Rosaleen said, and allowed herself to be led into the great hall of Castle Gyer.

They knew who she was, of course, Rosaleen thought later as she blissfully sank farther into the large wooden tub, sloshing a little of the hot, scented water over the side and onto the towels that had been placed on the floor.

The chamber Lady Gyer had given her was lavishly beautiful, putting Rosaleen in mind of one of the chambers of state that she herself kept ready at Siere for the use of the king and any high-ranking nobility who might arrive without notice. She had become suspicious that the Lord and Lady of Gyer knew who she was when she had seen their reactions upon hearing her name, and the fact that she had been put in this grand chamber was more than proof that her suspicions were correct. Although Alexander Baldwin was possessed of greater wealth than she, Rosaleen's birth gave her an eminence far above the Lord of Gyer's; to be given a chamber such as this was in perfect accord with her due as the daughter of the Earl of Siere, and as the heir of her family's great name and title.

But if they knew the truth, Rosaleen wondered, then why had the Lord of Gyer not allowed his wife to speak it to Hugh? She knew full well that she was considered more as a valuable property than as a person. Alexander of Gyer, being a member of the nobility and having sworn fealty to King Henry, would surely feel it his sovereign duty to return her to her uncle, who was her royally approved guardian.

Why, then, had he not allowed the truth to be revealed? Perhaps he had wanted to avoid an unpleasant disturbance before his people. Perhaps later, when there was more privacy, he would inform Rosaleen that he knew who she was and that he would be returning her to Siere. Or

perhaps, even worse, he had already sent a message to her
uncle informing him of her whereabouts. Whatever the
Lord of Gyer's game was, Rosaleen knew she couldn't
trust him. He and his wife were being very kind to her, and
she was truly grateful, but in spite of that she couldn't remain at Gyer and wait like a lamb about to be led to
slaughter. She had to get to London, and she had to see the
king before her uncle got to him first and poisoned her
chances with his foul lies.

Knowing it to be fully selfish, Rosaleen yet wished that
Hugh Caldwell hadn't turned out to be Hugh Baldwin. It
wasn't that she was not happy for him; indeed, she was
exceedingly pleased that he had been so well reconciled
with his family and that she, though unwittingly, had
played some small part in bringing that reconciliation
about. But, in truth, his turning out to be a member of the
nobility was a plaguing nuisance! How would she get to
London without a man like Hugh Caldwell to protect and
help her?

Pillowing her head more comfortably on the towel set on
the edge of the tub, Rosaleen fixed her gaze on the ceiling
and, with a loud sigh, began to think of what she must do.

Chapter Eight

"She's been beaten!" Lillis declared as she walked into her husband's working chamber, where Alexander and her brother sat talking. "That poor child's been beaten black and blue! The maids who were helping me ready her bath nearly took to screaming when they saw her bruises, and I almost became ill." She rounded on Hugh, demanding, "Who did such a thing?"

"It wasn't me." Hugh promised. "Don't look at me in such a way, I beg you. It was her uncle who did it, because she refused to wed the man he'd chosen for her. That's what set her on the run in the first place." He held his hands up as if proclaiming his innocence. "I'm simply the man she ran into. That's all, I swear it."

"Of course I didn't think you had done it, Hugh," Lillis assured him, unable to calm her anger. "But the man who did do it ought to have a whip taken to him!"

Her husband laughed. "And I imagine you'd like to be the one to wield it, would you not, my fierce wife? Calm yourself, sweeting, and come sit down. You look as though you're about to throw something for the simple joy of it."

Lillis plopped into the chair beside her brother. "You find it amusing, my lord, but if you'd seen the poor girl just now you'd be on your way to hunt the animal down,

I vow. I'm proud of you, Hugh, for helping Rosaleen as you have." She patted her brother's knee. "It was right and chivalrous."

Hugh cringed. "Please, Lillis, don't speak that word in my hearing, especially if you must attach it to my name. Besides, if you ask Rosaleen, she'll tell you a great many other words that would be more fitting. She never lacks terrible things to call me. I do believe that's what I'll miss the most about her."

His eldest brother fixed him with an interested gaze. "Miss her, Hugh? I had thought your relationship with Lady Rosaleen to be of a more permanent nature, and I expected you to tell Lillis and me of a possible future commitment."

"God's teeth, Alex!" Hugh uttered, horrified. "Tell me you jest! Rosaleen no-name is the most troublesome female I've ever known. I'd rather shackle myself with a she-bear."

"But, Hugh," Lillis protested, "she's quite sweet, and her manners are excellent. And you cannot deny that she's very beautiful."

"Well, there is that," he admitted. "She's a good-looking female. Did you see the look on Justin's face when they were introduced? I thought he was going to go down on one knee right there in the great hall and make a fool of himself."

Lillis giggled. "He was stricken, was he not? But, in truth, he has been looking for a wife. He determined only two months past that he will wed before he attains the age of five and twenty, and you know how seriously he takes such things. I fear he's approached the matter of marriage much as he would any other problem."

Hugh grimaced. "I can well imagine. Good lack! The boy has the personality of a rock. Why don't you send him to court, Alex? Or out into the world? Or anywhere other than Gyer. He needs a little adventure to liven him up."

Alexander sighed. "Like you did? From what we've heard about you over the past many years, Hugh, it seems that your life has been one adventure after another. You've been lucky not to end up in prison, or worse, have you not?"

Hugh felt an uncomfortable clutch of guilt.

"Yes. I've been lucky."

Lucky. The word throbbed in the ensuing silence like the resounding of a bell. He supposed he had been lucky. The past ten years of his life were one great blur to Hugh, a blur defined only by fleeting memories of fights and scrapes and near escapes. He had killed men, and gone hungry, and stolen, and fought both man and the elements in order to survive. He had made love with what now seemed like hundreds of women. He had made friends and lost friends. He had come to know everything there was about the basest elements of humanity, and he himself had embraced some of those lowly attributes in his struggle to survive. He had learned how to lie and cheat, how to take advantage of the trust of decent people, how to strike out and hurt before he could be struck and hurt first. But he had also learned about goodness, about the limitless boundaries of human kindness. He had known and experienced that goodness and kindness, and he had clung to them in his own effort to remain human. Thinking back on his life now, he felt ashamed to be in the company of his brother and sister, whom he loved too much to hurt with the truth of his own wretched behavior.

"Listen to me, Hugh," Alexander said. "Lillis and I will not ask for an accounting from you for the last ten years. Neither of us wants to hear of it. When you left you hurt us badly, I'll not deny that or excuse you for it. We all suffered for months afterward and worried constantly. I looked for you myself for many weeks, and kept half my army searching for you for longer than that. If I had found you then, I would have beaten you senseless for what you had done."

Hugh dropped his gaze, unable to meet his brother's eyes.

"I had to go," he whispered.

"I don't want to hear it, Hugh," Alexander said curtly. "I don't ever want to hear that from you. You didn't have to go, no matter what you thought then or think now. What we learned about Jaward and our father hurt all of us, not just you. Or did you think you were the only one who could feel pain? And if you didn't care what your leaving would do to the rest of us, the least you could have done was think of Hugo. Do you have any idea how he reacted that morn when he read your note?" Alexander's voice grew as grim as his expression. "He cried like a baby. For hours, while I held him." His eyes shut at the memory. "For months afterward, he wouldn't even step outside of Castle Gyer, not even to attend mass."

He wasn't going to cry, Hugh told himself very sternly. He was *not* going to cry. Except for the understandable lapse of that very afternoon, he hadn't cried since the day he'd learned the truth about himself, and he wasn't about to start now, no matter what Alex said, no matter what anyone said. He hadn't lost himself for so many years for naught.

He rose from the chair he'd been sitting in and walked to the windows that looked out over the gardens of the inner bailey. Several deep breaths helped to calm him, and he trained his eyes on the beauty of the gardens below.

"I'm sorry," he said. "I never meant to hurt Hugo or any of you. But I had to go. There was no choice for me,

Alex, no matter what you may think. You have said you don't wish to hear that, and, in truth, I haven't any desire to explain it to you."

"Hugh." A hand touched his sleeve, making Hugh wonder how Lillis had come up behind him so quietly. "It matters not. Truly. You are home. That's what Alexander and I care about. Do not count these angry words against him. You cannot blame us for what we feel, just as we cannot blame you. Please, Hugh, we must put the past behind us and start anew."

"I am *not* home," Hugh replied bitterly, shrugging at her hand to make her let go. "Gyer is not my home, now or ever. I'm only here because of that troublesome female above stairs. Now that Alex has promised to lend her aid, I'll be leaving. Tomorrow morn, in fact."

A brief silence followed his words, and then Lillis began to weep. Suddenly, loudly and uncontrollably. Both men moved toward her, but Hugh, being so close, caught her up in his arms before Alexander could take more than a step.

"Lillis! Don't cry," he begged, clutching her tight. "Don't cry."

She shook her head against his shoulder.

"It's my fault!" she sobbed. "All my fault! Aunt Leta tried to warn me what the truth would do to you, but I wouldn't listen! I believed you would want to know, but I was wrong, Hugh, so very wrong!"

Hugh didn't know what to say, because he did wish that he'd never learned the truth. He wished, as he'd wished a hundred times or more in the past ten years, that he had gone on in blissful ignorance, that he had never known who his real father was.

"It's all right, Lillis," he soothed. "You have said it no longer matters, and it doesn't. It's done."

"But still you would leave!" she cried miserably. "Stay with us, Hugh. Please stay at Gyer. This *is* your home!"

They would never understand, Hugh thought sadly. Gyer and Wellewyn were the wells of all his bitterness; he could never stay at either of them for long.

Helplessly, he glanced at his brother, only to be met by a furious expression that at once took him back to his boyhood, when he and Hugo had commonly managed to outrage Alex to just this kind of countenance. And he remembered, somewhat belatedly, that where Lillis was concerned Alex was rather sensitive. More than sensitive, actually. When Lillis was involved, Alex was easily brought to the point of mercilessness.

Remembering that, Hugh gulped, and hugged Lillis a little tighter for protection.

"Say you'll stay at Gyer," she begged. "Please say you'll stay, Hugh."

"I can't," he answered honestly. "Oh, Lillis, I can't. Please don't cry anymore. You break me in two! I cannot stay at Gyer." He chanced another glance at Alex, who was still glaring at him angrily.

He didn't have any choice. He had to take the easy way out, just to spare Lillis's and Alex's feelings.

"I can't stay because I've been given another fief to take care of," he said, and then went on to tell his brother and sister all about Briarstone and how he had come to possess it.

Alexander's fury was renewed.

"There's no need for you to tend the land of strangers, Hugh. There are several Baldwin fiefs that need caring for."

Stroking Lillis's white blond hair, holding her lovingly in his arms, Hugh replied, "Then you'd best send a Baldwin to manage them, Alex. Willem or Justin or even Candis should do very well."

The sound that came from his eldest brother was indescribable. It sent shivers down Hugh's spine.

"You," Alexander said tightly, "are a Baldwin." His expression dared Hugh to contradict him.

Gazing at him, Hugh realized with a deep sadness that his eldest brother no longer had the power to frighten him into submission. Too much had passed, too much had riven Hugh Caldwell's heart to make him feel any fear easily.

"I have lived by my chosen name for ten years, Alexander Baldwin," he said slowly, purposefully, "and I shall live under it the rest of my days. The only name I have a right to call myself. Caldwell." He eased Lillis away and made her look at him. *"Caldwell,"* he repeated to her disbelieving eyes. "And if you'll not take me as a Caldwell, then I'll leave this moment. Tell me and let me go, for I promise that I shall."

"No!" Lillis cried, gripping him. "I'll not let you go as you went before! I don't care what name you call yourself by! You're my own brother, and I'll not let you go!"

Hugh looked at Alexander, whose angry expression hadn't eased even slightly.

"No matter what name you go by," Alexander said, "be it Caldwell or Ryon or Baldwin, you will always be a member of this family. My father was your father, Hugh, in spite of every other truth. Charles Baldwin accepted you as his own son."

Alexander's words stunned Hugh. That man's name, that name he had forced with violence from his own mind a thousand times over, stunned him. It was the one thing, the one thought that he could not bear. He put Lillis away from him.

"I am Hugh Caldwell," he repeated, then gathered his breath to say more firmly, "Caldwell."

His own steps toward the chamber door beat loudly in his head. When he reached it, feeling sick and angry, he said, "I will never understand how you could name those two innocent children the way you have. Charles and Jaward! It's like some cruel jest!" he raged with a fury that he directed toward the door, unable to face either Alexander or Lillis with his most naked feelings. "You must think that by doing so you heal the misery those two men caused on God's earth, but you're wrong! *Nothing* could do that. You've done naught but damned your sons with the memory of two evil devils!"

Cold and stiff, wanting a fight, Hugh left the room.

His feet turned in the direction that he wanted to go before his mind realized his destination, and very shortly, having run all the way up the multitude of stairs leading to it, he arrived at the door to the rooftop hut where he and his brother had kept their birds so many years before.

Breathless, he pushed the door open, his entrance so sudden that the two boys occupying the partly enclosed shelter jumped with surprise.

"What in the—" Hugh was just as shocked as they were. He had expected to find the small shed empty of everything after all these years, including the cages in which he and Hugo had housed their birds, yet the place was remarkably unchanged. Not only were the cages still there, they were filled with birds.

Looking at his nephews, their surprised, questioning faces turned toward him, one of them holding a young sparrow hawk while the other attached a pair of jesses to the bird, Hugh could almost look back and see himself and Hugo doing the same thing, in just the same way.

"Hello, Uncle Hugh," one of them greeted cautiously. "Did you come to see our birds?"

Embarrassed to have intruded in such a way, and still feeling uncomfortable with them, Hugh replied, awkwardly, "Yes, I . . . guess I have."

"Mother said you and Uncle Hugo used to raise birds," the twin applying the jesses commented. "Uncle Hugo sometimes comes and helps us with ours."

Hugh wiped his hands nervously on his chausses and stepped farther into the room. Here was something else that looked smaller to him all of a sudden. There had been a time when this place had seemed big as a barn, yet now the top of his head barely missed scraping the ceiling.

"Well, your Uncle Hugo," said Hugh as he moved about the hut, looking in the various cages, "is one of the finest falconers I've ever known. You couldn't do better than having his help."

"That's odd," the twin holding the bird said. "Uncle Hugo says the same of you. That you're very good with birds. He tells us lots of stories about the things you used to do when you were boys."

"Does he?" Hugh smiled at the thought. "All good stories, I hope, about how well behaved and obedient we were."

The twins laughed. "No, he's not told us any like that. The stories he tells us are the kind that Father says gave him all his gray hairs."

"Father says that if we ever try some of the things that you and Uncle Hugo did," one of the boys said, grinning, "he'll make us rue the day we were born."

Hugh laughed, and the boys, finished with the bird, presented it for their uncle's inspection.

"Let's see, now," he said thoughtfully. "You've done a fine job with her talons. They've been nicely trimmed. The jesses are correctly placed, and you've belled her properly. Are her eyes seeled beneath her hood?''

The boys nodded.

"Father's head falconer sewed them shut for us," one of the twins admitted. "We've not learned how to do that yet."

"'Tis well," Hugh said. "It's always best to let a skilled man do the job rather than attempt it yourself before you're ready. You'd not want to hurt her pretty eyes, would you? She'd be of no use to you then." Carefully, he took the bird to his own wrist and bounced her gently up and down. "She's unsteady yet, but that won't take long to change. You've done well, lads," he said approvingly. "All she needs now is her leash and a perch and she'll be ready for training. She looks to be a fine bird once she's done. You'll be wanting to house her in the mews now, of course."

Again the boys nodded, much impressed by their uncle's knowledge of birds.

"We were just going to take her now," one of them said. "Will you come with us, Uncle Hugh?"

Hugh smiled at his handsome nephews. "I'd be pleased, lads. And on our way we'll stop at my chamber and fetch my own bird, Amazon. Have you seen her?" Carrying the sparrow hawk aloft, he headed for the door. His nephews eagerly followed behind.

"Yes, sir, we did see her," the one to Hugh's left replied quickly. "She's a beauty. We were hoping for a chance to see her more closely."

"We can do better than that," Hugh told them. "How would you like to have a try at handling her? We can take her to the north fields, where there should be plenty of small game for Amazon to play with."

This suggestion met with such joyful affirmation that Hugh couldn't help but laugh, and he had to be careful not to trip down the stairs as the two boys rushed him along.

"I would that you had seen them," Hugh said later that afternoon as he walked in his brother's gardens with Rosaleen, recounting his day with the twins. "Hugo and I were never possessed of such vigor, I vow. Those lads make me feel so old!"

Strolling beside him, Rosaleen offered Hugh a smile.

"You're enjoying this time with your family, are you not, Hugh Caldwell? I'm glad for you."

"It is good to be home," he admitted. "Strange, but good. I always knew that one day I must face returning to Gyer, though if not for you, I suppose I would have put it off awhile longer."

"I'm glad I forced you to it, then," Rosaleen told him. "The longer you put it off, the harder it became. Now you are reconciled and can enjoy your family just as you should, and they can enjoy you, if such a thing is possible," she added teasingly.

Hugh chuckled. "If it is, it will have to be possible from a distance, for I still intend to go to Briarstone."

"Yes, so Lady Gyer informed me. We spoke at length this afternoon. Your brother and sister are most unhappy about you leaving again. Your sister, supposing that I wield some kind of influence over you, though I cannot imagine why she should think such a thing, asked me to do what I could to change your mind."

"Did she?" Hugh asked with surprise. "Dear Lillis. I don't suppose I'll ever be able to make her understand why I can't stay at Gyer."

"You certainly won't," Rosaleen agreed, "for it is foolish and selfish beyond all measure. It has been ten years since your family has seen you, yet you would leave them again after only a day. Can you not sacrifice a little more of your precious time? Even a few days?"

"No," he replied bluntly, "I cannot. And I will remind you, lady, that this is no concern of yours, regardless that you're the one who caused me to return to Gyer."

Rosaleen made an impatient sound. "*Why* can you not stay with your family for a few days?" she demanded. "It cannot be as painful as you seem to think, and it would mean much to both your brother and sister, who love you well."

"I don't wish to speak of this, Rosaleen," Hugh warned.

"I don't care what you wish!" she returned hotly. "Are you some coward, then, Hugh Caldwell, that you cannot bide time with your own family? Are the memories of this place that painful?"

"My memories are mine and mine alone, sweeting. You could *never* understand what my feelings are for Gyer, or for my past."

She stopped, turning to face him. "I want to be able to understand, Hugh. I do. Tell me why you cannot stay here and let me try."

Enough was enough, Hugh thought furiously, and that sweet, pleading tone of hers was worse than enough. He stopped and turned, as well, raising his eyebrows in an expression that openly mocked her.

"You must learn not to intrude upon the privacy of others, sweeting. It is just the kind of coarse behavior that speaks of a lady's lack of breeding and training."

She'd known Hugh Caldwell only a few days, but already Rosaleen could tell when he resorted to insults in order to protect himself. He had a sharp tongue, indeed, but, she thought with a thin smile, it was a dull blade compared to hers.

"Oh no, my lord, my training was most complete, I assure you," she replied easily, falling into step beside him once more. "Unfortunately, I didn't have you to serve as my example for what true coarseness is. Thus, what I did learn of grossly vulgar behavior in my youth was a waste, as I'm sure you'll agree. I have been trying to remedy the lack by studying you closely these past many days."

Hugh couldn't help but admire her. She was something, his Rosaleen no-name. Reaching down, he took her hand and placed it on his arm, where he covered her fingers with his own.

"Rosaleen, my darling, you are the most unnatural female I've ever known. You were supposed to fall into tears at my words and proceed to make me feel like the veriest knave. Do you know nothing?"

"I have been told my understanding is very well formed, Hugh Caldwell," she said, "and be pleased to not flatter yourself, I beg. If you were naught but a knave I certainly should have treated you to a fit of tears. However, as I am loath to waste my time, I did not."

Hugh laughed and squeezed her fingers. "Do you know, Rosaleen, I don't think I've ever admired another female quite as much as I admire you. You've wit and beauty, the rarest elements to be found at once in a woman. Where shall I find my daily abuse after the morrow, I wonder?"

Smiling, Rosaleen said, "I was just thinking that myself, Hugh Caldwell. I wonder if I shall ever meet anyone who will be as wretched to me as you've been. I shall have to take up some form of penance to make up for the lack of it, I suppose."

Stopping once more, Hugh took Rosaleen's hand and brought it to his lips, where he kissed it gently. The surprise on her upturned face showed clearly, and Hugh felt an unaccustomed stab of regret. She had the prettiest eyes he'd ever seen, he thought for probably the hundredth time since meeting her, and she had the loveliest mouth he'd ever seen or kissed, and she had the smoothest skin that he'd ever seen or kissed or touched.

"I have been wretched to you," he admitted before he could think not to. "Kindness isn't part of my nature, I fear, but I do wish I'd been kinder to you, Rosaleen, for you have certainly treated me better than I deserve after all the insults I've handed you." He kissed her hand again, then offered a gentle smile. "I hope you'll not hold my bad behavior against me forever, sweeting."

For some strange reason, Rosaleen suddenly felt like crying.

"I think that perhaps I am the one who must apologize to you, Hugh Caldwell. I forced myself on you and made you return to a place you didn't wish to go, and I have been ill-mannered and mean-spirited. If you have behaved badly, it could only be because my own behavior has been so much worse. I have not even thanked you, yet I do want you to know how grateful I am for all you have done. Indeed, Hugh Caldwell, I shall never forget your kindness to me."

"Rosaleen," he murmured, "I've already told you that kindness isn't a part of my nature. And I wish you would not thank me." He smiled. "I much prefer it when you rail at me and call me all those dreadful things."

Rosaleen made no reply but continued to stare up at him, and Hugh, gazing back at her for a silent moment, finally spread his fingers gently across her cheek and neck and lowered his head to kiss her. There was nothing of passion in the kiss. It was warm, gentle and tender.

When Hugh lifted his head, he stared deeply into Rosaleen's eyes.

"How strange," he whispered, stroking his thumb across her temple. "I will miss you, Rosaleen."

Her hand slid over his, pressing it against the side of her face.

"It is odd, Hugh Caldwell, but I shall miss you, also."

A tiny light flickered in the depths of his green eyes.

"Rosaleen," he began with a great deal of uncertainty, "what would you think if... in a few months, when I've settled matters at Briarstone, how would you feel if I... what I mean to say is, I'll have to go to London eventually, for estate purposes, and while I'm there, what would you think if I... sought you out?" He sounded so unsure of himself, yet so hopeful, that it nearly broke Rosaleen's heart. "Would you care to see me again?"

Rosaleen swallowed with some difficulty and dropped her hand from his. Taking a step away, trying her best to sound as distant as possible, she said, "No. I wouldn't."

His eyes widened for the briefest of seconds, but long enough for Rosaleen to see the pain she had put in them. She wanted to cry out, to tell him that her words were false, but she couldn't. All she could do was stand there, steeling herself against the powerful desire to soothe him, and watch as he mastered his emotions with the ease of years of practice.

It took only a few moments for him to retreat behind his mask of indifference.

"You couldn't speak more honestly than that," he said, smiling.

"Hugh—"

"Let's not speak of it," he said without a hint of hurt or anger in his tone. Placing her hand on his arm again, he began to stroll through the gardens. "Tell me, instead, what it was that Justin was talking to you about when I found you together an hour ago. He looked as if he were laying his heart at your feet."

"In a manner of speaking, he was," Rosaleen replied miserably, wishing that she could think of a good excuse to leave him so that she could go to her chamber and have a good cry. "He was telling me of his many qualities, and explaining what he has to offer a bride and why he would make a good husband."

Hugh laughed harshly. "So he was blinded by your beauty and decided to win your heart, did he? How very foolish of him. Alex and Lillis told me that he's decided to wed as soon as he may, and you would do as well as any other woman, I suppose. Better even, for in spite of your cold nature, Rosaleen no-name, you do warm a bed nicely. More than that a man shouldn't desire from a woman. I never have, nor shall I ever."

Rosaleen winced at the sharpness of his tone but said nothing. Instead she turned her head away and forced her watering, aching eyes to look at the rosebushes.

"Why would you not let me tell Hugh the truth about Lady Rosaleen?" the Lady of Gyer asked her husband as they stood by the long windows of his working chamber, looking out over the gardens to where Hugh and Rosaleen were strolling together.

"Oh, I don't know," Alexander Baldwin replied, lazily running a hand over his wife's shapely back. "The poor girl clearly wants to keep the truth a secret. And who could blame her, with Simon of Denning and her uncle searching everywhere for her? That she and Hugh arrived safely at Gyer is a miracle, considering the small army that came here only a few days past asking about her. I didn't wish to make her feel foolish, I suppose."

"But Hugh will be furious when he discovers the truth. He thinks her naught but the daughter of a farmer and has treated her accordingly. Can you imagine what he'll think when he finds out she is Rosaleen Sarant, the heiress of Siere?"

"Mmm. Another reason I didn't wish to make such a revelation. Hugh probably would have strangled her, for it is certain he never would have offered her his aid if he'd known how valuable a property she is. He despises the nobility. He would have run from her as fast as he could. But—" he motioned toward the gardens "—look at him now. I've never known Hugh to be so happy in a woman's company before, save when he's had them in his bed." He grinned at his wife, who laughed.

"And what would you know of that, my lord?" she teased, before turning her attention back to the couple, who were so slowly making their way down yet another path in the gardens. "You speak the truth, my lord, for he does seem to enjoy her company. Does he love her, do you think? It would be strange were Hugh to become the next Earl of Siere, though I should be happy for him, of course."

"God forbid!" Alexander declared, pulling his lovely wife closer. "Can you imagine? We'd have to treat him like royalty, and I'll not spend the rest of my life saying 'my lord' to Hugh."

"It's impossible, I think," she said with a sigh. "He hates the nobility. He'll not even let himself be knighted, not even at the king's command. Still, I should love to see Hugh happily settled."

"As would I, my love," her husband agreed. "We must pray that he'll meet a more suitable maiden who will appeal to him as greatly as the lady Rosaleen does."

"Yes," said his wife, "though it is a shame. She is a lovely girl. Perfect for Hugh. If only she weren't so high-born."

Alexander of Gyer nodded but said, more practically and more grimly, "If only she weren't in so much danger."

Chapter Nine

Sir Larents Dassen and Sir Inghere Fitzwald thought they had died and gone to heaven.

And if they hadn't, they had at least come close to it. The angel before them was proof, and although she might be an unwilling angel, they fully intended to claim her as their own.

"I'll not be treated in such a manner!" Rosaleen said as firmly and as calmly as she could, speaking with all the authority of the heiress of Siere. "You gentlemen don't know who you have taken captive. I am a lady, and I demand to be treated as such."

"But we are going to treat you well, my lady," Larents said happily, holding the reins of her mare. "Very well, indeed. Are we not, Inghere?"

Inghere, a redheaded giant with the biggest nose Rosaleen had ever seen, nodded. "You've no need to fear us, mistress. We'll do you no harm, and we'll pay good coin after." He winked at his friend. "She'll be worth it and more, will she not, Larents? I doubt I've seen a comelier maid in all my days."

"You are mistaken," she told them, trying without success to regain control of her mare. "I am not what you assume. Be pleased to return the reins of my horse and let me pass."

Larents, holding her reins fast, chuckled. "We'll be pleased, pretty lady, and that I promise, but you must pay a forfeit first."

"A forfeit?" she repeated, gaping at the man as though he were the greatest fool alive. "I'll pay no forfeit to such as you. This road is owned by the king. No man save he can demand a forfeit for its use. Now give me back the reins to my steed or I'll...I'll scream."

"Aye, we'll make you scream, mistress," Inghere promised. "Take her over to those bushes, lad, and be quick about it. I'm eager to have her."

Rosaleen stiffened. "H-have me? Wait! I'm a lady, I tell you, not some whore to be taken without due!"

The two men ignored her and, flanking her, forced her little brown mare to the side of the road.

Frightened, Rosaleen groped about in her skirts to find the dagger she had secured there earlier. She was just in the process of pulling the sharp instrument from its sheath when the sound of horse hooves racing furiously toward them stopped her.

The same sound caught the attention of her assailants, for they stilled and, like Rosaleen, looked up to see who it was approaching them at such an express pace.

"God's teeth!" said Inghere, much amazed.

"Why, it's Hugh Caldwell!" added Larents with equal surprise.

"Oh dear," muttered Rosaleen, pushing her dagger back to its resting place.

"Good old Hugh!" Inghere said with a laugh. "Imagine meeting him on such a piteous road as this in the midst of England! Why, the last I saw of him, he was felling Frenchmen left and right at Agincourt."

"He looks as fit for battle this morn as he did then," Larents said. "I wonder who the poor devil is he's chasing after." He lifted a hand in greeting as Hugh neared them. "Hugh! Hugh Caldwell! Hail, good fellow!"

Hugh brought Saint to a halt several feet before them, and Rosaleen couldn't decide who was breathing harder, the horse or its master. One thing was certain, however. The look in Hugh's eyes as they came to rest upon her boded no goodwill. Swallowing, she attempted a tiny smile in greeting. Hugh glared hotly at her in turn and frowned.

"Aye, well met, Hugh!" Inghere agreed happily. "It's been a long while since we've seen one another, friend."

Not moving his eyes from Rosaleen, Hugh nodded. "Dassen, Fitzwald. It looks as though you've caught a pretty doe this morn."

"Aye, and that we have, Hugh Caldwell." Inghere laughed. "We were on our way to Drake, minding naught but ourselves, when what should come riding out of the mist but our very own angel."

"A right gift from God, do you not think, Hugh?" Larents asked, casting an admiring glance at Rosaleen, who sat rigidly in her saddle, trying to look at anything but Hugh Caldwell. "She means to make us work for our pleasures, I fear, but 'twould be an insult to the Deity to let her go without first showing our appreciation for His gift."

Both men chuckled, not seeing that their friend didn't share their jest.

"You are welcome to join us, if it pleases you, Caldwell," Inghere offered. He took in Rosaleen's full figure admiringly. "There's certainly enough to go around, would you not agree, Larents?"

"Certainly! Come along, Hugh, it will be like days gone past, though you'll have to put in your share for her pay after."

Still not taking his eyes from Rosaleen, Hugh replied calmly, "I'm sorry, my friends, to ruin your morning's sport, but you'll not be enjoying this lady's charms today, or any other day. It just so happens that she belongs to me."

A stunned silence followed his words, long enough for Hugh to bring his steed a few threatening steps closer to them. It was Rosaleen who finally spoke, angrily.

"Hugh Caldwell! What a thing to say! I do not belong to you!"

Both Inghere and Larents looked at the furious girl, then turned their eyes to their friend, memories of his fighting skills surfacing vividly in both their minds.

"Are you sure about this, Hugh?" Inghere asked regretfully. Belatedly he noticed the hot, possessive look that his old companion held on the girl.

"Quite sure," was the hard reply. "Had I come upon you too late, and found that you had already enjoyed yourselves upon her, I swear by all that is holy you would now be dead by my hand."

Swallowing, Larents gently handed the reins of Rosaleen's mare back to her. "We never touched her, Hugh," he assured him quickly. "Not one finger. Or hair. Did we, Inghere?"

"No, we didn't touch her in the least, Hugh."

"Good." Hugh nodded. "If you will be so good as to leave us, gentlemen, I will bid you Godspeed on your journey to Drake."

Knowing a reprieve when they heard one, the two knights turned their horses about and fled.

Hugh and Rosaleen sat glaring at each other until the sounds of the men's retreat drifted away, then Rosaleen gave vent to her anger.

"How dare you! I do *not* belong to you, you—you dissipate beast! And what did they mean, 'like days gone past'? Did you make a *habit* of raping every girl you found traveling without escort? Though *why* such a thing should astound me, I'm sure I don't know."

"Quiet!" Hugh commanded between set teeth. "Be quiet, Rosaleen, or I'll not answer for what I do to you." He rode closer and snatched the reins from her hands. Leading her mare to a nearby tree trunk, which came just to the level of her feet, he said sharply, "Dismount. You shall have to do it on your own, for if I lay a hand on you, we'll both regret the consequences."

Rosaleen dismounted quickly.

"Go and stand on the other side of the road," he instructed. "And if you value your skin, you'll stay over there until I tell you otherwise. And don't, Rosaleen," he warned when she opened her mouth to protest, "say one word to me until then. *Not one word.*"

Huffing, she walked to the other side of the road, then stood watching as he dismounted and tied the horses to a nearby shrubbery.

And she kept watching, forcing herself to remain silent, while he set to pacing back and forth, muttering to himself distractedly and occasionally running his hands through his long, untied hair.

Whenever he turned to pace back from where he'd just finished pacing she could hear snatches of his talk.

"I wake up...I go down to break my fast...I ask where Rosaleen is. They tell me that she's *gone*...I ask what they mean by *gone*...they tell me they don't know...she's just *gone*...I go riding out of Gyer so quickly that I leave Amazon behind...I didn't even bid my family farewell...I spend the next *four hours* searching every damned side road trying to find her...when I *do* find her she's about to be *raped*...."

At this point he shot her an extremely unpleasant look, then started up again, all over, as though he just could not believe it, as though there were something missing that he hadn't figured out yet but which was going to reveal itself to him eventually.

"I wake up...I go down to break my fast..."

He went through the entire litany twice more, finally falling silent and pacing more and more slowly. Eventually he stopped altogether, took several deep breaths, ran his hands through his hair a few more times, then nodded.

Going to the tree stump on which Rosaleen had dismounted, he sat down, looked at Rosaleen and, patting his lap, said, "Very well, Rosaleen. I have calmed. Come here."

She understood his intent at once and shook her head.

"N-no, thank you."

He raised an eyebrow at her. "Did you not hear me, Rosaleen? I said *come here.*"

"Why?" The word came out as a squeak, and Rosaleen unconsciously moved one hand protectively toward her bottom.

"Why do you think, Rosaleen?"

"You look as though you intend to punish someone."

"Rosaleen, your understanding truly astounds me," Hugh said with mock amazement. "You are quite right, sweet. I do intend to punish someone. Now, who could that be, do you wonder?"

Rosaleen gulped and moved her other hand to join the one behind her back. "But...but, Hugh, I don't wish to be beaten."

"I'm glad to hear it. If you enjoyed such a thing I'd be worried about the soundness of your mind. Now come here, Rosaleen."

"I'll not," she said. "You've no right to punish me, Hugh Caldwell. You're not my father or my guardian or my husband."

By the expression on his face, Rosaleen judged that those had been the wrong words to say.

"No, I'm not, thank God," he replied tightly. "But I am the man in whose protection you placed yourself, and I am the man who took two full days out of his life to escort you to the safety of his brother's home, and I am the man who is going to give you what you deserve for running away from Gyer without so much as a word."

"Please, Hugh, I know that what I did was unmannerly, but at least give me a chance to explain!"

"Have no fears for that, my dear. You may be certain you will explain everything to my satisfaction," he promised. "After. Now, come here before I come to fetch you." The look in his eyes promised just how much worse things would be for her if he had to go to such trouble.

Casting a glance up and down either direction of the road in a last hope that some source of rescue would appear, Rosaleen sighed resignedly and slowly made her way to where Hugh sat.

"It is not fair, I tell you, that men should be able to have their way simply because women are so much weaker than they! First my uncle tried to beat me into submission, and now you have the arrogance to punish me for something you've no right to!"

Hugh looked to where Rosaleen rode beside him and smiled, finally relaxed for the first time since discovering that she had run away.

"Cease your complaints, sweeting. I barely touched you. You should be thankful."

"Barely touched me!" she repeated angrily. "Thankful! You're not the one who has to ride with a sore bottom all day!"

That made him grin broadly. "You'll not make me feel sorry, Rosaleen. You deserved what you got, and worse, for running off as you did. What in God's name possessed you to do it? Did you not believe my brother when he said he would take you to London?"

"I believed him," she said, feeling even guiltier than when she'd snuck out of Gyer in the middle of the night. "And your family was truly most kind to me. But I...I felt that it would be best if I continued the journey on my own."

"Of course," he returned dryly. "Certainly you did. It was a different song you sang at the Red Fox Inn. *'But I can't go all by myself! I need protection!'*" he imitated mockingly in a high, squeaky voice. "I hope I've not been wasting both my time *and* pity on you, Rosaleen noname."

"No," she murmured, unsure of how to traverse this foreign ground with him.

"Explain yourself, then, and make certain to speak clearly, Rosaleen. I'd not want to miss a single word."

"I can't."

"What?"

"I said I can't. Hugh, please believe that I wish I could tell you why I left Gyer as I did. Truly I do. But I can't. I'm sorry."

Reaching down to grasp her horse's head, Hugh brought both animals to a halt.

"You will be sorry, Rosaleen," he threatened seriously, "if you don't tell me the truth, and right now. You convinced me that you were a damsel in need of rescuing, and against my better judgment I took you to my brother and sister, who took you in and agreed to help you without one question asked. You, in turn, repaid both them and me by running off like some thief in the night."

And, he raged silently, refusing to speak aloud this particular fact, she had given him the worst scare of his life. He had never experienced such fear for another living being as he had that morn when he'd discovered that Rosaleen was gone, and it had driven him wildly, relentlessly until the moment when he'd set eyes on her and seen that she was all right, that she was still alive and whole and unharmed. And in that moment, when he had seen her, he had realized an awful truth.

He cared for her.

He, Hugh Caldwell, whose absent heart had been a matter of great perplexity to almost every female he'd met in the past ten years, suddenly found himself *caring* for the most stubborn, wretched woman he'd ever known. Just thinking about it now almost sent his anger to the other side of the stars.

"Now explain yourself, Rosaleen, or I'll do worse than warm your bottom, I swear by God I shall."

As furious as he looked, Rosaleen didn't believe for a moment that he would truly harm her. The punishment he'd given her half an hour earlier had, despite her complaints, been laughably mild. He'd managed the whole matter through all her layers of clothing, clearly not wanting to damage more than her pride. She had humiliated him in front of his family by leaving as she had, and he had every right to an explanation. It had been a slim chance she'd had of his not finding her, though she hadn't had a choice, just as she didn't have one now.

Reaching out, she disconcerted him by grasping one of his hands.

"Hugh, I *will* tell you everything," she vowed, searching his eyes. "I promise I shall. But only if you take me to London. Once we are there and I've had an audience with the king, I vow by all that is holy I will explain everything to you."

Hugh didn't like this. He didn't like it one bit. He didn't like what he saw in her eyes, he didn't like the way her voice trembled when she spoke of the things she was hiding, and he especially didn't like the way she made him feel.

London. She was going to tell him everything, all the truth, once they reached London? No. London was where she said she didn't wish to see him again. London was where he was going to lose her forever. She'd made that clear enough. So clear that he had spent the entire night tossing in his bed and trying to keep from thinking that the following morn would be the last time he would ever see her. Except that she had already left before the morn had come, so that she hadn't even planned on seeing him then.

What a fool he had made of himself, asking her if she would let him visit her in London. The words had come from nowhere and had surprised him as much as they had surprised her. He had told himself afterward that he was glad she had so quickly put him in his place, for what man in his right mind would want anything to do with a shrewish female like Rosaleen no-name? She had given him a reprieve, and he was going to be grateful for it if it was the last thing he did.

He would take her to London without delay. That was what he would do. That was *exactly* what he was going to do. No one and nothing would stop him. He would take her to London and get rid of her and never, ever look back.

"We aren't going to London," he said abruptly. "I'm not taking you to London, Rosaleen."

Her eyes widened and she said, very slowly and very precisely, "What did you say, Hugh Caldwell?"

"You *are* deaf, sweeting," he replied, pulling his hand from hers. "You are in debt to me, lady, and I intend to have payment before I take you to London. Payment in full."

Angry color swept over Rosaleen's face. "You wretch! I owe you naught! How dare you speak to me of payment after what I suffered at your hands when first we met!"

"What *we*," he emphasized, "enjoyed that night at the Red Fox Inn was payment only for the money and care I spent on you while we were there. You're still indebted to me for what I've done for you since." Hugh leaned closer, looking her directly in the eye. "And I intend to collect in full, mistress. Set your mind to it."

"You know very well I've no money at present to pay you," she told him furiously. "If you would be paid, then you must wait until we achieve London."

Hugh shook his head. "Payment first, London second. And money is the last manner in which I wish to be paid. You've two choices, sweeting. You can either go to the nearest inn with me and spend the next three days and nights amusing me in bed—"

Rosaleen gasped. "I'd rather die!"

"Or you can come to Briarstone and work off your obligation there."

"What! Are you mad!"

"You aren't the first woman to ask me that," he admitted.

"I doubt I'll be the last," she said through gritted teeth. "I cannot go to Briarstone, you great fool. I *must* get to London. How many times must I tell you that? Have you no understanding at all?"

"Certainly I do," he said happily, releasing her horse. "I understand that you've just made your choice. You cannot go to Briarstone, so we'll find a comfortable inn and spend the next three days enjoying ourselves to the full. I must say, Rosaleen, as surprised as I am at your choice, I am truly pleased." He grinned lecherously at her. "I shall greatly enjoy teaching you the many pleasures a man and woman can share."

"Swine! I mean it when I say I would rather die than bed with you!"

Hugh lifted his eyebrows. "Then you are willing to come to Briarstone? You will work off your debt to me there?"

"How?" she asked suspiciously.

He shrugged. "From what I understand, the place is in want of governing. And if I've ever met a more governing female than you, Rosaleen no-name, I certainly don't recall it. All I need you to do is organize the household, while I tend to the livestock and fields."

That seemed easy enough, but Rosaleen didn't trust him. "That's all?"

Hugh laughed out loud. "What do you mean, that's all? Running a household the size of Briarstone is sure to be no small task. It will require a little more than the skills you possess of feeding pigs, my dear."

Rosaleen worked hard to keep a smile from her face. If he only knew how restful the task of running an insignificant fief the size of Briarstone would be to a woman who'd overseen the several estates belonging to Siere, he would surely be surprised. But let him have his little fun for now. He would learn the truth soon enough.

"For how long will I be in service to you at Briarstone?"

A warmth lit in Hugh's heart, and he had to turn away to keep her from seeing how glad he was.

"Three months, Rosaleen. Three months of your service in running my household, and then I will personally escort you to London."

Three months! Rosaleen thought with distress. Three months would surely bring her uncle or Simon of Denning knocking at Briarstone's door. And three months would be that much longer before she could lay her case before the king.

Hugh understood Rosaleen's silence exactly for what it was, and he pressed his case.

"Three months or three days, Rosaleen. The choice is yours."

Three months or three days.

She looked up at him, pleading, "Hugh, please . . ."

His heart was too full, for the first time in ten years, for him to let her go so easily.

"Three months or three days," he repeated sternly. "Let me know now, for we'll either go backward or forward, whatever you decide. Backward, we'll go along to Drake, where a very comfortable inn reminds itself to me. Forward, we'll go to Briarstone, and there we will remain, together, regardless of what we find awaiting us, for three months. Tell me your decision now, sweeting, else I'll make it for you."

She knew what his decision would be, for already he was straining his reins in the direction that led back to Drake.

Staring at him, meeting his eyes and wondering anew at how beautiful they were, Rosaleen gave a loud sigh.

"Forward," she said, resigned.

Triumphant, Hugh smiled.

"To Briarstone then, my lady. To Briarstone we go."

Chapter Ten

The manorhouse that Hugh Caldwell had expected to find at Briarstone didn't exist. Standing in the place where that humble dwelling was supposed to be was instead a large, crumbling castle, which showed every evidence of having once been as fine and impressive as Castle Gyer now was. It was not as large as Gyer, certainly, and had no surrounding village to give it any significance, but it was definitely larger than what Hugh had expected. What was left of it, anyway. From this distance where he sat atop Saint, Castle Briarstone looked more like the ruins of a castle than a castle proper. There were four large towers, one at each corner of the square-built outer wall, a smaller gate tower set over the massive wooden gates at the entrance to the place, and beyond that, in what Hugh assumed must be the inner bailey, was the keep, rising above the walls and displaying an uncertain rooftop.

God's toes, Hugh thought grimly, what had he gotten himself into? If John Rowsenly were still alive he would gladly kill him for shackling him with this . . . this incredible relic. Too embarrassed even to look at Rosaleen, he waited in silence for her disparagement of his new possession.

"Just look at those fields of wheat and barley!" she exclaimed with awe. "God's mercy, Hugh Caldwell! You're a wealthy man, or soon will be if all that land belongs to Briarstone and if it can be brought safely to harvest. And over there, look! Oats! And farther on, by the river. Is that not rye? And all those lovely, lovely oak trees, as well. Oh, it's beautiful, Hugh. You must be most pleased."

He'd been so busy suffering over the decaying state of his new home that he hadn't actually looked at the rest of what he'd won. He did now and felt a surge of hopefulness. Rosaleen was right. The castle of Briarstone was a wretched mess, but the surrounding fields would have done Gyer proud. The vassals of John Rowsenly had clearly labored hard in the master's absence, and Hugh sent up a silent prayer of thanks.

"Of course it's beautiful," he said to Rosaleen, adding, haughtily, "What did you expect?"

"Not this," she replied honestly. "But it is a relief, is it not, Hugh Caldwell? Admit that you've been worried at what you would find."

He laughed. "Very well, I admit it, but only to keep you from badgering me. 'Struth, it is a relief to see that the place isn't a full loss. But look at where we'll be living. Not a pleasant sight, is it? The barns at Gyer are probably more habitable."

Tilting her head consideringly, Rosaleen gave the keep and outer walls of Briarstone a fair appraising. They *were* in bad disrepair, and there was no denying that the next three months would require a great deal of hard work on her part, but, really, other than the year or two it would take a number of masons and carpenters to fix the actual structures, the task ahead wouldn't be all that difficult.

"I imagine it looks worse than it is," she stated positively. "And you needn't worry about it, Hugh Caldwell," she added, looking up at him. "You're to take care of the fields and livestock. I'm the one who must worry about setting your home to rights. Remember?"

Her words stung Hugh with sharp guilt, and he wondered if he should release her from their agreement. He had believed Briarstone would be no more than a small manor with a few fields and some vassals. Rowsenly had never mentioned that the place was so big, so...vast. What could a little village girl like Rosaleen possibly know about running a castle the size of this? She would be overwhelmed and terrified when she finally realized just how great the task would be.

"Listen to me, Rosaleen," he said kindly, "I didn't realize the dwelling would be so large, and I certainly don't expect you to be able to oversee it as well as someone like...well, as someone like Lillis could. You must not try to make everything perfect at once."

Rosaleen turned her head away to keep him from seeing the smile on her face, and she bit her lip to keep from laughing out loud.

"Why, Hugh," she managed to say, barely constraining herself, "that's very thoughtful of you. I know my skills in organizing a household aren't very good, but I promise I'll do my sorry best to keep my part of our agreement."

Hugh felt even worse. She had turned her face away to keep him from seeing how badly he'd hurt her feelings, and she sounded as if she were trying not to cry. Her breaking voice made his heart ache with remorse. Gingerly placing a hand on her shaking shoulder, he said, "Don't feel badly about being so lacking in domestic skills, Rosaleen. I know you weren't raised in a truly noble home. But all will be well. I'll help as best I can, and perhaps some of the vassals can be spared from the fields to help. Once you've become used to it, you'll find that managing a household this size is a very simple matter."

Her shoulders shook even harder, and all she could do was nod.

"Rosaleen . . ." he said with real worry.

She put a hand up in the air to silence him while she struggled to control her laughter. After a moment, during which she called upon years of training to keep her expression even in every kind of circumstance, she turned to him, presenting him just exactly the flushed countenance he'd been expecting.

"Thank you, Hugh. I do feel so much better."

"That's a mercy," he said. "I'd hate to have a weeping female on my hands."

Smiling sweetly, Rosaleen returned, "Has anyone ever told you, Hugh Caldwell, that you've no manners?"

"Now, Rosaleen . . ."

"Because if they have, then they're wrong. You do have manners. The manners of a pig."

Hugh grinned, relieved to have her behaving normally again.

"And who would know better than you, Rosaleen, with all the experience you've had with such creatures?"

She grinned in turn. "The only experience I've had with swine, Hugh Caldwell, has been since I've met you. Having been in your company for so long, however, I expect I am now an authority."

Laughing, Hugh was about to make a suitable retort, when the shrubberies surrounding them suddenly began to shake and rustle.

Hugh's sword was unsheathed before Rosaleen could speak a word, and just in time, for the next moment found them faced by three men who'd ridden out of the bushes to flank them.

One of them, a short, plump fellow, brought his frail and bony mount to a stop in front of them.

"Halt and surren—!" he began, pulling at the sword sheathed on the belt around his waist. "Halt and surren—!" he tried again, tugging relentlessly without success. "Fiend's foot!" he swore, taking his eyes off Hugh and Rosaleen and using both hands to pull at the stubborn weapon. "I said" he grunted, tugging, "I said, halt and surrender!" The sword swooshed free of its scabbard at last, the force of its loosing sending the man right over the side of his horse and down onto the damp earth.

"Oh dear," said Rosaleen.

Hugh, leaning forward on Saint, peered down at where the man lay sprawled. "Hope the little fellow's all right," he said.

"Damn you, John!" one of his companions said angrily, moving his equally frail steed toward his friend. "I told you ter keep yer yap shut till we had 'em good 'n' ready!"

The third fellow, a dirty young man, nudged his horse next to Rosaleen's and held his sword out threateningly. Brushing his lanky blond hair out of his gray eyes with his free hand and staring at Hugh, he said quite seriously, "You. Toss down your weapon and your gold, else I cut the lady's throat."

Resting his own heavy sword on his knee, Hugh gazed evenly at the boy. "I don't think so, lad. This lady is the loveliest creature you or I will ever set eyes on in this life, mostlike. No man who calls himself a man would willingly mar her perfection."

Thinking of her uncle, who had more than willingly marred her, Rosaleen frowned. The boy, seeing her unhappy expression, swallowed loudly but held his place.

"Then . . . then, if you'll not drop your sword and hand over your gold, we'll take her and...and have our way with her!"

Hugh snorted with disbelief. "I should like to see you do it! This lady is possessed of a tongue so sharp she could easily sever you in two, lad. If you steal her it will be your life I'll fear for, not hers."

Drawing a shaky breath, the young man made one more attempt.

"Alan! John! Mark your swords on this fellow. Now, sir," he addressed Hugh again, holding his sword to Rosaleen's throat, "will you throw your weapon down, or shall we wrest it from you by force and take both your gold and the lady away with us?"

Looking with mild interest at the two men standing beside Saint, who now held their weapons pointed at him, then turning his own magnificent sword lightly in his hand, Hugh said, pleasantly, "I'll not throw my weapon down, boy. I shall throw it up, instead." Hefting his sword until the sharp tip of it pointed upward, he set its heavy hilt in the palm of his outstretched hand. "Watch, now," he advised, keeping his eyes on the sword. "You'd not want to miss this."

With a sudden, sharp movement he sent the sword flying, like an arrow, straight into the air above his head. It flew upward for several feet, then, just as surely, made a wildly spinning descent.

Everything happened so quickly after that that no one, save Hugh, was able to say how it had come about. One moment the sword was spinning dangerously through the air, and the next it was held before Rosaleen's face, disarming the boy mounted beside her and coming to a halt just in front of his nose. At the same time, their other two assailants found themselves knocked to the ground by a kick from Hugh's booted foot.

Rosaleen, having shut her eyes when she'd felt the buffeting movements of Hugh's sword in front of her face, now opened them to find the sharp edge of the sword's blade an inch or less away. Eyes crossing from the nearness of the thing, she allowed her gaze to follow the path of the sword all the way to its end, where it held the complete attention of a thoroughly surprised and frightened boy.

The young robber held two shaking hands up in a gesture of defeat, but Hugh pressed the point of his sword toward him a little closer.

"You are fortunate, *boy*, that I'm in a good mood today," he said sharply, his earlier tone of complacency vanished, his voice filled with suppressed anger, "else you would now find yourself singing sweetly with God's angels. Any man who threatens a lady as you have done this day deserves to have his idiot head severed from the rest of his fool body. And should I ever, God forbid, come across your sorry carcass again and find you engaged in such an activity, I swear on my own mother's soul I shall personally perform the separation, and without," he promised quite clearly, "a moment's hesitation."

"Y-yes, my lord," the boy whispered, leaning as far away from the sharp blade as he could.

Rosaleen was also leaning away from the blade's edge, and found that her neck was beginning to ache.

"If you do not mind, Hugh, I believe you have quite rescued us."

He withdrew his blade with care and slowly sheathed it.

"You and your friends may take your weapons and your horses and leave," Hugh invited tersely. "If I ever see a one of you near Briarstone again I shall cut your ears off. Now go."

The short, plump man named John and the taller, lanky fellow named Alan had picked themselves up and were in the midst of dusting themselves off when he spoke these words.

"But, m'lord," said John, surprised, "we can't not go near Briarstone."

"Be quiet, John!" the boy, having regained his composure, demanded.

"But 'e's right, Chris," Alan put in. "Whur else would we go to? There's nowhur else."

"It matters not. Be quiet!"

Having listened to this short exchange, Hugh raised his eyebrows.

"Do I understand, from your words, that you live nearby?" He addressed all of them, but he looked at the boy, their apparent leader, as he spoke.

Sighing, the boy nodded.

"Yes, sir." He shot an angry glare at his companions.

"God's feet," said Hugh. "We are to be neighbors. How…amusing. Still, I mean what I say. If you value your lives, keep as far from Briarstone as possible and never even think about trying to waylay travelers on my land again."

Rosaleen wasn't sure which of their assailants seemed more shocked at these words, though she thought perhaps it must be the boy beside her, who looked about as confounded as a person could.

"*Your* land!" he repeated. "Briarstone is *your* property? *You* are Hugh Caldwell?"

And then Rosaleen realized she'd been too hasty. The most shocked being present was without a doubt Hugh Caldwell.

"This is Hugh Caldwell, in truth," she informed them, since that man had once again lost his voice. "May we assume that you gentlemen are residents of Briarstone?"

"Gawd's toes!" Alan swore. "Now we've gone and done it! We've 'eld up the new master."

"Well, it weren't *my* idea!" protested John. "Yer the one said we was runnin' low on supplies." Looking at Hugh, he repeated, "It weren't *my* idea, m'lord."

"God's my life, Rosaleen," Hugh murmured in a dazed tone. "Briarstone is a den of thieves."

Resisting the almost overpowering urge to tell him that he should feel right at home, then, she put out one hand and patted his knee assuringly. "I'm sure it's not as bad as it seems, Hugh Caldwell. These gentlemen must have a reasonable explanation for their behavior."

"That we do, m'lady," Alan replied quickly, while John added, "It weren't *my* idea!"

"If you think starving a reasonable explanation, my lady," said the boy named Chris, glaring hotly at his new master, "then that would be it. Forgive me, my lord Caldwell, but where have you been? We've looked for you for more than ten days now and had nearly given up hope."

Although he knew he should be affronted by his young vassal's forward speech, Hugh wasn't. One look at Rosaleen's embarrassed expression more than made up for whatever discomfort he himself had been feeling.

"I was waylaid by a damsel in need, lad, and had to do my chivalrous duty by her." He ignored the unladylike snort Rosaleen made. "Regardless of that, I cannot believe that anyone at Briarstone is near starving. The fields spread before us say otherwise."

The boy shook his head in silent disgust and replied, "Come down and see how matters stand for yourself, my lord. The women have labored hard to have the master's chamber fit to welcome you. John, Alan," he said, addressing the men standing on the ground, "ride ahead to tell the others that their lord has arrived and has brought with him his—" he glanced at Rosaleen "—very beautiful lady. I'll bring them down the main road that they may better see the fields."

Rosaleen wanted to correct the young man about his wrong idea of her relationship to Hugh, but she held her tongue for the moment and watched as the two men did as they were bidden. It was impressive, she thought, that the boy was able to command the obedience of men older than he. And yet there was that about him, the quality of leadership as well as maturity, though he couldn't possibly be older than ten and eight years of age. He had clearly been educated, for his speech was cultured, far removed from the low jargon of the other men, and although he was as dirty and ragged as a beggar, Rosaleen saw that he held himself as nobly as an earl. He was a handsome lad, his finely cut features holding all the promise of one day making him quite as attractive as Hugh Caldwell.

"What is your name?" she asked as she and Hugh turned their steeds to follow the boy's poor mount.

"Christian," he replied, not looking at her.

"Christian?" she repeated in the same tone she used on unruly servants, a tone that indicated displeasure at having been purposefully half-answered.

"Christian Rowsenly," he answered more respectfully.

"Rowsenly?" Hugh repeated. "John Rowsenly never mentioned any relatives. Are you his cousin? Brother?"

"Half brother," the boy replied, "and bastard born." He offered both Hugh and Rosaleen an emotionless face. "I'm not surprised John didn't mention me." Turning again in his saddle, he pointed toward the long, beautiful valley of ripening fields spread out below. "To the right," he said, "there are nearly three thousand acres of wheat. We planted most of the land in wheat, as it's the most valuable crop. Farther on there are six hundred acres of oats. To the left, by the river, we've seven hundred acres each of rye and barley. Of course, all of the fields have been sown in the proper ridge-and-furrow fashion. Half the ridges are planted with beans, the other half with peas."

Rosaleen, who understood such things better than Hugh, approved heartily. "Very good, Christian Rowsenly. You've made certain to keep the fields well drained?"

"Aye, my lady, and they were marled before we started planting. These are the first crops planted at Briarstone in more than seventy years, so we were able to use all the land without having to let any of it rest. Next year we'll begin to alternate the crops."

"The first crops in seventy years!" Hugh said with disbelief. "By the rood! Hasn't this been the Rowsenly estate for longer than that?"

Unexpectedly, the boy laughed. "No, my lord. Briarstone was a Rowsenly estate for less than two years, as that was when my brother, God rest his soul, acquired it in the same manner that you did. Before that, Briarstone lay abandoned."

"But the damned fellow told me it was his family estate!" Hugh insisted.

Christian shrugged. "He had planned on it being so, before he went to serve the king." He shook his head. "Only a few English killed at Agincourt, but John must be one of them. It's just like him, God rest his soul."

"So that's why there is no village," Rosaleen said thoughtfully, "and no vassals or villeins spread out over the land to tend it. What a wretched waste! This land is as rich as any I've ever seen. I cannot fathom the king letting it lie untended so long." She looked at Hugh. "The first thing we must do, Hugh Caldwell, is determine what Briarstone's future will be. There must be a village someday, else the land will fall into ruin again. A goodly area near the castle must be set aside for it, and we must plan for the vassals who will be wanting their own homes and fields to manage." Her gaze moved back to Christian, who was nodding at her in agreement. "I assume that the present vassals of Briarstone live within the castle walls. How many are there?"

"We've a little more than fifty in all, my lady," he answered. "More than half are men, the rest are women and children. I don't suppose," he said hopefully, looking at Hugh, "that my brother explained to you how he gathered his vassals together, did he?"

Hugh shook his head, fighting down a sense of dread.

"Ah well, I didn't imagine he would have," the boy said, adding with an unhappy sigh, "This should prove interesting."

The gates were already open when they reached the castle, and they rode directly inside. There was only one large bailey to the place, but that was kept beautifully clean and clear, much in contrast to the decaying state of the surrounding structures.

"Where are the stables?" Hugh asked, looking around and trying to get his bearings.

"There, my lord." Christian pointed to a tiny stone building with a sod roof.

Hugh frowned grimly when he saw it. God's teeth! He couldn't house Saint in that! It looked older than Methuselah, and just about as sturdy.

Old. Everything about the place looked aged.

Slowly, he moved his gaze from the stable toward the square-shaped keep, taking in the details of the outer structures. There were no mews that he could see, no dairy, no chapel, no separate kitchen. There was nothing in the grassy bailey save the keep, the decrepit stable and a well that looked as if it hadn't yielded water in more than a century. On the keep Hugh saw no windows, only arrow loops, and on the outer walls were empty spaces from which explosives could be dropped on an attacking enemy, or from which boiling oil or water might be poured to discourage anyone trying to scale those same walls. They were two of the oldest methods of defense that had been built into castles and had long since been improved upon.

Eyes narrowing, Hugh asked, "How old is Briarstone, Chris, lad?"

Dismounting, Christian replied, "It was begun in the year of our Lord 1004 by Hyweld the Goodsworn, who was descended of Aethelstan and well favored by Athelred the Unready."

He moved to help Rosaleen dismount but was pushed aside by Hugh, who had dismounted, as well, and who lifted his hands to circle Rosaleen's waist and pull her from her saddle. He didn't release her when her feet touched the ground, but instead took her hand and interlaced their fingers, pulling her along as he followed Christian Rowsenly toward the enormous castle doors.

"It was completed in 1025," Christian continued. "It was one of the finest castles of its day, at that time, and even William the Conqueror found it praiseworthy. Shortly after the Conqueror's invasion it was given as a prize to one of William's favorite nobles, a baron named Dellaroix, who already had vast estates in Normandy and who eventually deeded Briarstone to one of his cousins, Laurent Dellaroix. Laurent Dellaroix managed the estates well and Briarstone enjoyed great prosperity." They reached the base of the five steps that led to the doors, and Christian began to mount them while Hugh and Rosaleen followed.

"There were over thirty thousand acres of land attached to Briarstone at that time," he continued, "and a village bearing the castle name, which was one of the busiest trading centers in England. In 1289, however, the Dellaroix family fell out of favor with King Edward, and Briarstone was given by the king to a distant Dellaroix cousin, who had modified his name to Dellard and who was also, as it turns out, a cousin of Queen Eleanor's." Christian stopped in front of the keep's doors and turned to speak more directly to his rapt audience of two.

"The Dellards are the ones responsible for Briarstone's present condition. Allan Dellard was the first to lay claim to the fief, though he never lived here. His most memorable involvement with it was selling off most of the land. He died in 1340 and his son, William Dellard, inherited what was left. William did live here, but as a hermit. He did naught as lord. He never married nor had children and, save for a woman who did his cooking, lived alone until his death in 1402. By that time, with all but these five thousand acres of land sold and with neither guide nor care, the village had died away and Briarstone had fallen into ruin. After William Dellard died, what was left of Briarstone was inherited by yet another cousin, a man named Robert Dellard, who two years ago gambled it away to my brother, John, who subsequently gambled it away to you, my lord. And that," he said, grasping one of the large iron rings attached to a heavy oak-and-iron door, "is the history of Briarstone. Now, please, my lord and lady, prepare yourselves for what you're about to see. It may, I fear, greatly surprise you."

Chapter Eleven

Surprise, thought Rosaleen, after she had crossed the threshold of Castle Briarstone's keep, was an apt word for what she felt. And if the amount of squeezing that Hugh Caldwell was applying to her hand was any indication, it was an apt word for what he was feeling, too.

The great hall of Castle Briarstone was magnificently huge. Everything within it was easily seen, for although there were no real windows as such, much of the back wall of the building was gone, letting in as much light and air as a person could desire. The effect this absent wall presented was odd, Rosaleen thought, for it made her feel as if she were passing from one outside to another, with only a door in the way to make a difference. But that was not entirely true. The back of the keep was missing, but there was still a roof overhead, and other floors above as well, if what she had observed from the outside was true.

But as startling as the missing back wall was to a newcomer's entry, it was as nothing compared to what the scene before them offered by way of surprise.

Rosaleen, sweeping her astonished gaze from one end of the hall to the other, felt as though she had walked into some kind of excessive jest.

"Hugh," she whispered.

"Steady," he murmured. "Don't go all faint on me now, Rosaleen."

Dimly, Rosaleen thought with some ire that she certainly wasn't going to faint. It was far beneath her dignity, as the heiress of Siere, to faint.

The trouble was, she couldn't make any sense of the spectacle before her. What in God's name were those creatures? Cows? No, they were too big to be cows. They were ... oxen.

She closed her eyes and shook her head to make them go away. But when she opened her eyes again, they were still there—a dozen or more oxen, standing at the far end of the great hall, as happy as you please, contentedly munching fresh barley stalks.

Merciful God in heaven, she thought, perhaps she was going to faint.

"Hugh," she began again, certain she had lost her mind.

"I see them," he said softly, like a warning. "I see them, Rosaleen."

Near the oxen, in uneven rows, sat several crude benches and long tables, and beyond them, as far away from the gaping hole of the back wall as possible, was an indoor camp. There were pallets and blankets and beds made of hay strewn all about, with no organized pattern, as though the occupants who slept there fell together in a tumbled heap at night.

Set at the very back of the room, next to the open wall, was a crude kitchen, where even now several small fires burned beneath huge pots from which drifted the pleasant and welcome smells of stews and sauces.

"I believe we're supposed to greet my new vassals now," Hugh informed her, setting an arm tightly around her waist.

Vassals? Rosaleen dragged her gaze back across the hall again.

Standing before them, lined up in a straight row and looking as nervous as though they were about to be introduced to the king, was the most ragged, dirty group of people Rosaleen had ever set eyes on.

Christian Rowsenly started at the nearest end and began introducing them, one by one, while Hugh supported Rosaleen down the line, nodding and smiling and saying hello to each new face. Rosaleen, calling upon her years of training, stumbled along as best she could.

"And this is Alec Berry," Christian announced when they reached the twentieth man in line. "His specialty was robbery."

"Is that so?" Hugh replied pleasantly, gifting the middle-aged man with the same relaxed smile he'd gifted the previous nineteen with and receiving the news of his former criminal activities just as easily.

Thus far they had met thieves, murderers, forgers and just about every other manner of criminal possible, and Rosaleen was filled with admiration for Hugh Caldwell's ability to respond to these stunning introductions with such perfect calm. She herself was doing very badly, but, then, none of her training had ever included how best to greet a man who could boast of having stolen two gold plates out of White Tower.

"I'm surprised you weren't involved in today's encounter," Hugh said to Alec Berry. "Our assailants could have used an expert."

A nearly toothless grin split the man's face.

"I wisht I'd been there, too, m'lord, fer it'd be a real honor to hold up a great lord like yerself. But me'n 'arry—" he nodded in the direction of the man next in line

"—was busy fetchin' the evening meal, m'lord, an' we couldn't be in two places at once, could we?"

Hugh raised his eyebrows at the man standing beside Alec Berry.

"This is Harry Stoote, my lord," Christian introduced quickly. "We have Alec and him to thank for the lamb we'll be eating this night."

Extending an arm, Hugh clasped the man's hand in greeting. "It's good to meet you, Harry Stoote. You oversee the sheep at Briarstone, then?"

The happy expression on the man's face was replaced by one of confusion, and he sent a nervous glance toward Christian.

"No, m'lord. We don't got no sheep, 'n' I wudn't know whut t'do wiv' 'em if we did 'ave."

"Briarstone possesses no animal stock, my lord," Christian explained in a taut voice, "save those oxen over there and the few horses you saw earlier this day. Alec and Harry stole the lamb from one of our neighbors in preparation for your arrival. We have grown used to eating poorly, but your vassals didn't want their new lord to have vegetables and oatcakes as his first meal at Briarstone. Alec and Harry stole the lamb, Ivan and Peter are responsible for the two pigs, and Carl for the chickens."

Rosaleen's smile felt so suddenly brittle that she thought it might splinter into tiny pieces at any moment. Trespassers! Thieves! God's feet! Stealing animals was a crime punishable by death! What kind of place had she and Hugh Caldwell come to?

Christian Rowsenly stood there, staring at them with disdain, his arms crossed over his chest, clearly waiting for them to speak ill of the illegal deeds that had been done in their honor.

Hugh responded almost at once, reaching out his hands and clapping Alec Berry and Harry Stoote on their shoulders.

"Good men," he said with feeling, "the lady Rosaleen and I thank you. All of you," he added, looking down both directions of the line, "for making our welcome at Briarstone so very...memorable."

A murmur of approval rippled through the line.

"Don't forget the girls, Chris," one of the men piped up.

"Girls?" Hugh repeated with interest.

Farther down, just past the last of the men, seven young females were leaning over, trying to get a better look at their handsome new lord. Seeing him glance their way, they blushed and giggled and straightened.

Christian gave them a reproving look. "I'll not forget them, Robert," he said, and continued to introduce the men still left in line, while Hugh dragged Rosaleen along.

When they had finally passed the very last man, thirty-three men in all, they came to the first of the women of Briarstone.

The sight of them made Rosaleen's already stiff person stiffen even more, if such a thing was possible. It wasn't that the creatures were attractive, for they weren't, though dressed as they were in ragged garments that left little to the imagination, they did possess a certain crude allure that almost set her teeth on edge. No, it was something else about them that bothered her.

They were whores. It made perfect sense, of course. After all the criminals they'd just met, what could be more fitting than that the women of Briarstone should be whores?

"This is Alice," Christian began, and in quick succession introduced Kate, Ada, Jehanne, Beth, Maggie and Helen. Helen, the last, was heavily pregnant.

Smiling widely, Hugh Caldwell looked at the giggling women like a man who had just discovered a vastly valuable treasure, and Rosaleen felt like kicking him.

"The girls are responsible for the good wine we will enjoy this night," Christian said. "They earned it ten nights past, when we thought you might arrive."

"They earned it?" Rosaleen asked, wondering what had caused her to ask such a foolish question.

Christian nodded. "Yes. There is a small village, Stenwick, about two miles' distance from here. Since coming to live here at my brother's invitation two years ago, the girls have occasionally bartered their skills in exchange for food and money." He smiled at the females with genuine affection. "We never would have been able to make it without the girls. They do the cooking and the cleaning and the caring for the children." He motioned to the end of the line, where a dozen or so dirty urchins waited with ill-concealed excitement to have their turn at being introduced.

Hugh Caldwell's expression was all admiration, and he quickly loosed Rosaleen so that he could more properly greet his new vassals. "Sweet angels!" he declared, kissing each of their hands in turn. He graced the enchanted females with his most charming grin. "How fortunate we are to have such kind, lovely ladies at Briarstone."

The angry sound of a throat loudly being cleared drew everyone's attention to Rosaleen.

Hugh Caldwell was far too pleased with his new vassals, she thought angrily, watching him. Especially the female ones. But she would be damned if she would sit by for the next three months and watch as he and his newfound friends pursued a life of crime and lecherous, fleshly pleasures. He'd dragged her here to run his household, and by the rood, she was going to run it!

Pulling herself up to her full height and lifting her chin ever so slightly, Rosaleen approached the women who would now serve as her ladies. They fell quiet as she surveyed them, taking in their filthy clothing and their filthier persons. Not a one of them either looked or smelled as if she'd had a bath in more than a year. Vaguely, Rosaleen wondered what it was that men like Hugh Caldwell saw in such creatures, but with a slight shake of her head pushed the unworthy thought away. These women were under her direction now, and their bathing habits would shortly be altered, as would those of the entire household of Briarstone.

"You are Alice?" she asked the first girl.

Cowering beneath Rosaleen's steady stare, the girl made an awkward bow.

"Yes, m'lady."

"How many years are you?"

"Ten 'n' five, I think, m'lady."

"You think?"

"Yes, m'lady."

"You are an orphan, then? You do not know the year of your birth?"

"Yes, m'lady. I mean, no, m'lady," the nervous girl corrected quickly. "I don't know when I come about."

"We shall leave it at ten and five then, and we shall count the date of your next day of birth as October the first. That is three months from today, is it not? Shall you like that?"

The girl smiled. "Yes, m'lady."

"Very well. You shall be ten and six years of age on October the first, and we shall have a celebration in honor of the day and of the harvest and of one other very important event, as well." Rosaleen looked meaningfully at Hugh, who made her a mock bow.

Alice looked confused, but Rosaleen ignored her and moved on to the next girl.

"You are Katherine?"

The young girl turned bright red.

"Kate, m'lady."

"Kate is a lesser form of Katherine," Rosaleen told her, "and I do not approve of the use of such. From this day forward you shall be called Katherine, just as Beth shall be called Elizabeth and Maggie shall be called Margaret. You will answer to no name other than Katherine, else I shall be most displeased. Now, how many years are you, Katherine?"

And so she went down the line, finding that Ada, at ten and seven years, was the eldest and that Elizabeth, at ten and three, was the youngest. When Rosaleen came to Helen, she reached out and placed a hand lightly on the girl's protruding stomach.

"You are far along, Helen, and shall birth this child soon," she said with a smile. "It will be a pleasure having a babe among us. Who is the father of this little one?"

Helen, ten and six years old, grinned at her new mistress, showing the many gaps in her smile where teeth should have been.

"Oh, we don't know yet, m'lady. Could be any one of the lads. We're waiting till it comes to decide." Ignoring her mistress's suddenly pale face, Helen eagerly went on. "I got two other little ones, m'lady, just down there." She pointed to where a child about two years of age held her younger brother by the hand. "That's Ralf and Menna. Aren't they pretty, m'lady?"

"Your children are lovely, Helen," Rosaleen replied truthfully. "All of these children are lovely. Do they belong to all of you, then?" she asked the women.

They did, as Hugh and Rosaleen saw when each child broke from the line and moved toward his or her mother. The eldest child looked to be nearing five years of age.

"When my brother realized that there were no vassals belonging to Briarstone," Christian Rowsenly explained, "he went to London and offered anyone who was interested five acres of land in exchange for five years' labor. The girls are expecting land, too, for though they don't labor in the fields, they take care of everything else, as I said earlier."

Nodding, Rosaleen said, "And so they should. From what I see of the keep, it looks as if it has been kept quite clean, a remarkable feat, considering the lack of most of one wall and the presence of a herd of oxen."

The girls in the line beamed openly, and Helen remarked, "Oh, m'lady, the beasts aren't so bad to put up wiv', really. They're a bit of work, but they're all the worthies we got, so we got to take good care of 'em."

"All the worthies you've got?" Hugh repeated, looking at Christian for translation.

"Without the oxen we couldn't work the fields," the boy said. "Without the fields we can't survive. Everything depends upon the fields. They come first. Always." Looking suddenly aged and weary, Christian ran his solemn gaze over his ragged mates. "We've gone hungry because of the fields and have labored hard in every kind of weather. If they don't come to harvest, my lord, there will be naught left for any of us."

Rosaleen frowned. "One harvest, even one as rich as what these fields give promise of, will not be enough to set

Briarstone to rights, Christian Rowsenly. It will be years, many years, before this estate can be made profitable.''

"Aye, that is so, my lady," he admitted, "but now that our lord has arrived, all will be well." He looked at Hugh. "We have vowed to work as long and as hard as we must to bring Briarstone about. All we need is someone to guide us and to lend us support."

But that wouldn't be enough, Rosaleen wanted to insist aloud, knowing full well that what Briarstone needed was money, a great deal of it, as well as expert management. Without those two essentials the estate would fail, and all the labor and support in the world wouldn't save it.

She was about to speak, to make this point in as gentle a way as she could, when she was stopped by the expression on Hugh Caldwell's face. He looked, quite plainly, as though he was about to bolt.

"You are fortunate then, people of Briarstone," she addressed the assembled, wondering as she did where the words were coming from and why she couldn't make them stop, "for Hugh Caldwell will guide you well. Indeed, better and more ably than any other man on God's earth could do."

What in God's holy name was she *saying?* she wondered with horror. Hugh Caldwell's face mirrored her thoughts exactly, and she wondered if he was going to reach out and strike her to try to bring back her senses.

"Thank you *so much,* my lady," Hugh replied stiffly.

Katherine spoke up suddenly.

"We got a chamber upstairs readied fer you, m'lord, but we din't 'spect fer you to 'ave a wife." She blushed hotly. "So we don't got nothin' ready fer you, m'lady."

"She's not my wife," Hugh told her, and Rosaleen said at the same time, "Oh! I'm not his wife!"

Everyone looked at them.

Hugh and Rosaleen exchanged glances.

"The lady Rosaleen is my, uh..." Hugh began, unsure.

"Sister!" Rosaleen replied, just exactly as Hugh announced, "Cousin!"

They exchanged glances again, a bit hotter, and both opened their mouths to speak.

"Sister," he said.

"Cousin," she said.

Hugh lifted a hand and set it firmly over Rosaleen's mouth. He looked at his perplexed vassals and explained, "It's a confused lineage in our family. Suffice it to say that the lady Rosaleen is *not* my wife."

Rosaleen shoved his hand away with a huff, and the seven women of Briarstone looked at their master with renewed interest.

"As well," Hugh continued, "I would ask that you call me Hugh Caldwell, or even Hugh, but do not name me as either sir or lord, for it suits me not."

The people of Briarstone gaped at him.

"But are you not a knight?" Christian Rowsenly demanded.

"No, thank God," replied Hugh. "And, unlike the lady Rosaleen, I've no claim to nobility. I am bastard born, and naught better than one of the king's paid soldiers."

Christian Rowsenly, staring hard at the big man who was now the master of Briarstone in place of his dead brother, had some difficulty reconciling these words with his memories of the bold, skilled man who had so easily bested three robbers earlier that day. He shook his head.

"Very well, my...Hugh Caldwell. It shall be as you say, though you must give us time to become used to it."

"Of course," Hugh replied. "You will find me a tolerable master, I think."

Christian frowned, and some indefinable emotion passed briefly over his handsome features. When he swung his head to look back at the girls, Rosaleen thought she saw a great deal of sadness in his eyes.

"Let us show Hugh Caldwell his chamber," Christian said, "and find a fit chamber for the lady Rosaleen." He walked toward the uneven stone stairway, and Hugh and Rosaleen followed. "There are more than twelve chambers above stairs," he said, "but we do not use them. None of the fires work, save one in the great hall and one in the master's chamber, so we remain in the hall, where 'tis warmer, in spite of the missing wall." He set a foot on the bottom stair and, with a resolute glance into the darkness above, began to climb. "I think you will be pleased at how well we have learned to live with the little we have at hand."

Chapter Twelve

Lying in the darkness, his head pillowed atop his clasped hands, Hugh tried, for the fifth time, to make himself sleep. He closed his eyes tightly and began counting.

"One, two, three, four, five, six, seven, eight..."

No, that wasn't right. He opened his eyes and tried to recall what his mother had told him when he was little. Her soft voice and even softer hands were easy to recall; he would never forget her tender gentling of him after he'd waken from one of his bad dreams.

"Count back from one hundred, Hugh," she'd say, stroking her beautiful fingers slowly through his hair, "and before you reach one you shall be asleep."

It had always worked. He would begin to count aloud, and she would stay beside him, stroking his hair, keeping him safe, until he'd unwittingly fallen to sleep.

He closed his eyes once more and tried again as he now remembered it should be.

"One hundred, ninety-nine, ninety-eight, ninety-seven..."

"It's all right, my Hugh. It's all right, son. Go ahead and cry."

"No," Hugh said aloud, and began counting more loudly, "Ninety-six, ninety-five, ninety-four..."

It didn't work. His mother was gone. Dead. Strong arms circled him in his memory, holding him close, rocking him, soothing him while he cried and cried and...

"No!"

He sat up.

"Damn!" he swore, swallowing hard and trying to force his breathing to slow. He worked at calming himself for several long moments, then he lay down again, shut his eyes and took up counting from the beginning.

"One hundred, ninety-nine, ninety-eight, ninety-seven, ninety-six..."

He tried to force his mind to concentrate on the numbers, but still the memories rose up to torment him.

A long arm reaching out to hug him, the warm, deep laughter, the words. "You rascal, Hugh Baldwin! I should turn you over my knee for giving me such a fright!"

And him laughing...laughing as if he had a right to laugh with this man. "You were scared, Father! You were scared!"

"I'm never scared!"

"You were scared for me!"

More laughter. Why had he ever laughed with that bastard?

"I wasn't scared," his father had insisted, "I just didn't like the thought of my Hugh being up so high!" Then he'd taken Hugh up in his strong arms, hugging him and shaking him with violent affection so that his skinny little-boy legs had whipped back and forth until he had laughed... laughed...

"No!" he shouted into the darkness, bolting up in the bed again.

Hugh didn't let himself think this time. He threw the covers aside and got out of the bed.

Standing by the only opening in the room, a small window more suited for defense than for letting in light and air, he drew in his breath with forced slowness, calming himself, easing the pain of his body and mind.

What he needed, he thought as he ran his damp hands through his tangled hair, was a fight...a good, hard, wearying fight. That would fix him for a while, or at least would tire him enough so that he could sleep.

Of course, there wasn't much chance of finding a good fight in this rotting castle he found himself stuck with...a good fight or anything else he might want. There was no ale, no gaming. There weren't even any women available to him, if the look Rosaleen had given him earlier when he'd innocently dallied with the ladies of Briarstone was anything to judge by.

The wretched female! It was *her* fault that he was in such painful need of a woman. The least she could do was turn a blind eye while he relieved himself with the more than willing wenches who had been such a welcome surprise in the midst of the rest of this mess.

Briarstone! God's mercy, what a fool he'd made of himself these past many months with all his hopes and dreams about being his own man with his own estate. He rubbed his eyes in misery. No wonder King Henry had been so pleased to grant his request. No one, no sound-minded person, could possibly want to find himself possessed of this ancient pile of rocks.

He'd wanted to run. He had taken one look at the wreck they'd walked into and had wanted to grab Rosaleen, drag her back out to their horses, mount up and ride away.

And he might have done just that if he hadn't made the fatal mistake of glancing at the people standing in that long, straight line. It amazed him still, as he thought of it now, how that one brief glance had done him in. The great, immovable Hugh Caldwell, conquered in a moment by the grimy faces of the most ragged group of beings he'd ever set eyes on. The looks on their faces . . . the eagerness, hope, even relief, had felled him more surely than any sword could have done.

He had nothing to offer these people; less than nothing, in truth. No money, no husbandry skills, no morality...nothing. Almost anyone would be better able to help them than he. But he couldn't leave. Not now. Not after he'd seen the way they'd looked at him, as though he were the answer to all their prayers, as though he were their savior finally arrived. In a moment his desire to run had changed into a fierce desire to stay and to make this wreck of a place into something. If such a thing were possible.

So now they were stuck with each other. He with a crumbling ruin and a number of vassals the likes of which he doubted any other man had ever possessed, and they with a mercenary who had neither birth nor fortune nor any decent qualities to redeem him.

Well, perhaps that wasn't entirely true, he thought, trying to be generous with himself. He did know how to hunt, and would spend the next several days using that knowledge to fill the empty larder of Briarstone as best he could. And he had brought Rosaleen to these needy people.

He'd been mistaken about her, he had realized very quickly after their arrival. The way she had taken charge of the people of Briarstone, easily commanding their respect and obedience, made it clear that she'd have no troubles running his household. She knew what she was doing, and he knew full well that her admirable skills couldn't have been learned in any lowly hovel.

The thought made his forehead crease with displeasure. If she wasn't the lowly daughter of some small landed lord, then just who, or better yet, what—was she?

A soft rap at his door drew his attention.

"H-H-Hugh?" Rosaleen's voice came trembling through the darkness.

An unbidden smile bloomed on his lips.

The door opened a little more. "Hugh? May I c-come in?"

It was so dark that Hugh could barely make out her slender, white-clad form. "I'm here by the window, Rosaleen. Come."

He thought he heard a sound of relief just before she shut the door again, and he watched as, feeling her way with both hands on the chamber's stone wall, she made her way toward him.

When she got within reach, he stretched out a hand and drew her shivering body to him. She surprised him by not stopping just in front of him, as he had thought she would, but by moving until she actually bumped up against him, wrapping her arms about his waist and pushing her face against his shoulder as if she were a child seeking shelter.

"Why, Rosaleen," he murmured, sliding his arms about her, "you're frightened. What's happened? Did you find rats in your chamber?"

"Of course not!" she replied indignantly, her voice muffled against his bare skin. "I'm not frightened. I never get frightened."

"No? Then why do you shake so?"

She sniffed before answering, "I'm cold."

He laughed. "Of course. In the midst of summer with the rest of us sweating, you somehow contrive to be cold. You are the most contrary female on God's earth, Rosaleen no-name."

Rosaleen didn't laugh. "My chamber is so dark and . . . cold." She sniffed again, and Hugh reached up a hand to touch her wet cheek.

"God's mercy," he whispered with dismay, "you're crying!"

"No." She shook her head against him. "I'm not crying. I never cry."

"Oh, sweeting." He rubbed his hands over her slender shoulders in a soothing caress. "You are frightened. Because you are weary? Because of the dark? There's no shame in that. This old keep is as dark as the Fiend's soul. If we had some candles, it would be a little better."

"But we haven't any candles." Rosaleen sniffled once more. "Oh, Hugh, what can we do? There is much to be done here and naught to do it with."

"Is that what makes you weep?" he asked softly, drying her cheeks with gentle fingers. "You've no need to fear, sweeting. I'll not let you suffer either hunger or harm."

Her delicate fingers wrapped around his wrists, stilling him.

"I know that, Hugh Caldwell, but I am not your only care. These people have so little, not even a decent well for water, and the few things they do have are so meager and poor. Other than the oxen, the bed in this chamber is the only item of any value."

"John Rowsenly's one allowance for his comfort," Hugh admitted, thinking of all the dreams that had died with that man.

"What are we going to do?" she asked again, worry heavy in her voice. "I feel at such a loss. Without money, what can we even hope to do?"

He cradled her face in his hands, unable to reason why he should want so much to comfort her.

"We'll do what we can, as we can," he said, striving to speak with a confidence he didn't feel. "It shouldn't be so bad. For the next few days we'll work to increase our supply of food. I'll take some of the men hunting on the morrow and will send Alex a missive, asking him to send Amazon to me as soon as may be. Once I've got her back I'll be able to keep meat on the table. Meat we'll not have to steal, which should prove a relief to our neighbors. Then we'll turn our attention to repairing the well, or to digging a new one if necessary."

"And then?" she pressed.

"Then," he said with a weary sigh, moving his hands to rest on her shoulders, "we wait three months until the harvest, and pray each morn and eve that the fields we saw this day fulfill their promise of riches."

"It will not be enough," Rosaleen said sadly. "Whatever money you receive from the harvest will be needed to prepare for the next harvest. There will be naught left for repairs, for anything."

"We'll have to hope there will be," he replied. "Or we'll have to survive with what we get."

"There is a better way, Hugh Caldwell. Better and much more reasonable."

He lifted his eyebrows. "Yes, I suppose there is. I could organize and train the men a little better and we could make a good living as highway robbers. And the girls might be willing to make the place a whorehouse. I daresay Briarstone could make a small fortune in a year's time."

"Or you could write your brother and ask him to help you," she put in as quickly as she could, trying to ride on his good humor.

The painful squeezing of his fingers on her shoulders told Rosaleen that his humor had flown.

"And why would I want to do such a foolish thing, Rosaleen? I think you must have lost your senses."

"It's not foolish," she insisted, pushing at his chest to make him release her. "You have a right to a portion of Gyer..."

"I have no right to anything of Gyer!"

"You do!" Shoving free, she faced him, hands on hips. "As a younger son you have a right to a share of your father's and brother's estate!"

"Charles Baldwin was *not* my father!" he shouted with sudden rage. "And don't ever," he warned when she opened her mouth to argue, "suggest that that bastard acknowledged me as his son. Indeed, Rosaleen, you would be well advised never to speak his name in my hearing again."

Drawing in a breath, Rosaleen tried again, more calmly. "Notwithstanding what that man may or may not have felt for you or you for him, Hugh Caldwell, you still have a claim to a portion of the Baldwin estates. Your brother, the Lord of Gyer, made that quite clear when we were with them."

"My *half* brother is a good and benevolent man," Hugh stated angrily. "He is as charitable to the bastard son of Jaward Ryon as he is to his vassals and villeins. Do you ask me to take advantage of him because he was born with such unruly faults?"

"By the rood!" Rosaleen swore. "You are beyond understanding! You impugn your kind brother and yourself all in the same breath! But no one is safe from your venom when your pride is threatened, are they? You keep running from what you are, refusing to accept the truth, and when you can't run fast enough you fight to keep from thinking. What will you do now, Hugh Caldwell? Will you stay at Briarstone and watch these people starve and suffer because you were too proud to help them, or will you run again to keep from thinking of them?"

He glared at her through the darkness and Rosaleen could see the harsh movement of his chest.

"Briarstone is my estate, Rosaleen, and you are naught but my servant for the next three months. Don't speak to me of it again, and don't mention my noble brother again, either, if you know what's good for you."

Rosaleen stiffened. "*Yes*, my Lord Caldwell. *Certainly*, my Lord Caldwell. Please forgive your lowly servant for being so forward as to make a sensible suggestion to you, my Lord Caldwell. Please continue to let your people starve, my Lord Caldwell. Please continue to behave like an idiot, my Lord Caldwell. If you will but pardon your lowly servant, my Lord Caldwell, I shall take my leave!" And with that she began to stumble in the darkness, furiously, in what she hoped was the direction of the door.

Strong hands grabbed her before she could take more than three steps, and Rosaleen found herself gasping for breath as Hugh slammed her up against his hard chest.

"That sharp tongue of yours, Rosaleen," he said softly, "will be the end of one of us yet."

His mouth came down on hers before she could make a reply, and one strong hand held the back of her head so that she couldn't escape him.

The first kiss was hard, painful, and Rosaleen whimpered with fear. Hugh lifted his head at once, then lowered it and kissed her again, gently this time, with an unexpected tenderness that melted Rosaleen's rage like a handful of snow under a hot sun.

He was so needy, so wanting. She couldn't deny him. She loved him . . . loved him so that the feeling was an agony rather than a pleasure, as she had always thought love would be. She loved him, aye, the truth of it ran deep in her as his kiss grew demanding and as his hands began to move over her thinly covered body. She had loved him for days now, for so long she didn't even know when she had started.

When he lifted his head, Rosaleen discovered that her arms had somehow gone around his neck.

"You will never mention this matter to me again," Hugh told her between breaths. "And you will never mock me again in such a manner."

"I will," she replied between her own labored breaths. "I will do so whenever it pleases me. And if you will not write your brother on behalf of these people then I shall, Hugh Caldwell. I swear it!"

He kissed her again, long and deeply, until Rosaleen's legs had turned a consistency similar to that of boiled oats.

"If you do, mistress," he warned when he lifted his mouth once more, "I shall lock you in the highest tower at Briarstone. You know the one I mean. That crumbling one at the northern corner of the outer wall."

"Hah!" she scorned. "I shall scream loudly and without ceasing until every neighbor within five miles is at Briarstone's door begging you to set me free."

"I'll gag you before I lock you up, then. Now be quiet, Rosaleen, and give in to me."

Somehow Rosaleen found herself lying on Hugh Caldwell's soft feather bed, with Hugh Caldwell himself beside her, kissing her and holding her and trying to undress her.

"Please, Hugh." She struggled to get away from him. "I—I'm frightened."

He chuckled, the action puffing warm breath against her ear before he gently kissed it. Moving his fingers from the laces of her chemise, he sought her hand and clasped it.

"You're frightened," he murmured, drawing her hand up to press it against his chest, "and I'm frightened." He pressed her fingers flat at the place where his heart beat, and feeling the wild movement there, Rosaleen stilled. She looked up in the darkness and met his eyes, so close to her own.

"What is it between us, Rosaleen?" Hugh asked quietly. "What is it?"

She shook her head slightly, confused.

"From the beginning, it has been there," he went on, stopping her words. "Deny it if you can, Rosaleen. Tell me you have felt nothing between us."

She wanted to deny it, so very much, but he spoke the truth. There was something between them, something she had never felt with another living being. It was a rightness, a completeness, a deep, immeasurable understanding that supplanted the need for words. He had never been a stranger to her. She had known him at once.

Mute, she shook her head again, telling him that she could not deny his words.

He pressed her hand against his chest more firmly. "I've never been as afraid of anything or anyone as I am of you. I've been a free man these past ten years," he said fiercely. "*Free*, Rosaleen. Do you understand?"

Hot tears stung her eyes. "Yes, Hugh," she whispered. She loved him, but there was no future for him in her life, just as there was no future in his for her. "I understand."

He lowered his mouth and began to kiss her again, fully and hungrily, while his hands went back to unlacing her shift. This time she lay passive beneath him, accepting the skilled, sensual caresses of his tongue in her mouth and the gentle touches of his warm hands on her flesh and trying to commit every feeling he gave her to memory. He pulled her chemise past her shoulders and breasts until it was rolled around her waist.

"Rosaleen," he murmured, gazing at her in the darkness, touching one breast reverently with the tips of his fingers. "You are so lovely. That first night, when I saw you, I could scarce believe how perfect you are."

"You are very beautiful, also, Hugh Caldwell," Rosaleen said, lifting a hand to touch the softness of his long, amber-colored hair. "And I'm still frightened."

"Don't be," he whispered, kissing her gently. "I want only to give you pleasure, love."

His hands moved on her, causing Rosaleen to shift restlessly beneath his touch.

"I . . . I don't know what's happening."

"Good things, darling," he murmured, his breath warm against one breast. "These are good things happening between us." He touched her hard nipple with the wet heat of his tongue, and Rosaleen gasped with pleasure and surprise.

He chuckled. "Like that, do you? You'll like this even better." His mouth closed over her, suckling, and Rosaleen cried out and writhed beneath him.

"Hugh!"

"Yes, sweeting." He moved to caress her other breast in the same manner. "I shall love all of you."

"Hugh." She tugged at his hair before becoming lost in the pleasure of his touch. "I . . . I don't wish to lose my maidenhead. I can't, even if I wished to."

Hugh lifted his head. "Of course you don't wish to lose your maidenhead," he said softly. "All maidens are frightened the first time, just as you are. But I'll not take your maidenhead from you. Not now. Not tonight. Tonight I only wish to touch you. That's all, Rosaleen. That's all." She squirmed with fright, but Hugh held her tight with one arm, while with his free hand he began to caress her belly.

"Hush," he murmured, kissing her mouth with soft, quick kisses, seducing away her will to resist him. "There are many ways to find pleasure that will leave you a maiden, and I shall teach you all of them." His fingers moved to stroke the soft skin of her thigh.

"Hugh..."

"This is but the beginning for us, Rosaleen. I'll not let you hold yourself from me again after this."

"Hugh..."

"Hush."

Chapter Thirteen

"My darling. My sweet, darling baby. Did you miss me, little love? I missed you. Yes, I did. I missed you very, very much."

This, followed by several kissing noises, brought Rosaleen awake.

"But we'll never be parted again, will we, my darling? No, we'll not. Never, never, never."

It was sickening, Hugh Caldwell's baby talk, and Rosaleen sat slowly, wondering why he should be doing such a thing. The only living creature she'd ever heard him speak to in such a foolish manner was his...

"Bird," she said aloud, opening her eyes fully.

Hearing her, Hugh glanced toward the bed.

"You're awake, at last," he said, standing from where he'd been sitting by the window and carrying Amazon to the bed. "Look who arrived this morn with her own escort of four of my brother's finest knights." He sat on the bed with a thump, Amazon squawked in complaint, and Hugh kissed her beak soothingly. "There now, my sweet," he crooned. "I didn't mean to startle you."

"'Sbones, Hugh Caldwell, the way you treat that... creature...is beyond belief," Rosaleen said, rubbing her eyes.

"Is that so?" he asked, setting Amazon on the bed's wooden end. Turning back to Rosaleen, he captured her wrists and pressed her flat on the mattress. "And what of the way I treat you, sweeting?"

Full of shame and not a little remorse for what had passed between them the night before, Rosaleen turned her head away.

An angry sound rumbled out of Hugh, and he nipped the soft skin beneath her ear, just sharply enough to startle her.

"Never turn from me, Rosaleen." With his tongue he soothed the sting away. "You gave yourself to me, and now you are mine for the next three months. I'll not be waylaid by fits of maidenly fear. Set your mind to it."

Briefly, she struggled, but he was so much stronger that she knew at once it was futile. Keeping her head turned, Rosaleen spoke through set teeth. "I came to Briarstone to oversee your household, Hugh Caldwell, not to be your whore."

He had the nerve to laugh. "Whore?" he repeated, kissing her ear and lightly touching the center of it with his tongue. "You'll never be any man's whore, beautiful sweet. But we'll discuss this matter later. Tonight, in fact," he said with certainty, sitting up and releasing her.

"Tonight," she informed him, "I'll be staying in my own chamber."

"Of course," he replied easily. "Now, have you any interest in what else my brother sent?"

"No."

He gave a sigh. "I'll have to read the missive he sent you myself, then."

"What!" She bolted upright and grabbed Hugh's tunic. "Your brother sent me a missive?"

"He did," Hugh confirmed, taking the opportunity to slip his arms around her waist. "Would you care to read it?"

She looked at him as though he were mad. "Of course I wish to read it. It is for me, is it not?"

"It is."

"Well, then?"

"Well?"

"May I have it, please?"

He smiled. "May I have an appropriate morning's greeting?"

Rosaleen was confused. "I suppose you might. Good morning, Hugh Caldwell."

"Rosaleen, my sweet, surely you know me better than that."

Her eyes narrowed. "Only too well, Hugh Caldwell. Tell me plainly what you want."

Hugh lowered his head. "Open your mouth, Rosaleen, and give me a proper kiss."

"I'll do no such thing! I'll not make payment for something that already belongs to me! I'll not—"

Hugh's mouth closed over hers, stopping whatever else she meant to say. By the time the kiss was done, Rosaleen found herself lying on her pillows again, with Hugh Caldwell looming over her, a look of male satisfaction on his face.

"Do you want your missive, Rosaleen?"

"Hmm?" She gazed at him dreamily.

"Your missive, do you want it?"

"Very well," she said pliantly, sighing.

Hugh chuckled and pressed a sealed parchment into her hands. "Here, then. Read it and get yourself up and dressed. I've brought warm water for you, over there." He nodded toward a small wooden tub set before the fire. "Be as quick as you can. I mean to ride to the village this morn with a few of the men to buy whatever we'll need for the next few months, and I want you to prepare a list."

Rosaleen was surprised. "You've sufficient money for that? Briarstone's needs are great."

He shrugged. "Enough to purchase those few necessities we'll not be able to gather for ourselves, I believe. And if I don't, a visit to a tavern should fill our purses a bit more thickly."

"Of course," she said. "You'd rather gamble than write your brother a simple request. I should have expected such from you, Hugh Caldwell."

"Rosaleen," Hugh said wearily, standing, "you walk a narrow ledge by speaking of matters best left unspoken." He took Amazon on his wrist, then perched her on his shoulder. "We'll expect you downstairs within the half hour, so that we may all break our fast together."

She watched him leave, then directed her attention to the missive in her hands. Turning it to look at it from all angles, she briefly wondered how it was that the Lord of Gyer had known she would be at Briarstone, and whether he was writing to inform her that her uncle now knew of her location, too.

Breaking the seal, she unfolded the thick sheet of parchment and began to read.

To Rosaleen Sarant, Lady of Siere,
Forgive, I beg, my boldness in believing you to be under my brother's care at Briarstone. I have known Hugh these many years, thus I felt certain he could meet with naught but success when he set out to find you a few days past.

My wife and I regretted most truly the sudden conclusion of your welcome visit to our home, though we understand the circumstances that made you feel it necessary to depart. It is our great hope that you will honor us with your presence again in the future, my lady, when matters presently distressing you have been set right. Until that time, please be certain that we stand ready to serve you at any time and in any manner.

Information has arrived from London that I believe will be of interest to you. Your uncle has informed the king that you have been taken captive by unknown assailants and that a search carried out by him and your betrothed has failed to locate either you or your captors. Sir Anselm has vowed to continue the search, and the king has sent many of his own knights throughout England on your behalf, as well.

Lady Rosaleen, should you desire to travel to London very shortly, I would be honored to escort you there if you will but send word, and thus I make my pledge before God to maintain you against any threat of danger.

Please remember my lady and I to our wayward brother, and may God have you both in His keeping.

Sir Alexander Baldwin

The missive fell from Rosaleen's hands, and she stared at it, stunned.

Uncle Anselm meant to kill her.

God's mercy! He meant to kill her if he could find her, and had set his plan in readiness by telling the king that she'd been taken captive. No one would question her death, not even if Uncle Anselm took her body to display it at court, for one and all would accept his word that she had been killed by her captors. And if he didn't take her body as proof, the king would wait only a few months be-

fore declaring her death as fact, thereby making Uncle
Anselm the Earl of Siere.

Damn the man!

She took the missive up and read it through once more,
thanking God above that the Lord of Gyer had set his fealty on her rather than her uncle. It was too late for regret, of course, but Rosaleen silently berated herself for
having so impetuously run away from Gyer.

She must get to London, now more than ever. She had
to protect her family's name and titles and estates. They
were her responsibility, and assuring their continuance was
what she had been born to do. Everything, her father's
honor, his lineage, depended on her and on her alone.

And yet at the same time, there was no use trying to deny
that she wanted to stay with Hugh Caldwell, especially after what had passed between them in the night. It had been
wrong, yes, she knew that as well as she knew her own
name, but she'd not lie or pretend that she hadn't wanted
him then or that she didn't want him again, even if she
could have only that very little bit of him that they had already shared.

She loved him, and when this was over, when Siere had
been restored to her and when she had done her duty as the
heiress of Siere, she would never be able to see him again.
For all the years to come she would have only her memories of this time with him from which to gather as much
happiness as she could.

Throwing the covers aside, Rosaleen got up from the
bed, strode to the fire and threw the missive into it.
Watching as it burned, she made her determination. For
three months she would stay with Hugh Caldwell. She
would love him and help him and cherish every moment
she had with him as if it were her last, and she would carefully store each memory away in the corners of her heart.

When it was all over she would go to London; she would turn from Hugh Caldwell and would never look back.

If, of course, her uncle didn't find her first.

"Did my brother write you a proper scolding, sweet?" Hugh asked as he tied Amazon's leather strap to his wrist.

"In truth," Rosaleen replied with a haughty grin, "he thanked me for my visit and invited me to stay again at Gyer whenever it pleases me."

With a laugh, Hugh began checking Saint's saddle and reins. Although they were standing in the great hall of Castle Briarstone, they were surrounded by horses, where Hugh had decided the beasts should be housed alongside the oxen.

"Poor Alex," he said pityingly. "I told you he's possessed of too much charity. Chris, lad—" he turned his attention to the boy, who was readying one of the three skinny horses Briarstone possessed "—has the lady Rosaleen given you a list of what we'll need?"

"By word, yes, Hugh Caldwell, for we've no parchment or writing instruments."

Casting a wary glance toward Rosaleen, Hugh said, "Recite this list to me."

Rosaleen cursed under her breath and Christian looked thoughtful.

"Twelve geese," he began carefully, "twenty capons, twenty pigs, six milking cows, two dozen laying hens, three hundred new eggs—"

The people of Briarstone, who were gathered in the great hall, began to murmur excitedly.

"—seventy-five bushels cleanly milled flour, no pebbles or vermin, else the lady Rosaleen will personally see the miller jailed, fifty bushels cleanly milled oats, two bushels salt, one bushel pepper, five bushels each sugar and raisins, twelve barrels good ale—''

The men of Briarstone gave up a small cheer.

''—twelve barrels good wine, preferably Italian—''

Hugh raised his eyebrows at Rosaleen, and Rosaleen blushed.

''—one hundred yards heavy cloth, twelve spools waxed thread, seven pots dye in the following colors, red, green, blue, yellow, orange, brown and black—''

The ladies of Briarstone aahed with delight.

''—twenty sewing needles, strong and sharp, sixty pounds good wax candles, ten pounds scented soap, preferably French—''

Hugh looked at Rosaleen again, and this time she simply looked away.

''—twenty sheets parchment—''

Hugh frowned.

''—twelve writing quills, five pots ink—''

Hugh scowled.

''—two pounds sealing wax—''

Hugh made a growling sound.

''—and twelve boards and sets of pieces to comprise complete games of chess.''

The loud cheers following this recitation were earsplitting, and no one save Rosaleen heard Hugh when he said to her, ''I'll see you outside, woman. *Now.*''

''But, Hugh, there's so much work that needs to be done and—''

He grabbed her by the elbow and dragged her toward the doors. A moment later Rosaleen found herself standing in the bailey with a furious Hugh Caldwell facing her down.

''You will explain yourself, mistress.''

Clasping her hands together, Rosaleen gazed at him innocently.

"Explain, my lord?"

"Rosaleen . . ."

Hearing his tone of voice, Rosaleen wisely gave up pretending.

"I don't know why you are so angry, Hugh Caldwell. You told me to make a list of the things we needed, and I did."

Hugh gritted his teeth. "Your list, my sweet, would pauper a king. I can easily understand the wheat and oats and candles and soap and even the cloth, but by the Fiend's foot, what made you list the other? You know very well I haven't the funds to purchase even a tenth of what you listed."

Rosaleen met his gaze steadily. "I listed them, Hugh Caldwell, because those are the needs Briarstone must have met, and if you will note, I listed nothing frivolous such as spices or even milk or cream. You asked me for a list and I gave you one. An honest one."

Hugh didn't know whether to laugh in disbelief or weep with frustration. "Nothing frivolous? *Italian* wine, *French* soap, twelve sets of *chess!*"

Rosaleen's expression was blank, as if she didn't understand what could possibly be wrong with those items being on her list, and Hugh did his best to keep his already hot temper under control.

"You made that list to set my back against a wall and to make me look a fool before my people when I return from Stenwick with less than what they are now so happily expecting. I am sorely tempted to set you over my knee again and teach you a much needed lesson."

"I didn't know that you would ask Christian to repeat the list I'd given him!" she protested. "I only wished to give him as complete a list as possible. From that I thought you would purchase what you thought best."

He laughed bitterly. "I don't believe you, sweet. By giving him such a list you meant to shame me into writing my brother. But you've failed, Rosaleen. I may be the bastard half brother of the great Lord of Gyer, but I will *never* lower myself to begging to him. Not to a Baldwin," he added with hate-filled fury, stalking Rosaleen as she backed away from him. "I'd rather scrape and slaver to a goddamned Ryon than ever ask a Baldwin for one half groat of charity, and don't you ever, *ever*—" he grabbed Rosaleen by the arms and shook her "—think otherwise again!"

His grip was so harsh that tears stung Rosaleen's eyes.

"I wasn't trying to shame you! I meant only to make you know how great the needs of the people of Briarstone are. Hugh, stop!" She shoved at him and he loosed her. Stepping back, rubbing her arms, she cried furiously, "Men! God help me to understand a one of them! If there was a way for your people to live off that incredible pride of yours, they'd never go hungry again!"

They stood glaring at each other in silence, until Rosaleen said, "Write your brother and ask him to make a loan to you, then. A loan you'll repay as soon as Briarstone shows a credible profit. It will be a business matter, nothing more, nothing less." Her voice took on a tone of daring. "You need not even view the Lord of Gyer as a relative, but only as a banker from whose source you have drawn. Even the lowliest estate owner makes such contracts for the good of his lands and people. Has not the Lord of Gyer arranged such loans with his own vassals?"

Hugh nodded, but when he spoke, the words had nothing to do with either money or loans.

"There is something about you, Rosaleen," he said very slowly, very calmly, "that bothers me greatly."

Rosaleen's eyes widened first in surprise and next in bewilderment. Finally she looked down at herself, at the filthy clothes she hadn't had a chance to wash yet, and, spreading her arms wide, said, "Well, I know, Hugh, but I did try to bathe as best I could this morn, though there wasn't any soap. Once I've had a proper bath and have washed my clothes, I'm sure that I'll—"

"R-Rosaleen," Hugh managed to say, trying and failing to keep the sudden laughter out of his voice, "that's n-not what I meant, and you damned well know it! God's teeth, woman! Can you never let me stay angry with you for more than a few minutes?"

Perplexed, Rosaleen stood still as he neared her.

"What I meant," he clarified, lifting his hands to gently rub those places on her arms where he had earlier hurt her, "is that I am bothered by the fact that you are not in truth what you pretend to be."

When all the color drained out of her face, Hugh knew he had been right and, strangely, the knowledge made his heart ache.

"You promised that you would not press me until we reached London," she whispered. "That was our agreement, else I never would have come to Briarstone with you."

He frowned, and his hands moved in gentle circles over her tender skin. "I'll not break my word to you, Rosaleen. It has simply become clear to me that your knowledge of estates is much greater than I'd thought. I cannot help but wonder who you are in truth, or how wellborn."

"Will you write to your brother, Hugh Caldwell?" she asked, unwilling to speak of such things.

He gave her a very odd, considering look. "No," he said finally. "I have said I will not and I'll not, but we shall make a bargain betwixt the two of us, if you like. Your idea of a loan appeals to me, though I would, in truth, prefer to receive money from a source other than my brother. However, I realize that none of the London banks would be willing to take a risk on Briarstone as immediately as my brother would, and it would please me to prove my sufficiency to him by repaying such a loan with interest.''

''Oh, Hugh! You will write to him, then?''

''No, I said we would make a bargain, and that the idea of asking my brother for a loan is not entirely repugnant to me.''

''But what...''

He placed one hand beneath her chin and held her very still. ''A bargain, sweeting. An exchange. I will agree to let you write my brother, requesting a loan made not to me but to the people of Briarstone, to be repaid with interest. In return for my allowing this, you will agree to give me perfect obedience for the next three months.''

Stunned, she stared at him. She was the heiress of Siere. She owed obedience to no man save the king.

''Complete, total obedience, Rosaleen,'' he said. ''No speaking against my will, whatever it may be. No making me look a fool before my vassals.''

''I did *not* try to make you look a fool this morn,'' she insisted.

''Do we have a bargain, Rosaleen?''

''Never! I'd have to be mad to make a pact with such a devil! You would take unfair advantage at every turn!''

''Rosaleen!'' Hugh spoke as if she'd mortally wounded him and dramatically placed a hand over his heart. ''How can you say such a thing?''

''Easily,'' she muttered, and made to move around him to return to the keep.

"Very well. But remember, Rosaleen," he said to her retreating back, "you could have saved the people of Briarstone needless suffering but didn't."

Rosaleen whirled around.

"That's not fair, Hugh Caldwell! You're the one who makes them suffer, not I!"

"We both do, then," he replied with a slight shrug. "But we can both put an end to it, can we not? You have asked me to make a sacrifice, one that is more than a little unpleasant for me to make, and I have asked you to do the same. If that's not fair, I don't know what is."

Her expression was grim. "You will make me suffer if I make this bargain," she accused. "You will punish me endlessly."

He shook his head. "I'll not, Rosaleen. I swear it before God. There are many things I should like to do to you, darling, but making you suffer isn't one of them."

"I won't be made to give up my maidenhead simply because you demand it!"

His face showed real surprise. "God's toes, Rosaleen, you make your virginity sound like royal goods."

Strangely enough, she thought, he wasn't wrong about that. The virginity of the heiress of Siere, or rather the absence of it, was a matter that could seriously affect any marriage alliance she might make. The heiress of Siere must go to her marriage bed a maiden, else the parentage of the possible future Earl of Siere might be in question.

"I cannot lose my maidenhead," she repeated stubbornly.

Hugh pinned Rosaleen with a look that made her feel warm all over. "I want to be inside your body, Rosaleen," he said softly. "Tonight. Today. This very minute, in fact. And you want to feel me inside you just as badly. How long do you think we can share a bed without

quenching the fire that's been building between us since the
moment we set eyes on one another?''

His words made her shake so badly that Rosaleen
thought she might stumble to the ground and, seeing her
weakness, Hugh took advantage, going to her and pulling
her body against his own.

"Rosaleen," he murmured, laughter in his voice, "you
are so damned innocent. I could seduce you with words as
easily as with touches, little sweeting." He kissed her
trembling mouth gently.

"Oh, Hugh, don't do this to me," she begged, putting
her arms around him and pressing her face against the
warmth of his neck. She wanted him with all the violence
of a virgin's desire, so passionately that it was painful. "I
cannot lose my virginity, save to the man I wed. I will do
anything else you ask. Anything, I swear it, but don't make
me do that."

He groaned loudly. "God's feet, I hate making promises I'm not certain I can keep." With both hands he
cupped her bottom and pressed her softness up against his
aching manhood. "Can you not feel how much I want
you? Do you think that feeling is pleasant, especially when
the only ride I've got to look forward to is the one to Stenwick?''

The giggles that came out of Rosaleen were unstoppa-
ble.

Hugh sighed. "Very well, let us make our bargain and
have done with it. My vassals have bitten their nails to
naught by now, mostlike." He put Rosaleen from him and
looked into her beautiful face. "I promise to do my best
not to take your maidenhead, Rosaleen, but that is the
most I can promise. If you start begging me one of these
nights, I'll not answer for what I do. Now, what of you?''

"I promise not to take advantage of you, either, Hugh Caldwell."

Hugh gave her a stern look, and Rosaleen laughed.

"Very well, wretched man. I promise to be as obedient to you as possible, but that is the best that *I* can promise. I'll be no man's slave, of that I give you fair warning."

He kissed her again, licking her lips with his tongue when he finished, and enjoying the way she melted against him.

"Mmm, very nice, Rosaleen. I believe you'll make a very good, uh, servant."

She put her hands on either side of his face and looked him in the eye.

"The missive to your brother, my lord?"

"You will write it this eve, and I shall attend."

Rosaleen was sure she hadn't heard correctly.

"I'll not have you looking over my shoulder, my lord."

"You will."

"I'll not!"

"Rosaleen," Hugh said wearily, wondering at how quickly she had forgotten her vow of obedience, "you will."

Chapter Fourteen

"Do you know, my love," said the Lord of Gyer as his wife looked up from the tapestry on which she had been working, "I have just received the most extraordinary missive from the lady Rosaleen."

"Have you?" said Lillis, setting her needlework upon her lap and looking up into her husband's intent face. After ten years of marriage she found him almost more attractive than when they had first met, and with appreciation let her eyes wander over his handsome face and muscular body. Although he was a man of great physical activity, he was also a man of business, and it was rare that he should leave his working chamber to visit her in the garden solar, which was her own daily retreat.

"Mmm," he affirmed, frowning at the missive in his hand as he settled next to his wife on the cushioned bench on which she sat. With a careless hand he pushed the tapestry aside, sending it to the floor, and leaned over to kiss her. Just as absently he sat up again, slipped an arm about her to draw her closer, then set his eyes to the missive once more.

"I shall read it to you," he said, "verbatim."

"To Sir Alexander Baldwin, the Lord of Gyer,
"I am grateful to you, sir, and to your very good lady

for your kind support of my most difficult situation. Should I require assistance greater than what your brother can provide, you may be certain I shall send word to you at once. As well, I would ask your forgiveness for my unmannerly departure from Gyer. Although my reasons seemed good to me at the time, there is verily no excuse for such coarse behavior, especially after one has received such kind and thoughtful courtesy as you and your lady extended to me during my visit with you.

"As you guessed, I have indeed accompanied Hugh Caldwell to his new estate and have agreed to remain here in his service for three months. Lamentably, Briarstone and its people are in a distressing state; thus the need for this missive. I am writing this under duress, I might add, as your unmannerly brother has set himself guard over me at present and is swearing so loudly at every other sentence I write that if you happen to be out of doors at the moment you will no doubt be able to hear him all the way to Gyer.

"The purpose of this missive, my Lord Gyer, is to arrange for the people of Briarstone to obtain an ample loan from you, said loan to be repaid with interest during the next five harvests Briarstone completes. This loan will be made in provisions, household items, livestock and working men, the cost of which shall be determined and accounted by yourself and made known to me at the time of delivery of goods. The present rates of the London markets will be acceptable.

"I shall list our needs by category.

"Provisions:"

Alexander stopped and squinted at the parchment. "It becomes more difficult to read after this, for it looks as though Hugh has gone back and scratched over a great deal of what Lady Rosaleen wrote, but I shall read it as best I can."

He proceeded to recite the same list that Rosaleen had previously given to Christian Rowsenly, although the amounts requested were much greater. Several of the items had two or three different amounts listed, as Hugh had gone back and changed them before the document was sealed, and Rosaleen had waited until he had left the room before she unsealed the document, rewrote the figures and resealed it before Hugh had returned.

Finishing "Provisions," Alexander began working his way through "Household Items."

"Fifty trestle tables crafted of oak from the forests of Kythem, with chairs or benches fashioned of same oak to seat one hundred. One high table made of cherry wood from the orchards of John Smith of Bandoewn, large enough to seat thirty, with matching chairs fashioned of same wood—"

He gazed hard at the document. "This is difficult to make out with all Hugh's scratches," he told his amused wife, and then he continued, slowly and with many starts and stops as he worked out the words.

"—ornamented with carvings depicting the riches of the harvest, carved by Newton Bessick of Camdentown. One complete set of goods suitable for a lady's bedchamber, including—"

He shook his head. "This one word has been so heavily scratched out that I can't be certain. I shall assume that it reads 'bed.'" He looked at Lillis. "I cannot imagine why Hugh should not wish to have an extra bed in his household. Can you, my love?"

"It seems a reasonable request, my lord, especially if it is for Lady Rosaleen's comfort."

"Very strange," said Alexander, before reading from the list once more.

"—including bed, dressing table and matching chair, four clothing chests, low table and two matching chairs for leisure, set with hand-embroidered cushions. All goods are to be crafted of imported Italian rosewood and ornamented with carvings of various spring flowers, especially roses."

Both he and Lillis broke into laughter.

"She writes with the knowledge and authority of a queen," Lillis said. "I doubt Eleanor of Aquitaine was so commanding."

Chuckling, Alexander agreed, "She writes like the future Countess of Siere, and rightfully so. God's pity, the forests of Kythem! I'd not find her regal demands so amusing were it not for thoughts of how Hugh must be suffering at her hands."

Lillis shook her head. "I'm not sure who is suffering more, she or Hugh, but one thing is certain . . . this list of hers will cost you a fortune! And why could Hugh not write and ask himself? Does he not realize that you would willingly give to him without asking recompense?"

"He knows, love, and all too well, but you have not let me finish this. Lady Rosaleen added something when Hugh had left the chamber. Let me read it to you. It is just past the place where she has listed all of the masons and carpenters and husbandmen she requires.''

"My lord, this must be quick, as your wretched and beastly brother has finally taken himself away for a few blissful moments. He has watched over my shoulder all this time, reading and arguing over every word I write, so that I have not been able to write as I wished. You must dismiss what I wrote earlier of Briarstone repaying this debt. I shall make payment as soon as my rights as the heiress of Siere have been established. I would not have you fear for recompense. You shall have it in full, and more, with all my gratitude, as well. This, from Rosaleen Sarant, Lady of Siere.''

With one last smile Alexander set the missive upon his knee.

"She is very kind," said Lillis. "She would aid Hugh without harming his pride. I think it most sweet."

Reaching out to caress the smooth skin of his wife's cheek, Alexander said, "I think it most foolish, for should Hugh discover the truth, he would turn her over his knee." He chuckled. "But I think I must go and make myself busy, love, rather than sit here longer and enjoy myself."

Standing, he added dolefully, "If I'm ever to fulfill this list, I must send missives at once to the master of the forests of Kythem and to John Smith of Bandoewn and Newton Bessick of Camdentown. I am certain Lady Rosaleen would be able to command their immediate attention to her needs had she been able to do so directly, but I, being so much less a personage," he teased, "must rely upon my wealth to do so."

Smiling, Lillis bent to pick her tapestry off the floor.

"Aye, that you must, my Lord Gyer, being so much less a personage."

"Lillis..."

"I but jest, my lord," she assured him, her eyes filled with amusement as she gazed at him. "I have never heard such foolishness. There is naught about you, Alexander, that could ever be named—" her eyes moved over him appreciatively "—less."

Alexander tossed the several pieces of parchment that made up Rosaleen's list onto the floor.

"Madam wife," he said, settling himself comfortably beside her again and pushing her tapestry back to the ground. "I am a fool, full dumb and void of reason. You must explain what it is you mean by such speech." He kissed her lingeringly. "In minute degree," he whispered against her mouth. "Good lady, I do beseech you."

Chapter Fifteen

The late summer sun beat down upon the fields, powerfully, unmercifully, causing even the most tolerant workers to frequent the water barrels set out at the ends of the rows of wheat and oats and barley and rye. Hugh Caldwell, stretching full height for the first time in more than an hour, wiped the drenching sweat from his forehead, then took his bucket and headed for the nearest barrel. The daily irrigation of the fields was nearly finished, so he felt no guilt whatsoever about filling his bucket and dumping the water over his head.

Refreshed, he rested his hands against the sides of the barrel and surveyed his lands with pride. The fields were ripening beautifully, and with only one month left before the harvest the success of them seemed sure. The feeling this gave Hugh was so strong and pleasurable that he almost wondered at it.

If matters could stay as they were, Hugh imagined that he would be the most content man on God's earth. Or at least close to it. And it wasn't simply the prospect of being wealthy and independent that made him think this; it was the satisfaction of success, the feeling of belonging and of being wanted, the pleasure of small daily activities that had never before held any import to him. And more, it was Rosaleen.

He thought of the day two months past, so long ago, it seemed, when Rosaleen had written her letter. The anger he'd felt then had taken days to dissipate, and just when it had, an incredible train of goods had arrived from his brother, inflaming his fury anew. Thinking of the things he'd said to Rosaleen on that day and of how, in his anger, he had left Briarstone and gone on a drunken revel for half a week even now made him shake his head with regret.

What a fool he'd been! Even his people's delight with the costly items Alex had sent hadn't softened him. Only gradually, after he had seen what a difference the goods made at Briarstone, had he finally begun to accept what Rosaleen had known all along. The provisions, the tables and chairs and other such goods, the cloth with which she and her ladies labored long hours to create new clothes for all the people, the candles and sets of chess, the bathing tubs and privacy screens, the improvements that the workers Alex had sent were making to Castle Briarstone, everything, all of it, had brought dignity and comfort and happiness to the people there. Gone were the wretched, ragged, half-starved vassals who had greeted them on the day of their arrival. In their place were warmly dressed, well-fed and contented men, women and children, all of whom took newfound pride in themselves and in their appearances, and all of whom displayed a health and happiness that made Hugh feel near to bursting with pride whenever he thought of it.

So many gladdening memories filled his head that each crowded the next. There was the night when he'd returned from his angered flight to find Rosaleen demonstrating the proper manner of bathing to his people, all of whom had been standing around her. Rosaleen herself had been on her knees, sleeves rolled up to her elbows, her dress more wet than not, instructing in that firm, commanding way of hers while at the same time struggling to maintain control of a most unhappy child. She had seen him standing in the shadows, watching her, and had ignored him, lifting her nose and continuing her lecture as though he weren't there at all.

But later that night, as he'd paced his chamber, repeating all the words he'd spent two full days readying to speak to her, she had walked through the door and gone directly into his arms and had loved him, not letting either of them speak until afterward. She had lain silent through his whispered apology, then had moved on top of him and begun kissing him, sending his mind to flight all over again.

And there was the memory of her teaching her ladies how to sew, a few days after the bathing incident, on the same night when she had insisted that he, Hugh, instruct the menfolk how to play the game of chess. He had countered that he would teach them dicing instead, but the expression on her face had quickly killed that idea. It had been so soon after their reconciliation that he had given in, though only God knew how he'd wondered at what good it would do men like these to acquire skills at such a game. Now, of course, he understood the value of it very well, as each and every night since had found his people, even the ladies, amusing themselves after the evening meal with the gentilesse of highborn nobles. To a one his people loved chess and had even begun holding tournaments to establish the best player among them.

And, of course, he would never forget the afternoon when Helen had gone into labor. Some of the older children had come running through the fields to fetch everyone back to the keep, but by the time Hugh and the men had arrived, Rosaleen had finished delivering Helen of a healthy boy. The sight of her standing there, covered with blood and birthing fluids, her face flushed and damp, triumphantly holding a live babe in her arms, would remain forever impressed on Hugh's memory. She had met Hugh's eyes and smiled, so that Hugh hadn't been able to keep from taking her in his arms, babe and all, and kissing her. In that moment he had wished that the child was theirs and that she was his wife and that they had the rest of their lives to look forward to moments such as these.

There were many other memories, too. There was the night when Alex's workers had finished digging two new wells, one in the bailey and one inside the keep itself, and Rosaleen had had a special meal prepared in honor of the event. It had been a feast compared to the stark food they had been used to eating, but it hadn't compared to the celebration she'd arranged when the oxen and other animals were finally moved out of the keep and into the new stables. On that occasion she had dipped lavishly into Briarstone's larder, and the people of Briarstone had eaten and celebrated as they had never dreamed possible.

Rosaleen had been so happy on those two occasions that he could only imagine how she would feel when the hole in the back of the keep had finally been repaired, as it soon would be, or when the new dam gate was completed so that the fields could be easily watered with the labor of only a few men, or when all of the chimneys in the castle had finally been cleaned, repaired and readied for use, or when the new buttery, larder, pantry and kitchen had been completed, or, most of all, when all of the windows and open spaces she had requested had finally been built, letting in the fresh air and light she so craved, and which

Hugh craved for her, knowing how much those things meant to her.

Of course, these things would take years to complete, and she would only be able to enjoy them if she stayed with him for longer than the three months she had originally agreed to. Hugh had every intention of making certain that she did. In truth, there wasn't any reason for her to leave, or at least not any that he could see, regardless of all her worries about her uncle. As long as she stayed with Hugh she needn't fear that bastard; he would keep her safe. She was happy at Briarstone, and happy with him, and that was the way things were going to stay.

"There now, that is much, much better." Standing back, placing her hands on her hips, Rosaleen surveyed the outcome of the afternoon's work with approval. Around her stood her ladies, save Helen, their expressions set with worry.

"I don't think the men'll like it, m'lady," said Jehanne, tucking a stray wisp of blond hair beneath her head covering.

"Certainly they will," Rosaleen replied confidently, brushing her hands together to dust them. "All people enjoy having a place to be private and to keep their treasures. It is a quality shared by both man and beast."

Gazing doubtfully at the multitude of screens that now partitioned the farthest half of the great hall into several small rooms, the women all nodded slowly.

"It'll be strange not to see ever'one else, though, m'lady. It was real nice to talk wiv' each other at night."

"I'm goin' to feel like a rabbit in a cage," said Katherine. "All closed up."

"Don't be foolish," Rosaleen admonished. "You will feel no such thing. And as to the other, you will still be able to hear one another. Those partitions are made of linen and wood, not stone.''

"But the men won't like it!" Jehanne insisted again, unwittingly causing her mistress to grow angry.

Rosaleen knew very well that the women of Briarstone still entertained the men of Briarstone with their peculiar talents, and quite willingly so. This fact had been bluntly proved on the night when Helen's son Neddy had been born. The child had come out of the womb with a bright shock of red hair. Helen had smiled at Henry Bascombe, the only redheaded man at Briarstone.

"Why, 'enry, it looks like he's yours," she'd announced happily, and cheers of congratulations had gone up for Henry as though he'd won some game of chance.

Rosaleen had helplessly rolled her eyes, and Hugh had come up and laughed at her and given her a lavish kiss, right there in front of all his people, so that, embarrassed, she'd been obliged to push him away.

But right after that he had carefully taken the baby and, as the master of Briarstone, had proudly presented the child first to his people and then to Henry, who with shaking hands had accepted his son and promptly burst into tears even noisier than the infant's.

"I really do not care what the men think," Rosaleen replied tautly. "Now," she went on, firmly changing the subject when her ladies looked as though they would argue, "we will next set up partitions for the workmen, over on this side of the hall. But I think that can wait until the morrow."

Her ladies, as one, sighed with relief, which Rosaleen understood very well. Raising up partitions was tiring, but with the men being occupied with the all-important fields, such heavy tasks as these fell to the women. Unfortunately, the need for Alexander of Gyer's workmen to have a separate sleeping place was a necessary one, and so Rosaleen and her ladies would have to labor hard again when the next day came.

Alexander of Gyer had sent a little more than fifty workmen—carpenters, masons, husbandmen—and from the moment of their arrival they had contended with the men of Briarstone for the attention of the women. Occasionally they had been successful, and that had caused strife, strife that Hugh Caldwell had been hard-pressed to bring under control. No one had been killed yet, but if matters continued on as they were, that event wouldn't be too far off. The residents of Briarstone had to eat together, they had to share their bathing and evening hours, but they *didn't* have to sleep together. Her ladies had been strictly told to have nothing to do with any of the men, either of Briarstone or Gyer, unless the man in question made known to Hugh Caldwell his intentions for a formal union. Otherwise they were to stay in their own beds at night.

She knew it was hypocritical to give such commands when she herself could not keep from going each night to the man she loved, and especially when her ladies were fully aware that she did so. She wondered, at times, whether any of them still believed Hugh and her to be related by blood, and, if so, what they made of it.

"We must prepare for the evening meal," she stated, turning toward the area of the great hall still used for cooking and casting a quick glance as she did at the many workmen rebuilding the missing back wall of the keep. This was always a bothersome time of the day, the cooking time, for the carpenters and masons never lost an opportunity to dally with the women.

"Alice, go and see if Helen has finished nursing Neddy, and if she has, bring the older children down from the nursery to help."

The nursery was the first chamber Rosaleen had had created out of the dark, gloomy rooms above stairs. With enlarged windows and a working fire, it was a comfortable place for the children to spend their afternoons, and soon, when the tutor she had written to Alexander of Gyer about finally arrived, it would also serve as their place of schooling.

Alice dutifully did as she was told, and Rosaleen next turned to Ada, who, being a gifted cook, supervised all meals. "I thought roast lamb tonight, with several farsed hens and perhaps some of those fresh cod the Lord of Gyer sent us boiled in wine and herbs."

Ada nodded thoughtfully. "Yes, m'lady, 'n' p'raps potatoes wiv' peas 'n' onions, 'n' leeks in broth and some arbolettys."

"Are there enough eggs and cheese for the arbolettys? Very well, then some fried squash and sallat and some manner of fritter should finish the meal. And parsley bread, also, I think."

"And black pears for last!" Margaret begged.

Rosaleen laughed. "No, we've not enough pears, Margaret. A tri-cream for the last course, Ada, with currant tarts."

"Yes, m'lady."

Two hours later, as Rosaleen gratefully soaked in the warmth of one of the large wooden tubs Alexander of Gyer had sent to Briarstone, she allowed herself to think of Hugh Caldwell. And thinking of him, as much as she did, wasn't a pleasant activity. She had long since passed the half mark of her time with him, and now that she was on the shortening end of it, the hopeless end of it, there was naught to look forward to but saying goodbye. That was a painful contemplation.

She would never be sorry for the past two months, or for the month to come, for they had been the happiest days of her life. But love was such a painful thing...and she loved Hugh Caldwell with every part of her. The wonder and beauty of the emotion amazed and enthralled her so that sometimes Rosaleen wondered how she would live without all the feelings Hugh Caldwell gave her; the pain of love gave her such misery that sometimes she wondered how she would make it through another day.

The worst of it had struck her on the day when the goods from Alexander of Gyer had arrived. Hugh had been angry before that, though his anger hadn't followed them into his bed at night, and Rosaleen had understood and even sympathized with his feelings. But when the goods actually arrived, some deep, uncontainable fury had released itself within him, so powerfully that Rosaleen, watching him, had almost been able to see it unfold. He had wordlessly packed his things, taken Amazon, mounted Saint and ridden out of Briarstone even while Rosaleen had been greeting the first of the workmen at the front gates.

The confusion of the people of Briarstone at their master's abrupt departure, the disorganization of the workers and goods arriving and the frantic, sick feeling of abandonment Rosaleen experienced as she watched Hugh Caldwell's tall figure riding farther and farther away, all of it had nearly brought Rosaleen down to tears. Never, even on that morn when her uncle had approached her, smiling with anticipation, holding his whip, had Rosaleen felt such despair. Had it not been for Christian Rowsenly's innate leadership ability and her own stoic training, she would have been lost.

When he had finally come home, his face swollen with bruises from the fights she'd known he would seek, that damned grin spread on his face, she'd been torn between the desire to scream at him and the need to throw herself into his arms. Later that night, when she'd gone to him, her desire had triumphed.

All had been well until a few days later, when Hugh had taken her strolling in the summer night air after the evening meal. They had been walking very companionably, speaking of common matters, when they had passed the old shed that had once served as a stable and heard someone sobbing within. Exchanging glances, they had fallen silent, and at the same moment had realized who it was.

They had moved at the same time, Rosaleen to speak aloud and Hugh to clap his hand over her mouth to keep her quiet. Picking her up, he had carried her across the bailey until they were well away from the stables.

"You will not try to speak with him, Rosaleen," Hugh had firmly informed her as soon as he'd lifted his hand from her mouth.

Furious, she'd pushed him away. "You wretched beast! How dare you smother me in such a manner!"

"I mean it, Rosaleen," he continued as if she'd never spoken. "I'll not have you making Chris feel like a foolish child."

"I would never do such a thing!" she returned with offense, laying one delicate hand over her breast. "The poor boy is simply overcome by the arrival of the king's missive this afternoon regarding his late brother's bravery at Agincourt. It is perfectly clear that he loved John Rowsenly, much as he tries to deny the idea. I see nothing wrong with giving him comfort."

Hugh was so angry his eyes glittered. "You can't begin to imagine what that boy is feeling, and I'll not have you making him feel even worse with your well-meant comforting.'' His hands moved to grip her shoulders. "He loved his brother, aye, and deeply, but John Rowsenly never felt the same. He never said a word to anyone about his little bastard sibling. Not one word, Rosaleen. The man was a damned fool!" Hugh's expression grew hard as stone. "If I had a brother the likes of Christian Rowsenly," he vowed, "I would crow of it to the heavens as oft as I could."

In the end Hugh had reminded her of that wretched vow of obedience she'd so stupidly given him, and like an imperial prince to a slave, he had ordered her back to the keep and had gone alone to see Christian. Rosaleen had sat with her ladies, unable to think on the needlework in her lap, until Hugh and Christian had returned to the hall an hour later, both laughing aloud at some private jest. Christian had looked perfectly well, as though a sad thought had never troubled him, and with a grin he had sat with Hugh to play a game of chess. Later that night, Hugh had made love to her with a fever that had frightened her, just as everything he had done to her in his bed had frightened her, a little.

The things she had learned at his hands! The things she had done! God's mercy, if her parents could have known of it all, they would have turned in their graves. After the coarse insults she had suffered at the hands of Simon of Denning, and after all the whores Uncle Anselm and his friends had entertained at Siere during their visits over the years, Rosaleen had thought there would be little left regarding the physical relationship of a man and a woman that would surprise her overmuch, but she had been far, far wrong. Hugh Caldwell had surprised her time and again, and had coaxed her into performing such amazing acts that just to think of them made her blush. And the things he had done to her...with his hands...and mouth! God's teeth, even her toes turned red at the memory.

Tucking her legs and arms fully inside the tub, as if to hide them, Rosaleen sank a little farther in the warm water. But that only reminded her of the night Hugh had made a bath for them in his room, when with warm, scented water he had bathed her, and she had in turn bathed him, and they had afterward sunk into the water and...

"M'lady?" Margaret called over the partition. "Do you need a fresh towel?"

Rosaleen had to clear her throat to answer. "No, I thank you, Margaret. I brought one with me."

"Very well, m'lady. Call out if you need me."

Margaret went away, and Rosaleen sighed, grateful that the girl hadn't come around the screen to see her blushes.

"God's feet, Hugh Caldwell," she whispered, "what have you done to me? Is it not enough that you occupy my nights? Must you occupy my every waking thought, as well?"

But there was one thing Hugh Caldwell had never done, and never would do. He had never spoken of love. In all the nights they had lain together, pleasuring each other in every way possible save the one that kept her a maiden, not a word of any emotion deeper than affection had ever passed his lips. For Hugh, their coming together each night was normal and expected. It was to be enjoyed while it lasted, and nothing more.

Chapter Sixteen

"God's my life, Hugh Caldwell, you've done well for yourself."

Smiling lazily at Peter Brenten, who with Stewart of Byrne had arrived unexpectedly at Briarstone three hours earlier, Hugh drew a sip of red wine into his mouth, swallowed it slowly and, with an air of satisfaction, sighed.

"'Struth, Peter, lad. 'Tis indeed the truth."

He wondered if this was the way his brother Alex felt whenever he sat down with guests in the great hall of Gyer.

Here he was, the master of his own estate, sitting at the head of a richly crafted table, enjoying an impressive meal from the bounty of his own lands and from the full larder of Briarstone, and entertaining his friends in a style and manner that he had never conceived possible. On one side of him, in her place as the lady of the household, sat Rosaleen, managing the progress of the meal with the ease of a skilled hostess and looking so beautiful that he couldn't help but swell with pride. On his other side sat his friends, appropriately impressed with their surroundings. Below him, spread out in the neat rows Rosaleen had ordered to be arranged, sat all the people of Briarstone, as well as the workmen Alex had sent, eating their meals in comfort and conversing quietly.

He felt, quite honestly, as happy and content as a king overlooking his subjects, and just as regal.

"Will you have more wine, Stewart of Byrne?" Rosaleen asked in a manner so charming that that man looked up at her with an expression of enchantment.

"Thank you, my lady," he said, like a sigh, and watched Rosaleen as she motioned to one of the servers to refill his goblet.

"Do you know, Lady Rosaleen," he said, continuing to gaze at her with an open admiration that annoyed Hugh, "I find it difficult to believe you are the same lady whom we met so long ago at the Red Fox Inn. You are as lovely as a queen, and not in the least what any of us assumed you to be when we first set eyes on you."

"Aye, you are most lovely indeed, my lady," Peter Brenten quickly agreed, not wanting to be outdone by his friend. "I only wish I'd been quicker than Hugh in stepping forward to rescue you, for then you might have come home with me, instead."

Forcing a smile, and thinking that at Siere these men would have been whipped for speaking to her in such a forward, familiar manner, Rosaleen replied, "You are very kind."

Hugh, however, frowned darkly. His friends were quick to compliment Rosaleen, yet it was clear they still thought her a common woman who had merely come to Briarstone to live as his mistress. The way in which they called her "lady," as though the title were a jest, made him want to shove their teeth down their throats.

"You've not yet said why you're on your way to London—" Hugh spoke slowly, willing his taut muscles to relax "—only that you're meeting Gerry there. Never tell me there's another war somewhere that you're off to."

"No, thank a merciful God!" Stewart declared, setting aside his eating dagger. "But we're hiring out just the same. Gerry was called to London by Simon of Denning, and he sent us word as soon as he found out what Simon wanted. He would have sent you word, as well, I imagine, if he'd not thought you too busy with your new estate to come along."

"He was right," he said, and, having felt her stiffen beside him, glanced at Rosaleen. She had gone quite pale, he noted with concern. Swinging his eyes back to his friends, he prodded, "What soldier work has Gerry found with Simon of Denning, then?"

"It's about his betrothed," Peter replied, swallowing a mouthful of parsley bread. "Do you remember how he told us he was going to marry some duchess or countess or some such as soon as he returned from France?"

Hugh shrugged. "I remember, but Simon was a common boaster... it was hard to know when to believe him or not."

"That's true enough, but he spoke the truth about that particular matter. Trouble is, the girl was stolen before they could wed. Simon is hiring men to search her out."

"Stolen?" Hugh repeated with disbelief. "Why in God's Holy Name would anyone want to steal something that belongs to Simon of Denning? It's as sure as signing a death warrant, I vow."

Chewing a sweet, roasted onion, Steward nodded. "But this lady is a rich heiress and supposedly very beautiful. Whoever has her must believe Simon will be willing to pay dearly to have her back."

Hugh shook his head. "Poor old Simon. That's a bad turn for him, and he's a good enough fellow, especially in a fight. How did he manage to betroth himself to an heiress, I wonder? He's rich enough, of course, but a cruder devil I've never met. God's teeth, when I think of the way he used to treat his women! Perhaps the heiress ran away to avoid wedding him.''

"God help her if she did," Peter said, "for Simon would kill her when he caught up with her."

"W-would anyone like more wine?" Rosaleen asked suddenly, too loudly.

Hugh turned to look at her again, already aware that she was as taut as a hard-pulled bowstring. The sight of her beautiful face, pale and distressed, sent shivers of warning down his spine. Reaching out beneath the table, he touched her knee lightly and felt her jerk as though she'd been shocked by a lightning bolt. She jumped up, knocking her wineglass over in her haste and scraping her chair loudly on the wooden dais.

"Forgive me, please," she whispered in a voice that trembled. "I must be excused from table. I...I must go and see to the last course."

"Rosaleen, whatever is the—"

But she had already turned and walked away, hurrying toward the back of the great hall where the makeshift kitchen lay.

"Ah, the women of France!" Peter Brenten kissed his fingertips in a gesture of tribute. "They have no equal on all of God's earth!"

Stewart of Byrne laughed. "Nay, lad, but you're wrong," he said, and lifted his tankard into the air. "Here's to the women of Spain! Hot-blooded, fiery beauties, every one of them!" He winked at the group of men who were sitting close by, listening raptly to the conversation taking place by the fire. "You'll never find sweeter, more willing wenches in any land, lads," he assured them. "'Tis God's truth, I vow."

Clearing his throat loudly and wishing that his friends would lower their voices, or at least take a look around to see that the men of Briarstone weren't the only ones listening to them, Hugh said, "Now, good fellows, you both speak falsely. 'Tis the English beauties who are the best and loveliest of any women on earth." He sent a cautious glance to where Rosaleen sat with her ladies, only to be met by eight pairs of female eyes bearing expressions so chilling they could freeze a man solid. "The, uh, noblest, bravest...ahem...uh, kindest, wisest and *certainly* the most understanding women ever created by God's own hand."

He hoped the words would soothe the women, but he knew matters had probably gone beyond that. It was now several hours since the evening meal had ended, and somehow things had gone from bad to worse. First Peter and Stewart had wanted to gamble, and in an effort to be a gracious host Hugh had let them bring out their dice, though reluctantly, for he knew Rosaleen despised the sport. Next they had drunk themselves into a sorry state and had started gazing with warm interest at the women, until Hugh had had to remind them that they were far outnumbered by the men of Briarstone, who tended to be possessive about their females.

In their drunken state, Peter and Stewart had been indignant and had complained at such inhospitable treatment at the hands of their old friend, but Hugh had diverted them into recounting tales of their battles and conquests, much to the pleasure of the men and children of Briarstone. Somehow, though, the conversation had wandered toward the many sexual adventures they'd enjoyed together during their mercenary years, and Hugh found himself sinking further and further into the unpleasant mire of fury that the ladies of his household were now directing his way.

After hearing his statement, both Peter and Stewart burst into laughter.

"By the rood, Hugh Caldwell! I'll not dispute you," Peter said, "for if there is any man who knows about women, 'tis you, though all the lovely lasses you courted in France would tear your heart out to hear you say such a thing, I vow!"

"That's right, lads," Stewart said to the men of Briarstone. "Your master is as legendary with his female conquests as he is with his sword. The prettiest maids that followed our camp were ever throwing themselves at his feet. 'Struth! I swear it!"

"The prettiest maids!" scoffed Peter Brenten. "Even the ugly ones ran after him, and by my troth, he did his best to keep them satisfied, every one!" The two men laughed heartily. "A right kindhearted soul is Hugh Caldwell, never wanting to disappoint any of the wenches who'd a yearning for him."

The men of Briarstone gazed at their master with new admiration, and Hugh wished a hole would open in the floor beneath the rushes and swallow him up. He could almost feel the sharp points of the daggers Rosaleen was looking at him.

"Do you remember those twins who fought over him at Rouen, Peter? In the end he took them both to bed. God's toes, I'll ne'er forget the next morn when they came out of his tent. They could hardly walk, either of them, but still looked as pleased as two cats who'd got the cream!"

Hugh set his head in his hands and groaned.

"But that was naught compared to that night in Abbeville—" Stewart began enthusiastically.

"At that brothel!" he and Peter finished together.

Mouths gaping, the men of Briarstone leaned closer.

"God's my life," said Peter. "You were in rare form that night, Hugh. Rare, indeed."

Unable to lift his head from his hands, Hugh groaned again, though more loudly.

"That tournament you devised, Hugh!" Stewart nearly howled. "That j-jousting t-tournament!"

"Jousting tournament?" Christian Rowsenly asked curiously.

"Peter, Stewart . . . don't do this to me," Hugh begged weakly.

"Never in my life have I experienced such a time," Stewart went on heedlessly. "Only Hugh Caldwell could come up with such a game, I vow." He looked at his miserable friend with affection.

"In truth, it was more like striking a target than jousting," Peter explained, ignoring the sounds of agony coming from Hugh. "Hugh had all the tables in the place lined up against one wall, and then the wenches sat on the edge, you see, side by side, with their legs spread like this." He demonstrated with his hands.

The sound of distress Hugh made surpassed description.

"Each man lined up opposite the woman of his choice," Peter went on happily, "and got his 'lance' out and ready. That's why Hugh called it jousting, because at the signal, each man took off at a run and the winner was the one who could—"

Hugh shot up off his chair. "I think I'll take Peter and Stewart into Stenwick," he announced. "There's a good tavern there, with plenty of whores. What do you say, lads?"

The men of Briarstone protested loudly, but Peter Brenten and Stewart of Byrne, smiling and nodding, were already standing to leave.

Light . . . it hurt. God's mercy, it hurt. He tried to move his hand to cover his eyes, and that hurt, too. When was Rosaleen going to have some damned curtains hung over this damned bed?

He ached everywhere. His toes ached, his ears . . . even his teeth ached. Rosaleen, in her sleep, stretched and made the whole front of him ache.

"Mmm," she mumbled, and moved again. Her back was against his front, and she reached one hand around to touch his sex, caressing.

"Sweeting," he muttered, "go back to sleep."

She kept touching him and took one of his hands, drawing it forward to press against her womanhood. She was hot and very wet, and despite his misery Hugh felt himself hardening. She pressed his other hand against one of her breasts, and when his stiff fingers brushed against the hard nipple, she moaned and moved her soft little bottom against his erection.

"From behind, m'lord," she murmured, pulling his manhood between her damp thighs and moving rhythmically with it. "Put it into me from behind. Please," she begged, sounding breathless and not like herself. "Please, m'lord. Do it now."

It took his dulled brain a moment to understand, though his body was already far ahead. He felt her, Rosaleen, hot and wet and ready for him, wanting him to push himself deep inside her, at last.

"Yes," he groaned, a mixture of pain and ecstasy. "Yes, my beloved one." But he didn't want to take her like this. His Rosaleen was a virgin still, and when they finally joined their bodies he wanted the moment to be special. Despite the agony it caused him, he lifted himself up on one elbow and pulled her beneath him. "My love," he whispered as his mouth descended to hers. "My beautiful love."

But it was wrong. Something was very wrong. The kiss he gave her lasted only a moment, and then he pulled back, his drink-addled eyes opening with difficulty to look at her. She didn't taste like Rosaleen. Not in the least. Rosaleen's mouth tasted sweet...like fine wine mixed with honey. This mouth tasted horribly sour, like onions and rotted cabbage. While Hugh's eyes focused, his hands made other discoveries. The one buried in her blond hair felt a sudden coarseness...a coarseness that had never been there before; the hand resting on one of her breasts felt the smallness, the shapelessness of it...a smallness and shapelessness that didn't belong to his Rosaleen.

As he pushed himself a little farther away, furiously blinking his eyes to clear them, Hugh's nostrils suddenly came to life, and the smell that greeted them turned his stomach so violently that it was all he could do to keep from emptying its contents.

This foul-smelling creature was *not* his Rosaleen.

He was in bed with some strange, terrible female, and as his eyes focused, revealing a young, thin, pockmarked girl, Hugh laughed, painfully, from the strange humor of the situation. How had this girl come to be there? Where had she come from?

A short, strangled sound made him turn his numb head, and as he kept blinking he saw Rosaleen, standing in his chamber a short distance from the bed, staring at him in horror.

"Rosaleen," he croaked, feeling sick and miserable and wishing that this whole nightmare would go away and let him sleep his drunkenness off.

Her wide, shocked eyes took in the girl beneath him, so that Hugh, much more slowly, turned to look at the girl, as well. She was as barely awake as he, but enough to realize what was going on. Seeing Rosaleen, she grinned, revealing several missing teeth.

"Hope that's not yer wife, m'lord," the girl said, and Hugh suddenly realized, with slow-witted distaste, that he was still cupping one of her tiny breasts.

Moving so slowly that even he wondered why he couldn't do better, Hugh peeled his hand off her rough body and looked back at Rosaleen. Her mouth was covered with a trembling hand, and her eyes were filled with tears. The sight of her misery cleared Hugh's brain as nothing else could have done.

"Rosaleen," he said again, his voice thick, "this is all right." And he wondered, as he heard the words, what he meant by them. What he'd wanted to say hadn't come out the way it was supposed to.

He opened his mouth to speak again, to tell her that what he'd meant was that this wasn't what it looked like, but before he could utter one syllable, Rosaleen turned and fled the room.

She couldn't seem to control the sobs; they were so harsh they hurt. She couldn't stop the tears that burned her face, she couldn't even make her feet move, so she stood against the chamber door she had slammed only moments before and wept.

Bastard! she thought furiously, hitting her thighs with angry fists. He was a rotten, wretched bastard and she hated him! *Hated* him!

How could he have done it to her? And with that…that *creature*… that filthy whore! He'd even called the mangy girl his beloved. His love. Never once, in all the times she had lain with him, had Hugh spoken such words… not even carelessly. What further proof did she need that she meant nothing to him, nothing save as his servant…as his convenient whore! Hadn't he admitted as much just now? "This is all right," he'd said. Going to bed with her was all right, and going to bed with another woman was all right, and playing a game of "jousting" with a whole roomful of women was all right! Everything was all right to a man like Hugh Caldwell, and she had been more than a fool to let herself fall in love with him.

Breathing furiously, wiping her hot, wet face with the palms of her shaking hands, Rosaleen sternly told herself a few truths.

First, she was the heiress and future countess of Siere, the daughter of the third Earl of Siere and the descendant of a noble family. In her blood ran the legacy of a hundred great, courageous and famed ancestors. No one, not Hugh Caldwell, not Simon of Denning, not her Uncle Anselm, would make her bow her head in defeat.

Secondly, she was the lady of this household until the end of this month, and she would be damned to hell and back again if she would let a man like Hugh Caldwell shame her so openly in front of the people of Briarstone, or make her cower in her chamber like some wounded rabbit, afraid to face him or them *or* that filthy little slut he'd dragged home. She was going to go downstairs and hold her head high and behave like the lady she was.

Last, the most important truth of all, she was going to put this valuable lesson Hugh Caldwell had given her to good use.

Never again would she trust a man with her heart.
Never.

Chapter Seventeen

"Jehanne! Katherine! Ada! *Margaret!* Stop this at once!"

As Rosaleen descended the stairs into the great hall, her ladies turned to their mistress, their faces filled with fury.

"What is this commotion?" Rosaleen demanded, moving to where her ladies were holding four filthy, struggling females. "Alice, you will explain."

"Hugh Caldwell and his friends brought these dirty sluts back wiv' 'em from Stenwick," Alice said with clear disgust, pushing at one of the ill-smelling, raggedly dressed creatures and tossing a hateful glare in the direction of Peter Brenten and Stewart of Byrne, who were sitting together at a nearby trestle table, looking as though they wished they were dead. "They say Hugh Caldwell told 'em they could live at Briarstone, but we'll not have it, m'lady. We'll not!"

Hearing these words, one of the whores from Stenwick began to screech at Alice, and all seven of the women of Briarstone fell upon the four intruders with renewed fury.

"I said cease!" Rosaleen shouted sharply, and her ladies, with difficulty, let their victims go. "Such behavior is not worthy of the women of Briarstone. Christian Rowsenly!" she demanded. "Come to me!"

He was beside her at once, a thoughtful frown twisting his lips.

"What do these women do here, Christian?"

"What Alice said is the truth, my lady," he answered, perusing the sluttish females with a shake of his head. They were horrible things, these women. Why would any man want to put himself inside one? He preferred either Katherine or Jehanne, both of whom had been keeping themselves, of late, delightfully clean. "Hugh Caldwell and his guests brought these women home with them just after the dawn and promised them a living at Briarstone. That is what these men have explained." He nodded in the direction of Peter Brenten and Stewart of Byrne, who were groaning sickly.

In disbelief, Rosaleen shook her head, then drew in a steadying breath and approached the women from Stenwick.

They stared at her with clear defiance, and one of them, the girl who'd been in Hugh Caldwell's bed that morn, actually laughed at her.

"I understand that you have been offered a livelihood at Briarstone." Rosaleen spoke to them with stiff address. "I am the lady of this household, Lady Rosaleen, and if you would stay here you will answer to me. No one who lives here does so without earning his or her keep, and if you remain you will abide by the rules observed by the rest of those in the household. You will be obedient to Briarstone's master, Hugh Caldwell, and to me. You will observe a regular bathing schedule, you will be given proper clothing and will dress—" her eyes wandered with distaste over their bawdy attire "—as is fitting. You will assume a fair share of the work. If you are willing to meet these terms, you may stay at Briarstone and be certain of your meals and of a roof over your heads and of an eventual share in the profit of the lands. If you are not willing, you may return to Stenwick at once. What say you?"

Three of the girls gazed at Rosaleen with awe and not a little confusion. The fourth, the one who had been in Hugh Caldwell's bed, laughed again and placed her hands on her hips. Swaying, she moved to stand in front of Rosaleen and bared what few teeth she still possessed in a sneer.

"You're one to be telling us what to do," she stated insolently, eyeing Rosaleen up and down with contempt, "whatever it is you are, anyway. Long as I'm the one what's keeping the master warm in his bed, you answer to me, not the other way 'round."

Rosaleen struck the girl so fast and so hard that even she hadn't realized what she'd done until she saw the girl lying in a stunned heap at her feet.

Her voice, when she spoke, was sure and firm.

"I am the lady of Briarstone, and I will not tolerate such as that from anyone. Christian—" she spoke without taking her eyes from the shaking girl "—you will take these whores back to Stenwick and return them to the place from whence they came. You will do it now."

"Yes, my..."

"You will do no such thing, Chris."

Two warm hands closed over Rosaleen's arms, squeezing lightly, and Rosaleen felt Hugh's body press familiarly against her back.

"I am the master of Briarstone," he said calmly, his voice close to Rosaleen's ear, "and I have given these women my promise that they shall have a place here in trade for their labor. They shall stay. All of them. Erda," he said addressing the girl on the floor, "rise and beg your mistress's forgiveness and then we will all of us break our fast."

As she quit her tears, the girl's expression changed from abject fear to glad certainty and, rising, she offered Rosaleen a graceless smirk, then shifted her gaze to Hugh Caldwell, at whom she smiled intimately.

"Forgive me, m'lady," she said, suppressing laughter and grinning now at Hugh.

His fingers tightened on Rosaleen's arms, and she felt his body stiffen, but her feelings were so frozen that none of that mattered. Gasps from the assembled of Briarstone rang in her ears like crashing cymbals. Those gasps, those humbling, dishonoring gasps, struck her proud soul with shattering impact.

Jerking free of Hugh's grip, she faced the preening girl with all her pride.

"There is no need for you to beg my pardon," she said. "Come, I will show you the place the master of Briarstone has given you, Mistress Erda."

Reaching forward, she grasped the girl's bony arm with steeled fingers and drew her, amid the gaping of those present and in spite of Hugh Caldwell's foul swearing, toward the front of the great hall. The girl stumbled along behind her and struggled to loose herself, but Rosaleen, with cold fury, dragged her all the way to the long table, to the place of honor set aside for the lady of the household. To the place where only Rosaleen had ever sat.

Shoving the frightened girl into the ornate chair that had always been hers, she declared, "There, Mistress Erda, is the place your master has given you this morn. You must sit beside him, where his lady should be, where he has chosen you to be. Look now to all who stand before you." Rosaleen waved a hand toward those in the hall. "They are yours now to guide and care for, as you wish and as you will." Reaching up, Rosaleen tore the linen covering from her head, exposing the wheat gold of her hair. She threw the mantle of gentility onto the rushes and put her foot and heel upon it in a gesture of renunciation. "May you and your lord have the joy of your new duties."

With that, she turned on her heel, heading for the portal at the back of the keep. She held her chin high and her eyes forward, ignoring the dismay of those she passed. To one side, where she had left them, she could hear some of her ladies crying, like children frightened by the unknown.

She had only passed the partitions shielding the kitchen area before Hugh caught up to her, his long fingers closing painfully over one of her arms and forcing her around to look at him.

"By the Fiend's foot!" he swore vehemently. "What was that about? Have you lost your mind?"

She wrenched her arm free. "Don't touch me! Don't you *ever* touch me again!"

Hugh was momentarily stunned, but in spite of the pounding headache plaguing him, he regained his wits quickly and reached for her again. "Be quiet!" he demanded. "Everyone in the hall listens to us. Come here, Rosaleen. We're going back in there and you are going to—"

"I'll do nothing with you!" Pulling away once more, and with a glare of pure hate, she turned and made her way to the hole in the back wall.

Hugh watched, amazed, as Rosaleen hopped over the low repairs and stalked toward the nearest field, her strides long and purposeful. And he kept watching until the golden wheat of her hair became lost in the golden wheat of the field, the slight bobbing of her head the only mark of where she was.

"Women," he muttered thickly, shaking his throbbing head and regretting the action when it made him feel sick.

"God save me from every one of them. If there's a man on God's earth who understands the foolish creatures, I wish he'd explain them to me."

With a yawn and a scratch of his chest, Hugh returned to the main hall. If Rosaleen wished to make an idiot of herself, so be it: he was going to fill his belly and drink enough ale to make his head stop spinning. Later, when she had calmed, and when his brain had ceased to feel as if it were going to splinter into a thousand pieces, they would speak and settle the matter of her foolish behavior.

It wasn't until he'd taken his seat at the long table that Hugh realized how quiet the hall was, and when he lifted his eyes he saw with surprise that all his people were staring at him. Peter and Stewart had already moved to their places of honor beside him, so that he asked them, "What troubles them? Why have they not taken their places?" With slow movement, his dry, reddened eyes passed over the unoccupied tables. The food and drink were set out, yet the benches remained empty.

"Hugh," Peter murmured, sounding as sick as Hugh felt, "you…you humiliated Lady Rosaleen in front of all your people."

Hugh was honestly taken aback. "I? Humiliate Rosaleen? I'd never do such a thing. You drank too much last night and don't know what you say."

"And we humiliated her, as well," Stewart added miserably. "We brought those whores into Lady Rosaleen's household without any thought for her feelings. God's mercy, to have treated a lady thus. It's… it's the behavior of one ignoble."

Ignoble. That word penetrated Hugh's blurry haze like the crack of a whip. "Well, I'm not noble," he stated harshly, "so you'll place no guilt at my door. Neither of you had a care for Rosaleen's gentle birth yester eve. Why should you worry for her tender sensibilities this morn? By the rood, she's not the Queen of England. A little humbling will do that haughty female some good, if you ask me.''

With that, he turned his attention to filling his cup with ale, since none of those who served the table had yet come to perform that task for him. When he lifted the pewter goblet to drink, however, he was stopped by the silent perusal of the hundred pairs of eyes upon him. Their stares were condemning, and some of the ladies, including the newest arrivals, were still crying.

Helen, who was not crying, was the first to leave. Pinning Hugh with a defiant glare, she lifted her chin, grasped her two oldest children by their hands and marched out of the hall. One by one the other ladies followed, and then the men, all silently, until only Hugh, his friends, Christian and the newly arrived whores were left. Silence, but for the crying and sniffling of the females reigned for several long moments.

"Well, by my troth," Hugh muttered.

"We're sorry, Hugh," Peter moaned beneath the hands his head was buried in. "We'll be on our way after we've eaten."

Hugh shook his head. "It's of no matter, Pete, lad...Stewart. Never blame yourselves. Rosaleen is my woman and these are my people. They're my responsibilities."

"Hugh," Christian said, speaking so much more clearly than the other men at the table that all three of them looked at him with simple wonder, "perhaps I should take Mistress Erda to the kitchen with the rest of the females. The sooner they are bathed and have properly dressed themselves, the better."

It took Hugh a moment to make sense of what the boy was saying, and then he realized, for the first time, that the girl Erda was still occupying Rosaleen's chair. A deep frown formed on his lips, and he spoke roughly. "Erda, get up from there. What do you mean by sitting in your lady's place? Get up and go with Chris and don't dare to make so much of yourself again. You've made more trouble this day than most women do in a lifetime, and the sun's not yet crossed its half mark. If you go on in such a manner you'll be back in the whorehouse at Stenwick before you can count to ten. *If,*" he added caustically, "you can count to ten in the first place."

At this, Erda's tears of fright turned into wrenching sobs. With a disapproving look at his master, Christian touched the weeping girl's hand and indicated that she should follow him. Ignoring them, Hugh set his forehead gingerly against the palm of one hand.

"God's teeth, my head hurts," he said wearily.

His head didn't stop hurting until much later in the day, after Peter Brenten and Stewart of Byrne had taken their sickly leave of him, and after Hugh himself had returned to his chamber to sleep away the rest of the morning. Then, when he had woken and filled his belly with the food someone had kindly left there for him, he began to feel himself again.

He called for a bath, and while he belatedly bathed and shaved, he thought over the events of the previous eve and of that morn, though most of his memories proved dim, at best. As soon as he was dressed, he went in search of Rosaleen.

It was not long past the time for the midday meal. The people of Briarstone had already eaten and the men had returned to work in the fields, a fact that weighed heavily on Hugh's mind, for he knew he should be out working with them. Rosaleen, however, had not yet returned, he discovered when he questioned Jehanne, whom he found kneading bread in the kitchen. She answered his questions courteously, though stiffly, until Hugh finally gave up any attempt at being friendly and went to gaze out the open wall in search of Rosaleen. The masons and carpenters working there bid him a solemn greeting, and Hugh graced them with a halfhearted smile. It was clear that his people were as angry with him as Rosaleen was, yet Hugh couldn't concern himself with them until he'd made everything right with her.

When he saw no sign of her after a few minutes' searching, he began to worry, as well as to wonder about the soundness of his mind in letting her wander off alone without one of the men for protection. The very thought caused a clutch of that same unfamiliar fear he'd known when she'd run from Gyer to wrap around his heart, so that he felt he could hardly breathe.

"Jehanne, leave what you're doing and go fetch Chris. He's out in the northern fields. Tell him to come at once and ready Saint for me and a steed for himself. I'll be above stairs readying myself...."

In the distance, through the fields, he saw a slight bobbing among the stalks. Frozen, breathless, he watched as the movement drew closer, and then he said, "Go on as you were, Jehanne."

Jumping through the wall opening, Hugh ran all the way to where Rosaleen was wearily stumbling through the fields. When he came on her she looked up, her face stained with tears, full of misery.

"You little idiot!" he swore, seeing her exhaustion. "What were you thinking to do such a thing?"

She opened her mouth to speak, but no sound came out. Closing her eyes, she leaned forward and fell right into Hugh's arms.

When Rosaleen next opened her eyes it was to find herself lying on her bed, being tended gently by Hugh Caldwell.

"What . . . ?" She tried to sit, but he lightly pushed her back down.

"Don't move, sweeting. All is well. Go back to sleep."

His voice was low and soothing. Too weary to argue, Rosaleen obediently closed her eyes and relaxed upon the soft bed. A touch of wet warmth against one of her legs brought her eyes open again, and she realized, with some surprise, that Hugh was bathing her.

"Go away," she murmured. "I don't want you touching me."

"Do you not?" he asked, sounding slightly amused. "But you've not the strength to stop me, so you shall have to suffer it. Besides, sweet, this isn't the first time I've cared for you in such a way."

Turning her head away, she made no reply, and Hugh continued bathing her legs and feet in silence. When he lifted one of her arms and ran the cloth over it, he said quietly, "Rosaleen, we must speak of what happened this morn . . . about what you saw in my chamber and about what took place in the hall. I know what it must have looked like when you saw Erda in my bed, but I assure you it was not what you think. And as for the other, in the hall, I couldn't go back on my promise as the master of Briarstone, and I certainly couldn't let you gainsay me before all my—"

She groaned loudly. "Not *now*, Hugh Caldwell. Do you possess no mercy at all?"

With a frown, he began to bathe her face and said, "Aye, you are full weary and must rest. I know you were angry, but I wish you would have given me a chance to explain before you ran away in such a rage. Perhaps you meant to punish me, but you hurt only yourself. Do you not think it foolish to spite yourself so? To no good purpose?"

Yawning, she replied, "You would know the answer to that better than I, Hugh Caldwell, for you have spent the last ten years spiting yourself." She yawned once more and closed her eyes, drifting into slumber and leaving Hugh staring at her with a thoroughly confused expression.

Chapter Eighteen

"Rosaleen, sweet. Sweet Rosaleen."

The husky words were breathed against the tender skin just beneath her ear, followed by the moist, gentle pressure of a mouth, the light, hot lick of a tongue.

"You've been asleep all day, dearling, and I've come to the end of my patience. Come, my beautiful Rosaleen. Wake now. Can you not feel how much I need you?"

The fingers of Rosaleen's left hand were molded gently around a familiar length of rigid flesh, and with a sleepy moan she tightened her grasp.

"Mmm." She moved her hand slowly up and down the length of him, drawing out the stiff shudders her caresses always wrought from him. She turned on her side, toward him, seeking his heat, and was rewarded with the gentle warmth of Hugh's mouth closing over hers. His hands moved beneath her chemise, tickling her bare skin.

"Hugh," she murmured when his mouth moved to her throat. "Hugh." Her hand upon him slowed. "Hugh." Her hand stopped altogether, and her eyes opened.

Hugh found himself suddenly being shoved away, and in the next moment he was entirely bereft, Rosaleen having leapt out of his bed.

"What in the—"

"I do *not* believe you!"

Blinking, Hugh looked first at his empty hands, which had only seconds earlier been filled with sweet, warm flesh, then up at Rosaleen, who was standing beside the bed, hands on hips, glaring down at him.

"Is aught amiss, sweeting?" he asked.

"Your *mind* is amiss, you wretched beast! Or what little you possess that might be mistaken for a mind!"

She turned to go, but before Rosaleen could take one step she was caught by the wrist and dragged back onto the bed.

"Release me!" she screeched furiously, struggling in vain against Hugh's superior strength. "You cannot force me to share your bed!"

"Why are you behaving in such a manner?" he asked with honest confusion. "You're not still angry about this morn, are you? I explained about that earlier. Do you not remember? Or do you fear sleeping in this bed after Erda had her filthy person in it? In truth, she did leave some few fleas behind, but I bade Elizabeth change the bedclothes this afternoon, so all is well again."

"I would rather sleep with the fleas than with you!" Rosaleen shouted. "Release me, Hugh Caldwell. I want no explanations. Indeed, I want naught from you at all! If you need a woman so much, go slake yourself with your new whore!"

"With my *what!*" he returned, much offended. "You think I'd make a foul-smelling creature like that a whore of mine? God's mercy, Rosaleen, you should know me better than that after the time we've spent together."

She laughed, bitterly, and kept trying to gain freedom. As much as she tugged and fought, however, he only held her that much more tightly.

"Calm yourself, sweeting. You cannot truly think I have replaced you with any other." But the look on her face told him that she thought just that. "Rosaleen, you little fool..."

"If you do not take your filthy hands off me, I swear by all that is holy I shall scream the bricks from the walls!"

Oblivious to the precarious state of her emotions, Hugh grinned. "Why, Rosaleen, you're jealous. I never expected such an open declaration of your feelings, but I'm pleased. Most pleased, dearling." With an infuriating chuckle, he released her and sat up. "But there is no need to be so distraught. If you will only let me explain what happened last night, I vow you will find the tale most entertaining."

With a look of disgust, Rosaleen stood and headed once more for the chamber door.

"Stop, Rosaleen."

"Go rot in hell." She flung the words back at him, continuing her course.

"You vowed to obey me in all things," he reminded her. "Will you go back on your word now? Like one with no honor, Rosaleen?"

She stopped, her back rigid.

"My vow to obey you had nothing to do with sharing your bed," she stated furiously. "I have done so freely and of my own accord, but I choose to do so no longer, and I will not."

The sound of him getting out of the bed sent a shiver of fright through her. In another moment his hands gripped her shoulders, spinning her around. In the dim light their eyes met and held.

"You are mine, Rosaleen. *Mine.* What's between us has naught to do with vows or promises or any other damned thing. If you ever say such a foolish thing again I'll wring your neck!"

"I'm not yours!" she cried, torn between anger and hurt. "No longer. You brought that whore home and took her into your bed. You chose her above me!"

Amazed, Hugh shook his head. "Women are the most senseless creatures on God's earth, and you, my darling, are worse than most. Tell me why, please, I should want that wretched little girl when I already possess such a beautiful creature to warm my bed?"

"You seemed content with her this morn," Rosaleen replied tartly. "Indeed, you seemed more than content."

"If I did, it is because I thought she was you. That is God's truth, Rosaleen, I swear it. Last night in Stenwick, Pete and Stew and I got so soused that not a one of us could have told you our names. Pete and Stew took a liking to the tavern whores and decided to bring the wenches back to Briarstone, and somewhere along the way I must have offered them a home. I can't be sure of it, for I don't remember a moment of the ride, or even much of what took place at the tavern, for that matter." His voice filled with remorse. "I tell you true, dearling, I never meant to get so drunk, though I don't expect you to forgive me, for there is no excuse for letting myself get so far gone that I took another female into our bed."

"I don't know why it should bother you," she returned. "Indeed, after hearing of your many adventures last eve, I should think that servicing more than one or two or even three females at a time wouldn't turn a hair upon your head."

It took a moment, but Hugh managed to control the almost overwhelming urge to laugh out loud. Clearing his throat, he tried to speak as normally as possible.

"Rosaleen, darling, I cannot deny any of what my friends spoke last eve." Lightly, his fingers squeezed her arms and drew her closer. "I am not like my brother Hugo, more saint than sinner. You know that better than anyone, having been at my mercy from the very day we met. But those days are in the past, Rosaleen. I promise you they are. Now I want only one woman." He smiled and added teasingly, "At a time, of course."

Rosaleen knew he was only trying to make light of what was, for him, a most serious speech. She knew it, but the knowledge didn't soothe her. She had wanted her time with him at Briarstone, true, but the sight of him with Erda had forced her to face the truth. There was only one month remaining of her service to him, and after that she would leave. She loved him; for her the parting would be unbearably painful, for him it would be a small inconvenience. Perhaps Erda had been only a brief substitution, but she had been a substitution all the same, and the fact that Hugh Caldwell had taken the girl to his bed at all only proved how quickly and easily he would find someone to take her place once she was gone.

Not looking at him, ignoring the warm caresses of his hands on her arms, Rosaleen said in a small voice, "I am weary. I wish to return to my chamber."

Hugh raised his eyebrows. "Do you not believe me, Rosaleen? I tell you in all truth that I thought it was you who lay beside me this morn."

"I believe you."

"But you are not satisfied," he said, frowning at the sad sound of her.

"It matters not, Hugh—"

He was suddenly angry. "You are the only woman I want. The only one, I swear it. What more would you have from me?"

"To be let go," she begged. "To be left alone for the next month until I'm free to leave this wretched place."

"No," he said tightly. "No."

"Hypocrite!" she cried, hurt beyond reason. "You say you want me, only me, but you lie! Can you swear by all that is holy that you didn't join your body with hers last night? Can you?"

Meeting her pained gaze, Hugh replied, "No."

Rosaleen's head drooped forward. "Oh, God's mercy..."

His arms went around her trembling body, hugging her. "Rosaleen, what would you have of me? I cannot lie to you. I was so damned drunk...my memories are so few. I wish I could tell you that naught happened between Erda and myself, but I can't. It's been so long since I've joined myself to a woman's body, and lying with you night after night...wanting you so badly...it's possible...very possible that I joined myself to her, thinking she was you. And I think... Merciful God, Rosaleen, I think I did."

The sobs that came from her broke his heart, and he wanted to fall on his knees and beg her forgiveness. But he couldn't. It wasn't in him to do so...like so many other qualities he didn't possess. He could only do what he had always done—try to fight his way out.

"Damn!" he muttered, his anger directed all at himself but his words striking her. "I should have known to expect such as this from a virgin! If you didn't prize that maidenhead of yours like some kind of holy relic, I never would have done it! You're the one to blame for what happened, so don't think I'll keep pleading your forgiveness like some noble knight of the realm! I'm not noble and I'm not a knight and you damned well know it!"

When she made no reply but only continued to sob against him, he went on, heedlessly, thoughtlessly. "Damn all wellborn ladies! Give me a good whore any day and I'll be a happier man!''

Shoving free, she slapped him with a force that stunned them both.

In silence, they stared at each other.

''You gave me your vow...'' he warned.

''You'll never know what I gave you!'' she cried wrathfully, wiping her wet eyes with the back of her hand. ''But for all that, I honor my vows. I'll be your servant for the next eight and twenty days, my Lord Caldwell, but I'll no longer be your whore. If you want a woman, find one among the females from Stenwick, but leave my ladies and myself alone.''

Hugh gave her no reply, and Rosaleen turned and left the room.

Chapter Nineteen

Although he already knew what the answer would be, Christian Rowsenly looked down upon the bent head of his master and asked the question anyway.

"Will you be returning to the keep with us for the midday meal?"

Not looking up from the dark earth out of which he was pulling ripe beans, Hugh replied, "Not today. Have food sent back for me."

And that was that. The same as every day for the past two weeks. Not that Christian could blame his master...mealtimes at Briarstone had, of late, been unpleasant events. Gone were the relaxed chattering and easy comfort of the meals the people had enjoyed after the arrival of their new master and the lady Rosaleen, and in their place were stiff, quiet minutes during which everyone finished their meals as quickly as they could. Since the day that Lady Rosaleen had put the girl Erda in her chair, it had been thus, though Erda now sat with the other women of Briarstone while the lady Rosaleen rigidly took her place beside Hugh Caldwell.

They did not speak with each other any longer, Hugh Caldwell and Lady Rosaleen, or at least they didn't if they could avoid it, and when they couldn't avoid it, the words they exchanged were short and few. They no longer played chess after the evening meal or sat by the fire talking and teasing and laughing. They no longer sent secret smiles to each other or went for long walks in the cool of the summer evenings. They avoided one another, and their previously pleasant natures had become so unpleasant that the people of Briarstone did their best to avoid their master and lady, too.

This was the worst of it, Christian thought. Hugh Caldwell's insistent and daily desire to work himself to death. Perhaps, thought Christian as he considered his master's sweat-drenched back, this was Hugh Caldwell's way of keeping his surly temper under rein. He had snapped and growled at so many of the people lately that Christian fully expected him to lash out at the very next man to cross his path, including himself. The constant tension of Hugh Caldwell's body, the tautness of the muscles beneath his flesh, reminded Christian of an arrow set upon a hard-pulled bow, wanting only to spring wildly free at the moment of release.

"If that is what you wish," Christian said at last.

"It is," Hugh said, still not lifting his head. In another moment he heard a sigh, and then Christian turned and walked away. When he was certain the boy was far enough away, Hugh stopped his work, rested his forehead upon one knee and gave way to his misery.

Nothing he did soothed the ache inside him. Nothing. He could work himself into the grave or fight a hundred men or drink until he could no longer stand . . . none of it was going to help. He had run out of ways to escape his pain, and living with it day by day was worse than slow death.

There were so many thoughts whirling in his mind that he could no longer separate the pain of one from the other.

Rosaleen, the truth of his birth, memories of the man he'd called father and, worst of all, his dreams...dreams that had so blissfully disappeared during the months he had held Rosaleen in his arms but which now plagued him night after night after night until Hugh wondered if he would go mad from them.

Sometimes he thought he should release Rosaleen of her debt to him and send her away...to London, where she wanted to be and where he would no longer look upon her every day, wanting and aching for her and not being able to touch or even speak to her kindly. She hated and despised him. She'd made that clear on that night two weeks ago when she'd walked out of his chamber. If she'd been any other woman, Hugh never would have let her get away with it. He would have pursued her and forced her back into his bed where she belonged, but for once in his sorry life, he'd been unable to take what he wanted and had simply stood there and felt all the dreams he'd harbored of a future with Rosaleen drain out of his heart like sand pouring through his fingers.

Because he loved her.

He hadn't been able to pursue her because he loved her and because he'd hurt her. And if by some miracle she did stay with him, he would hurt her again and again. His soul was empty of good yet so full of bad. No matter how hard he might try not to, and in spite of the fact that he loved Rosaleen more than he had known it possible for a man to love a woman, he would hurt her. As sure as the sun rose in the sky each morn, he knew this was the truth.

And so he had let her go, and in two weeks' time he would let her go again. Forever.

Hugh shut his eyes and let the pain wash over him. A few deep breaths helped him through the worst, and when it had passed he told himself that a broken heart wasn't so unbearable once you began to get used to it.

"Hugh! Hugh Caldwell! Come quickly! Alec Berry is being beaten to death!"

Hearing Christian's panicked cry, Hugh reacted out of instinct, uncoiling like a snake from his crouched position and leaping through the tall stalks of wheat toward the sound of Christian's voice. Running fiercely, he briefly took in the sight of a giant man on horseback whipping Alec Berry. Not slowing, an animal cry tearing from his throat, he threw himself at the man full force, and the momentum and impact bore both men down to the ground, where they landed with a thud, Hugh on top, straddling the big man's body. The next moment Hugh raised both fists and smashed them into the man's face, cursing him roundly all the while, until the giant managed to free one of his own hands to start swinging.

The fight lasted only a few, wild moments before Hugh was dragged away from his opponent by several armed men who, using their combined strengths, overpowered and held him. Hugh's own men, he saw at once, were held at sword point by what looked like the rest of a small army.

"By God's holy bones, I swear I will kill you!" Hugh raged at the giant he'd left lying in the dirt, who with visible effort was trying to sit. "These are *my* lands and my people! You've no right to trespass and lay a hand to any of them! I'll go to the king and have your head!"

"God's teeth! It's Hugh Caldwell!"

In an instant Hugh found himself freed, the arms around him melting away like snow on a fire, and then, suddenly, he was surrounded by a sea of familiar faces.

Breathing hard, shaking his head to clear it, he gaped at the men.

"Stephan . . . Stephan Ayrell," he managed to say.

"Hello, Hugh Caldwell," that man replied with a grin. "It's been a long while."

Hugh kept looking around. "Roger Wade...Alan of Tyneham...Rob...Rob Barstett."

"Good to see you, Hugh," Alan of Tyneham said, laughing and extending an arm in greeting. "Leave it to Hugh Caldwell to attack his old friends like some wild beast come out of the woods! He's the only man who could do it and not be thought crazed."

Stiffening, Hugh pushed his friends aside and strode toward the man he'd left in the road. "Then who by the Fiend is this?" he demanded, stopping short as the giant, rubbing tentatively at his temple, turned his head to offer Hugh a wry smile.

"Damn you, Hugh! I think you broke my head. Must you ever be seeking a fight every moment of the day?"

Hugh lowered a hand and helped the giant to his feet.

"Simon of Denning! By the rood, I had no idea 'twas you!"

Laughing, still rubbing his sore head, Simon of Denning said, "I hope not, Hugh Caldwell, else I'd think our friendship over. Can you not simply greet a man with a hand grasp?"

Hugh frowned, remembering the sight of Simon beating Alec Berry. With renewed anger he grasped the bigger man's tunic and dragged him closer. "What do you mean by beating one of my men?"

"Calm yourself, Hugh," Simon advised, placing his own hairy hands over Hugh's and squeezing with a force meant to break bones. "I asked the man a question he refused to answer, and I paid him his due for showing his betters such a lack of respect." He crushed Hugh's hands more tightly, but to no avail. "A breach of simple law that I might remind you of, Hugh Caldwell. I could have killed him for it, if I'd wished, just as I could kill you for laying hands on one of your betters, if I wished."

With a strength born out of years of rage and bitterness, Hugh gritted his teeth against the pain of Simon of Denning's punishing hands and replied, "I may be bastard born, *Sir* Simon, and I may not be a grand knight of the realm, but at least I'm not ugly."

The fury that colored Simon's face gave Hugh all the edge he needed, and yanking his hands free, he delivered a blow to Simon of Denning's face, so powerful that it landed the giant on his back again.

Towering over him, Hugh met Simon's dark, outraged eyes. "Lay a hand to a man of mine again, Simon of Denning, and I'll not give a thought to all the times we fought side by side. I'll kill you outright and take the consequences. On that you have my solemn vow. Now, what are you doing here?" Reaching down, he helped the man to his feet once more.

"I think," Simon stated, dusting himself, "that you are the only man I'd let fell me twice and allow to live, Hugh Caldwell. You have saved my life on the field of battle too many times for me to slay you easily, but I, too, will make a vow. If you dare to lay another of your commoner's hands on me again, bastard of Wellewyn, I will kill you, regardless that you are the brother of the Lord of Gyer, and I'll not think of the consequences, either."

Hugh nodded. "Fair enough, Simon. Now tell me what you're doing on my land, then leave."

Simon scowled. "Come, Hugh, cry friends and walk with me, that I may speak to you in peace and see this new land of yours. I must say, I am impressed. I never expected you to make anything of yourself."

He started in the direction of the keep, but Hugh stood where he was, watching him distrustfully. He had been one

of few men to call Simon of Denning his friend, but it was
an uncertain honor. He liked Simon well enough as a soldier and as a fellow gambler, but there was no denying that
the man was an animal in every sense of the word, and
Hugh didn't trust him any farther than he could throw
him.

Looking back, seeing Hugh standing in his place, Simon prodded impatiently, "Come along, Hugh. I'll only
take a few minutes of your precious time, and then my men
and I shall leave. I swear it by God."

First casting a meaningful glance at the men, his friends,
whom Simon of Denning had bought with his money, just
as Hugh himself had been bought so many times before,
Hugh moved to follow.

"As good as it is to see you again, Simon," Hugh said,
keeping a careful distance between Simon and him, "it is
harvest time and my men and I are very busy."

"I understand," Simon replied easily, "but as I made a
special trip to Briarstone simply to see you, Hugh, the least
you can do is spare me a little of your time."

One of Hugh's eyebrows slanted upward. "What is it,
then? I suppose Peter Brenten and Stewart of Byrne told
you I was here. They stopped here two weeks past on their
way to London. They decided not to join you?"

Simon shook his head. "They have, but I've sent them
off with a separate army led by Gerry Walson."

"Ah, in search of your betrothed. Pete and Stew told me
she'd been taken captive, and I was sorry to hear of it.
That's a bad turn for you, Simon."

"More than you know, Hugh, more than you know."

The sadness in his tone surprised Hugh.

"God's teeth, never tell me you love the woman! I'd not
believe it! Not after all the years we've known one another."

Simon chuckled. "You think I've no heart, then, Hugh? Well, that may be true, but if I could love a woman it would be this one. She is beautiful, so perfect, so. . ." He thought for a moment, clearly trying to find the right words. "She's the kind of woman," he said at last, "who makes a man feel lost the moment he sets eyes on her. Do you know what I mean, Hugh?"

Grimly, Hugh nodded. "Aye, I know just what you mean." Then he tilted his head, regarding his companion. "She's a duchess, or so Peter told me. I must admit, I never thought of you as a duke, Simon. A damned weighty title, if you ask me."

"No, no, she's a countess," Simon corrected, waving a hand as if to wave away the misconception. "Or a future countess, I should say, though once we're wed she'll give away her right to that title forever. She'll be my baroness and no more. I've no use for haughty females who think they're better than I or any other man."

Without even knowing her, Hugh felt sorry for the girl and wondered anew if she'd run away rather than been taken captive.

"Her uncle," Simon went on, "who will inherit the title once we've wed, has his own army searching for her, and the king has his men out, as well, but none of us has found even a trace of her."

"There must have been something, surely," Hugh stated, "else how would you know whether she'd been taken rather than simply run off? Has there not been a ransom demand?"

"No, only the fact that she is gone. 'Tis her uncle, Sir Anselm, who insists the girl has been taken, and I believe it, for she knows full well what her recompense would be if she dared to run from me of her own free will. I would kill her if she did such a thing. I would put my hands around her soft neck and squeeze the life from her."

"Come, come, Simon," Hugh said, amazed at his companion's quick fury, "no woman on earth is worth getting that angered over."

"This one is, Hugh. By the rood, she is. There is no other woman like my beautiful heiress of Siere. I wanted her the moment I saw her, as I've never wanted another. Everything about her is lovely beyond belief, as though she were made from heaven and not earth."

Staring at his friend's lovesick expression, Hugh almost felt like laughing. Simon would change his mind about his heiress right quick if he could ever see Rosaleen, Hugh thought. No woman existed who could be more lovely than she.

"She's a stubborn wench," Simon admitted, "and needs a firm hand. I've not yet found the way to draw her tears, though God alone knows how I've tried, but that will be a small matter when we've wed. I will be master in my home, and she will bend her knee. On our wedding night she'll learn it, I vow, and 'twill be sweet indeed to see her lowered before me, a proper and obedient wife to be used for her husband's pleasure."

Hugh felt slightly sick. He'd known Simon of Denning long enough and well enough to know how brutally he used his women.

"If you've come to ask whether I've seen any sign of your noble maid, Simon, then you have wasted your time. Naught of her has come to my ear."

"That's a shame," said Simon, "though, in truth, I came to ask if you would join in helping me find her. A better man in a hunt I've never met than Hugh Caldwell."

Quickly and thoroughly, Hugh declined the offer and courteously resisted every counteroffer Simon made.

"You're certain, Hugh?"

"Quite certain. I'm finished with being a soldier for hire."

"I'll double the wages."

"Nay, I'm content at Briarstone."

"Well," Simon said with a sigh, scratching his bearded chin and turning to walk back toward his men, "'tis a pity, that's certain, but I can see you'll not be swayed. By the by, Stewart and Peter told me you've a lady of your own now who is extraordinarily fair. It must be she who keeps you tied to this place, for I've never known Hugh Caldwell to turn aside a chance for adventure in the stead of anything as dull as a harvest."

"She is extraordinary," Hugh agreed quietly. "And you speak truly when you say that I do not want to leave her."

Simon of Denning laughed. "I should like to meet this woman who has finally captured Hugh Caldwell. She must be a beauty, indeed. God only knows, every fair maid in France did her best to hold you. But I've no time to stay and enjoy your hospitality, Hugh," he said, ignoring the fact that Hugh hadn't extended any. "I must be on my way. I'm sorry for the trouble with your serf."

"With my vassal," Hugh corrected, wanting Simon to understand that none of his people were slaves to him. Offering a hand in farewell, he added, "I wish you Godspeed, Simon, and luck in finding your lady."

Simon of Denning grasped Hugh's hand and arm in a familiar gesture of friendship.

"Thank you, Hugh. God knows I'll need some luck. It may be a hard task, but I'll find her if it's the last thing I do. There's not another woman like Rosaleen Sarant in all of England, and one day, I swear it on my own soul, she'll either be mine . . . or dead."

* * *

"What lovely stitches, Leatrice. I do believe you've the makings of a fine seamstress."

"Do . . . do y' think so, m'lady? Truly?" Leatrice asked her mistress, looking up with pleasure.

"I do indeed," Rosaleen replied truthfully, gazing approvingly at the linen the girl held out for inspection. "You are talented after so short a time. Not every student would be so quick, I vow. I am most pleased. Now, Janet—" she moved to the girl sitting beside Leatrice "—let me see your work. Very good, very good. This portion does not need so much black. It is to be a dog, not a cow. Erda? How is your part coming along? Quite nicely, it seems. Be careful to keep these stitches on the center of each flower as small as possible, else the effect will be ruined. Alvina, let me see your work now. Good, good, very nice." Standing away, Rosaleen added, "You are all doing beautifully, and your master will be pleased. Perhaps in a few days I shall set you to work on the new castle banners." The excited expressions this news brought to the faces of the women from Stenwick amused Rosaleen.

The four new arrivals had settled in quickly, if somewhat tensely, after their first unhappy day at Briarstone, and even Erda had begun to behave as well as Rosaleen could want.

"I'd like you to put the tapestry away for now and go to the kitchen to help Ada and the others with the evening meal. If I'm needed I will be in my chamber, preparing ledgers for the upcoming harvest."

The women obediently did their mistress's bidding, until Erda, lifting her head at the sound of the keep's doors opening, said, "Master Hugh is coming, m'lady."

Whirling, Rosaleen saw that Hugh was indeed coming, in fact, he was striding toward them, a grim, set expression upon his handsome face.

As she watched him approach so purposefully, Rosaleen's heart began to pound. For two weeks they had lived like strangers, even like enemies, and for two weeks she had fully regretted the pride and anger that had driven him from her. Twice she had tried to apologize to him, for she had realized after only a few days that the little girl Erda meant nothing to him and that what had happened between them had all been a terrible mistake that Hugh honestly regretted. And more, Rosaleen had accepted that he'd been right when he'd blamed her for his lapse. Making love with him each night in the way that they had done, doing all save the final consummation, had been difficult for him. How could she have blamed him for something that had been natural, perhaps even necessary, to him? If he had made love to Erda, he had certainly not done it purposefully, for he avoided the girl as much—if not more—as he now avoided Rosaleen herself. And so she had gone to him to make her apologies, but each time he had sent her away without letting her say more than a few words. He didn't wish to speak to her, he said, and he wished that she would leave him be for the remainder of her time at Briarstone. She had reluctantly left him both times, feeling more hurt and humiliated than she could ever remember being, and so frightened that the few remaining days she had with the man she would always love would be fraught with anger and silence.

But it appeared as though the silence were about to be broken, for it was clear that Hugh Caldwell had something on his mind. The look on his face said that, and when he stopped in front of her, his hard mouth opened and confirmed it.

"I wish to speak to the lady Rosaleen alone," he told the women curtly, not moving his eyes from Rosaleen. "Leave us."

Nervously, Rosaleen glanced at the frightened, frozen women. "They are finished with their work, and it will only take them a moment—"

"Leave us!" he thundered, making all of them, including Rosaleen, jump.

"How dare you!" Rosaleen said angrily after the women had flown. "If you must behave as an animal you can do so out-of-doors! I'll not have you shouting at my ladies."

His expression, steely, hard, furious, didn't waver.

"Don't speak, Rosaleen. I've not come for that. I've come only to tell you something. Nothing more."

He was so angry, so bitter and tense that Rosaleen could only stare up at him. He was still dirty and sweaty from laboring in the fields, but in spite of the grime covering him he looked, in that moment, impossibly handsome.

"I have just sent Carl on his way with a missive to my brother, the Lord of Gyer, requesting that he come to Briarstone at once to escort you to London."

Ignoring the surprise on Rosaleen's face, Hugh went on. "He will be here in no more than three days' time, and by then I want you ready to leave."

"But, my service to you is not done for another two weeks!"

"I release you of it. I want you out of Briarstone, Rosaleen Sarant of Siere." He spoke her true name like a curse. "When my brother arrives you will be ready to leave at once, or I swear by God that I'll throw you out the front gates myself with naught but the clothes on your back!"

Finished, he turned and left the hall, slamming the heavy front doors loudly and leaving behind a pale, trembling Rosaleen, who stood alone, stunned, horrified and very, very frightened.

Chapter Twenty

"Hugh! Oh, Hugh, wake up!"

Rosaleen's desperate pleading penetrated his dark Hell, reaching Hugh, grasping him, pulling him back against the heavy tide, dragging him up and up and up....

He bolted upright in the bed, gulping for air like a man nearly drowned, his big body drenched with sweat and shaking violently.

Her arms were around him, keeping him, holding him safe.

"It's all right, Hugh. It's all right."

Half in hell and half out, panting with the effort to breathe, Hugh tried to still the spinning of the room, of his mind.

"Don't leave me!" he begged. "Don't leave me here, Rosaleen!"

"I'll not. I'll not leave you, Hugh."

She was crying...sobbing. He could hear it in her voice and feel it against his body. Slowly, with effort, he brought his arms up to circle her trembling form.

"Don't leave me," he repeated.

She shook her head against him, unable to speak beyond her tears.

A few minutes passed, and finally the terror left him. Working at it, Hugh managed to calm his breathing, and then, swallowing hard a couple times, he spoke.

"I was dreaming."

"You were screaming."

"I didn't mean to frighten you."

"Hugh—" she turned her tear-wet face up to look at him "—what was it? What could possibly have done that to you?"

"Nothing. A bad dream, no more. All is well now. You can return to your chamber."

Sitting up, moving a little out of the circle of his arms, she said, "Nay. I'll not leave until you tell me the truth. It was much more than a bad dream, Hugh Caldwell. You were screaming. And look at you." She placed both hands on his bare chest. "You're shaking."

"I'm cold. Go back to your chamber, Rosaleen."

"It's hot as a fire in here," she stated. "And I'll not leave until you tell me what your dream was about."

Briefly, he frowned, and then his features took on a familiar mocking expression. "If I was screaming, Lady of Siere, it was probably because I dreamed we were wed to one another. Can you think of a nightmare worse than that? I certainly can't. Now *go away.*"

Rosaleen made a sound of impatience. "I'll not, and don't speak such lies to me, you foul beast. I came here this night to face you one way or another, and I'll not walk out that door unless you either answer my questions or throw me out by force."

"Don't tempt me!" Hugh warned, pushing her aside and getting out of the bed. The fact that he was naked didn't seem to bother him at all, though the sight gave Rosaleen a moment of surprise. Her eyes followed him as he stalked to the open window and looked out, taut and edgy like a caged animal. "Get out, Rosaleen. Get out now."

"You said a word while you dreamed," she told him. "I could make it out plainly."

He made a low sound, and Rosaleen bit her lip.

"It was 'father,'" she said, and Hugh's body stiffened as though she'd whipped him.

"I can't," he whispered. "I cannot speak of it, Rosaleen. All these years... I can't..."

Rising, Rosaleen went to him, and when she placed her hands upon the strong muscles of his back he flinched, then settled.

"Hugh, you must speak of it. You have lived in torment these many years. You must speak of it and be freed."

Wordlessly, he shook his head.

"In three days' time I will leave this place," Rosaleen said quietly, moving her hands upon his body in soothing motions, "and we may never see one another again. Do this one thing for me, I beg you. If I have ever meant anything to you at all, Hugh, do this so that when I leave I will know you will be happy."

"There is naught..."

"You dreamed of your father... of the man you called father. Charles Baldwin. How you must have loved him, Hugh."

Hugh fisted his hands. "I hated him! The man was a devil. A God-cursed devil with no honor, no love, no pity in him whatsoever."

"That wasn't always true," she countered. "Hugo told me that you loved him when you were a boy."

"I hated him!" Hugh shouted furiously. "I despised him!"

"He loved you and Hugo better than your brothers and sister, and in return you worshiped him. His other children he treated with indifference, but you and Hugo he loved and spoiled."

"No!" Hugh insisted, his whole body tensing against the pain. "He didn't love Hugo and me. He used us. He made a jest of us...an insult! The bastard sons of his greatest enemy, Jaward of Wellewyn, living as the sons of Charles Baldwin. A jest, Rosaleen. Hugo and I were naught but a great jest!"

"That is not true!" she insisted, gripping him with her hands. "He loved you and Hugo and claimed you as his own sons!"

Whirling, Hugh shoved her away so violently that Rosaleen stumbled to the opposite wall.

"Do you not understand, Rosaleen? Can you not begin to understand? Jaward of Wellewyn was his enemy. He *hated* him. From my birth Charles Baldwin nurtured me on that hatred. My first words...my first thoughts...and Hugo's...were to *hate* Jaward of Wellewyn. To hate our natural father. To want to destroy him. If you only knew...oh, damn!" He turned away, striking the wall with his fist.

"Hugh..."

"He didn't love us!" he went on furiously, forcing his voice to work against the pain. "He used us for vengeance against his enemy. There was no other reason. He lured us with words and deeds, making us love him...trust him." Lowering his head, he closed his eyes. "How he must have laughed each night in his bed on how perfect was the revenge of having the slavish love of his enemy's sons!" He looked at Rosaleen once more, his eyes filled with rage. "That's all Hugo and I meant to him. *Vengeance!*"

"I don't believe that!" she cried. "I'll not believe it! Vengeance is only complete when a man's deeds are made known, and your father never flaunted you and Hugo before Jaward of Wellewyn. He never told anyone, not one person, that you were not his own natural children. Indeed, from what I've heard, Charles Baldwin never lost an opportunity to boast of his twin sons to any who would listen. Is that the behavior of a man seeking vengeance?"

"That counts as naught," Hugh muttered. "Charles Baldwin was perverse enough to enjoy his jest in private. He'd not want the world to know that he'd been cuckolded by Jaward of Wellewyn. I'm sure it was enough for him that he'd raised the offspring of his enemy with so much hatred for their natural parent that they would willingly have killed him simply to please the man they worshiped as their father." With a bitter laugh, he stumbled to the bed and sat upon it. "A most humorous contemplation, do you not think?" He buried his face in his hands, and Rosaleen's heart ached for him. Going to him, she knelt at his feet and placed her hands on his knees.

Slowly, Hugh lifted his head and met Rosaleen's gaze.

"So painful," he whispered, his voice wobbly and thick. "It's so painful."

Silent tears spilled over, coursing down his face.

"I l-loved him. How—" his voice broke as he searched Rosaleen's face "—how c-could he do it? How could he do it to us?"

One hand he pressed to his chest, at the place where his heart was, as though the ache there would shatter him forever.

She gently wiped the tears from his face. "Hugh," she murmured, "you torture yourself needlessly. If you would only think of the good times you had with your father...."

"No."

"Listen to me," she went on, taking his hands and holding them tightly. "There is much of your father's story that you have never heard or have somehow, in your misery, forgotten. I had a long talk with Hugo before we left the monastery, and with your sister, Lady Lillis, on the day we arrived at Gyer, and I have learned a great deal about the enmity between Charles Baldwin and Jaward of Wellewyn.

"You have said that your father and Jaward of Wellewyn were lifelong enemies, but that isn't so. At one time, during their boyhood, they were the best of friends. In fact, your Aunt Leta told your sister that the two men were closer than mere friends—they were more like brothers. They were fostered together and spent much of their time together. Even after your father and mother were married, Jaward of Wellewyn often visited at Gyer. He nearly courted your Aunt Leta, and he was your eldest brother's godfather until his falling-out with Charles Baldwin. Did you not know any of this, Hugh?"

Dazed and slightly bewildered, Hugh gazed at her as though she were speaking a foreign language.

"Father and Jaward of Wellewyn? Friends? No... it's not possible. My first memories... from the moment I could understand... he spoke of naught but hatred for the man. He... he—" Hugh blinked against the memory "—hated Jaward of Wellewyn so much that he raped his wife. He raped her and she killed herself."

"Yes, he did do that," Rosaleen admitted, gripping his hands more tightly when she felt a fine trembling course through him, "but you must listen, Hugh. You must understand this. Your father had lusted after Jaward of Wellewyn's wife for many years and made no secret of that lust. That is what brought the friendship of those two men to an end. There can be no excuse for what your father did, for nothing can allow for such a foul deed, but you, better than anyone, know that Charles Baldwin was neither a good nor decent man. That doesn't mean he was incapable of love. Hugh! You must listen to me!'' she demanded when he tried to pull away from her. ''You must try to understand that what happened between those two men so many years ago was between *them*. It had naught to do with what Charles Baldwin felt for you and Hugo.''

Feebly, as weakly as a child, Hugh struggled to be free of Rosaleen's imprisoning hands and searing words. He didn't want to hear these things. He couldn't. It hurt. It hurt so badly. Like a hot, sharp knife slicing all the way through his soul.

''Why do you find it so impossible to believe that he loved you?'' she persisted. ''Because you are convinced that he hated Jaward of Wellewyn and therefore must have hated you for being that man's offspring? You must accept the fact that they loved *and* hated one another. It sounds impossible, but it's not. For some people those two emotions, love and hate, are so joined that the difference can hardly be found. When Jaward Ryon and Charles Baldwin loved one another they loved as closely as brothers, and when something happened to change that love, neither could accept it as altered. It was a strong love, but not a malleable one. It could not be bent to a different form but could only be turned to hatred.''

He didn't believe her. He wouldn't let himself, and so he said, ''You speak madness.'' And yet, strangely, the ache in his chest began to ease.

''If this does not convince you that I speak the truth,'' she said, ''then nothing will. Your Aunt Leta told this to your sister Lillis, and Lillis told it to me. On his deathbed, your father told your Aunt Leta that the worst thing that had ever happened to him was losing the friendship of Jaward of Wellewyn. It was worse than his parents' death, worse than the suicide of the woman he'd raped and worse even than the death of his own wife. Do you see now, Hugh? Your father loved you not only for yourself, but also because you were the son of the man who had once been his closest friend. If he taught you to hate Jaward of Wellewyn, it was probably because he feared you would leave him should you ever discover the truth. He didn't want to lose either you or Hugo, because you were all he had left of the friend whom he had once loved so well."

Her words shocked Hugh to his very depths, and he slowly shook his head.

Disputing him, Rosaleen nodded.

"You can say the sky is green all you like, Hugh Baldwin, but that won't change its color."

It was the first time she had ever called him that... Baldwin. Always before Rosaleen had respected his decision to name himself differently. Yet he wasn't angered, for the first time in ten years, to hear himself called thusly. He drew in a long breath and felt his pain ease even more.

"You have spoken of memories," he said quietly, "and of the past, but you cannot know how such things have tormented me, Rosaleen. Since that day on which I learned the truth, my memories have haunted me, pursued me like demons.... I cannot even escape them in sleep unless I have worked myself into a state of weariness. Tonight the worst of them came to me. The very worst memory of all."

"Tell me," she whispered.

He drew in another breath and released it, then began to speak.

"My mother died when Hugo and I were ten years of age. It was very hard, for we loved her, but neither of us cried for her because Father had taught us that a man never cries, not for any reason, and we didn't want to anger or disgust him. At our mother's funeral, only Willem, our elder brother, cried openly. None of the rest of us dared to do so.

"Father was furious with Willem and said things to him—" Hugh shook his head woefully "—such things! And when Alex tried to comfort Willem, Father lost his temper, right there at the grave site." His face hardened with anger. "It was so wrong, Rosaleen," he said with feeling. "Willem has ever been a gentle soul, and he loved Mother so deeply. Father humiliated him before all those assembled. Before Mother's grave."

"Oh, Hugh. What an unfeeling thing to do."

The fire in his eyes died away, to be replaced by a deep sadness. "Worse than unfeeling," he said. "It was thoroughly unjust, an act of hypocrisy. But I must finish the tale for you to understand.

"That night, after everyone else had gone to bed, I sneaked down to the cellar. Father found me there. I was crying for Mother."

"Hugh," Rosaleen couldn't keep from murmuring.

"I was crying," Hugh went on, determined to tell her everything, "and when I saw him standing there, watching me, I was horrified. I wanted to die rather than have him see me crying. But he wasn't angry with me as he had been with Willem. He...he pulled me onto his lap and held me and he...told me it was all right. He told me to go ahead and cry." As if the pain eased with each word he spoke, his voice had grown wistful. "I have ever felt guilty for it, and the memory has angered me more than any other. But he called me his Hugh," he said with wonder, as if just remembering it. "He always called me his Hugh."

"He loved you," Rosaleen said.

It was too new, too amazing for him to believe. "No, he..."

Reaching up, she kissed him, gently, tenderly.

"He loved you," she whispered, gazing into his eyes. "Your father loved you, Hugh. In all the years you had with him, he made you and Hugo his own just as surely as though you had been his in truth. And perhaps more so. To his other children he gave only his seed, but to you and Hugo he gave his love, as best he was able. In an odd way, you and your brother were more his true children than his natural children were."

He stared at her, unable either to deny or confirm her words. Unable to do anything at that moment.

"He loved you," Rosaleen repeated.

He was beginning to believe her and smiled faintly, saying, "He was more saint than sinner, then, I think, for I'm not very lovable."

She set her hands on either side of his face.

"Oh yes, Hugh Caldwell, you are. For I love you with all my heart."

He stopped breathing.

"I love you," she said, pulling him down to her. "I will always love you," she murmured against his mouth, "and I shall never love another."

"Rosaleen," he said, stunned.

"Make love to me," she whispered.

"Rosaleen..."

"I want to be one with you, Hugh Caldwell, Hugh Baldwin, my own beloved Hugh. I care for naught else. Once, if only once, I want to be one with you."

His arms went around her. "Not once, but forever," he vowed. "Forever, for I have loved you longer than I have known life."

"Yes," she murmured as he kissed her, and then, when he had lifted his mouth, she said, "Make me yours."

His hands moved to pull the chemise from her body. "You are mine already, love," he told her. "You have always been mine."

Reverently, he placed her upon the bed.

"I have never made love to a woman before," he said, coming down beside her, smiling into her eyes as his hands moved over her warm, silken skin. "I have known many women, Rosaleen, but I have never loved one until this moment. I wish I knew better how to speak of my love for you. There are no words, I think, or if there are, I have never heard them."

He kissed her, then lifted his head to gaze at her once more. "There is something I want you to know. Something important. I never joined my body with Erda's. She told me, only yesterday, that I was so drunk that night when we came back from Stenwick that I did no more than fall upon the bed and commence snoring. Even when she removed my clothes I did not stir. She promised me that she spoke the truth. You can ask her, Rosaleen, and she will tell you."

With loving fingers she caressed his cheek. "I believe you, Hugh, and I am glad. But even had it been otherwise, I would not have held it against you. I was foolish to be so angry, and I have since been ashamed. If you had turned to another woman the fault would have been mine, for I selfishly wanted all you had to give and gave you so little in return."

"You gave me everything," he murmured, "but my hunger for you is so great that I was never satisfied, no matter how much you gave. And I never shall be satisfied but shall always need you as I do now, as much as I need air to breathe and water to drink. Rosaleen, let me fill myself full of you now . . . and again and again and again."

"Yes." The word was sealed like a solemn vow between their seeking mouths.

It was a mutual loving, for they had learned each other's bodies in all the long, sensual nights they had shared. Now, their hands and mouths touching the tender places, the pleasure-giving places, they loved one another surely and well.

When the moment of union came, Hugh held her close and whispered her name, sanctifying the joining of their bodies for the first time and forever.

It hurt more than Rosaleen had expected—his manhood seemed to want to tear her apart—and she couldn't stop the tiny yelp that escaped her.

Hugh, gripping her, groaning, heard her cry but felt useless to respond, having been suddenly transported into heaven. She was his now, forever and for all time and even beyond time. She was his and neither man nor God would come between them.

"Hugh?" Rosaleen's soft voice came, questioning his stillness.

"Shh. I want to remember this forever."

"You sound as if you've been running," she said, laughing nervously. He was crushing her beneath his weight, but Rosaleen ignored this and began to stroke the hot, damp skin of his back with both her hands. She wondered if it was all over, since he lay so heavy and still.

"I'm trying not to move," he said thickly, as if knowing her thoughts. " 'Tis a difficult task."

"Oh? Is there more?"

"Much, much more." His mouth was turned against her ear, and his breath and words pelted the soft skin there.

"But I want to remember this moment, when we became one, forever. I'm committing it to memory."

"I'm sure I'll never forget it," Rosaleen teased, thinking of the pain, which had blissfully receded.

He lifted himself above her, keeping his weight on his elbows. Grinning down at her, he moved his hips very slightly, very slowly, and gained the response of surprised pleasure that he had sought.

"Yes, love," he agreed softly, kissing her parted lips, "I vow that you will never, never forget this."

Chapter Twenty-One

Amazon's sharp complaints woke Rosaleen, and when her eyes fluttered open she saw that it was morning.

Pressed against her back, Hugh slept like a dead man, exhausted beyond salvation. Smiling, running one hand gently along the warmth of the arm that held her tight, Rosaleen understood perfectly well why that was so. Her own body felt battered and bruised from all the lovings they had shared and she, too, thought she would sleep several more hours.

But Amazon kept complaining, moving back and forth agitatedly upon her perch, and Rosaleen understood after a moment that the poor creature was hungry.

It took a little work to get Hugh to relax his tight grip on her, but eventually Rosaleen managed to slip out of the bed and don her chemise.

Alternately clucking and speaking to Amazon in what she hoped was an imitation of the pattern Hugh used on the creature, she tied the leather wrist strap to her arm, removed Amazon's hood and gently took the proud bird from her perch. Continuing to speak softly to the bird, who eyed her with perfect amiability the while, she carried it to the open window.

"Go and break your fast, madam," Rosaleen said as she lifted her wrist in a motion that sent the bird flying, "but be pleased to come home when your master calls you."

She watched the magnificent creature fly and listened to its fierce cries, and then, without warning, Rosaleen began to tremble. The import of all that had passed the night before crashed down upon her with shattering force.

She was no longer a maiden. She, the heiress of Siere, would not go to her marriage bed a maiden.

"God's mercy," she whispered, utterly horrified.

"You told me months ago that you had several birds of your own," Hugh said sleepily from the bed behind her, "and I thought you spoke lies. I wish I had let you handle Amazon then and seen how skilled you are."

Rosaleen turned and looked at him. He was lying against the pillows, magnificently naked, both hands behind his head, and he was smiling at her with eyes filled with love.

"You've only been out of bed for five minutes and I miss you already." He held out a hand to her, beckoning. "Come and lie with me again."

She stared at his hand as though it were an asp. "Hugh," she said, her voice shaking, "how did you come to discover my whole name?"

His hand dropped heavily on the bedclothes, and he breathed out a weary sigh.

"Simon of Denning was at Briarstone yesterday." At her frightened gasp he quickly added, "He does not know you are here. Indeed, for the space of half an hour, while we spoke with one another, I never realized who it is he seeks. It was only as he left that he said the name of his betrothed and I realized it was you."

"And then you decided to send me away?" she asked in a small voice. "Because you discovered who I was? Because of my noble birth?"

"Rosaleen—" he held out his hand once more "—come to me. Let me hold you."

She came, hand outstretched toward his, and let him grasp her and pull her into his arms.

"When I realized who you were," he began, "and that Simon of Denning and your uncle *and* the king were searching for you, thinking you'd been taken captive, I understood at once the danger you are in. I knew that you must get to London in order to be safe, and I knew that I couldn't take you myself. I've been trying to stay away from you these past two weeks so that I could bear to let you go when the end of the month came, but if we were traveling together, forced to be in one another's company for so many hours each day, and each night...do you not understand, love? I never could have kept my hands from you. I wanted you too badly. So I wrote Alex and asked him to come at once, with his army to protect you."

"That's why you were so angry when you told me he was coming?"

He hugged her tight and buried his face in the warm silk of her hair. "Yes," he admitted miserably. "That's why, and it was damned hard to carry out. The look on your face when I told you...it was worse than torture! I wanted to hold you and tell you the truth of how I love you, of how I have loved you for so long and never wanted you to leave." He pulled away and looked at her. "But what else could I do when I knew I had to let you go?"

Rosaleen searched his eyes. "And now what will you do? What will *we* do?"

With a gentle hand he touched her cheek, wanting to smooth away the anxiety stamped upon her lovely features.

"Do you not already know the answer to that? Did we not make a holy bond when we joined our bodies last eve?

You are my wife, though we have not yet taken vows, and I am your husband. Now that I know you love me as I love you, we shall be wed as soon as possible." He smiled as an idea came to him. "I'll write Hugo and ask him to come. He can perform the ceremony here at Briarstone. It will have to be done in the great hall, of course, since we've no chapel, but that matters not." His smile widened as he thought of it. "God's teeth! Wait until we tell those below stairs that you are to become their lady in truth, that you'll not be leaving Briarstone. What a celebration there will be!"

"Oh, dear God," Rosaleen murmured, trying to pull from him. "Hugh..."

Seeing her lost expression, Hugh held her fast.

"My darling! If it means so much to you, we'll go to Gyer and be wed. There's a beautiful chapel there, and Alex and Lillis will be glad to put on a whole celebration for us. I never thought I'd have to suffer through such as that, but if it's what you want, I'll manage to get through it."

"You don't understand! Oh, Hugh!" she wailed. "We cannot be wed!"

"Of course we can," he countered with certainty. "Never worry about your uncle or Simon of Denning. With a little help from Alex we'll be able to settle with them quickly enough, and they'll cause no more difficulty, I vow."

"No, no! Hugh, you must listen to me!" Rosaleen pulled away and grasped his hands. "I am Rosaleen Sarant, the heiress of Siere. I cannot stay at Briarstone. I must return to Siere and take my rightful place as lady there, and I must marry a suitable husband and produce the next Earl of Siere."

He frowned. "Simon said your uncle was to be made the next Earl of Siere when you wed. You were to become Simon's baroness."

"Yes, and that's why I ran away! As part of the marriage contract, Simon of Denning promised my uncle that I would give up my claim to Siere and to the earldom. I refused to make any such bargain, and when my uncle tried to beat me into doing it, I knew that I must somehow get to London and plead my case to the king. Once the king understands that my uncle and Sir Simon were forcing me into that unwanted bargain, I know he will take my side and protect me from them. My father was one of old King Henry's favorites and was as loyal to the throne as any man who ever lived. His son would never turn his back on my father's only child."

Hugh stared at her.

"I...I cannot marry a commoner, Hugh," she went on in a voice filled with misery. "There is no other choice for me, and the king would not allow it, anyway. I am the last living Sarant, the last of a great and noble family. It is my duty to carry that family's name on. Can you not understand?"

"I understand."

The emotionless tone of his voice made her want to weep. "I do l-love you, Hugh, but I have no choice in what I do. From my birth I was taught to put duty first. I cannot walk away from that, not for any reason."

"I see," he said.

"There is one possible answer for us, Hugh."

"Yes, there is one," he agreed.

Rosaleen swallowed before suggesting, gently, "You could become a knight, and accept the name and nobility of being a Baldwin. I cannot promise that the king would approve you as the Earl of Siere, but I'm certain he would not deny us marriage. And your eldest son would be the Earl of Siere. That would be something, would it not?''

The expression of disgust on his face answered her question.

''There is another way,'' he countered curtly. ''You could tell the king that you will deed Siere, along with your grand title, to your uncle. I'm sure Henry wouldn't mind letting you wed with a bastard commoner after that.''

Rosaleen gasped, shocked, and stood up from the bed.

''How could you suggest such a thing to me!''

''And how could *you* suggest such a thing to me?'' he demanded just as hotly.

''I asked you to give up little and offered you much!'' she shouted furiously. ''You asked me to give up all in return for naught!''

Hugh's eyes narrowed. ''Briarstone is *naught?* My love, my life, my children are *naught?*''

''Don't be foolish,'' she returned impatiently. ''I meant that Briarstone is as naught compared to Siere, and compared to what will come to you through marriage to me.''

Eyes blazing now, Hugh tossed the covers aside and stood. ''You wish to buy me like cattle and keep me as your legal whore, is that not what you mean? What will you do with me when I'm not engaged in warming your royal bed, Rosaleen? Will you keep your bastard husband hidden away as it pleases you? Will you bring me out on occasion to display to your people? Your obedient, dearly bought husband?''

''Hugh!''

''Or will you allow me the run of all your vast estates as long as I do nothing to disgrace you?''

''That is *not* what I—''

''And any children we might create, will I be allowed to have anything to do with them? If they'll be such damned highborn, noble creatures, you surely won't want their bastard father dirtying them with his commoner's ways."

"Stop!" Her hands closed into fists at her sides. "That was not what I meant and you know it very well! My offer was the highest honor I could ever think to bestow, while yours... God's mercy! Do you not know how you insult me, asking me to spend the rest of my life in this wretched little fief as the wife of a man who'll not even lay claim to a decent name?" She lifted her chin. "My ancestors hail back to the time before the Romans came to Britain and include kings, queens, royal princes and princesses, archbishops and cardinals and even a pope!"

Hugh affected a look of amazement and swept her a mocking bow. "God's mercy, I do beg your pardon, great highness. I wish you'd told me that last night before I took you to bed. I feel as though I've slept with the whole royal court and half the Holy Bible!"

"That's better than sleeping with only God knows what!" she flung back at him. "You don't even know what you are, Hugh Caldwell...Baldwin...Ryon, whatever else you may be! Why, you're naught but a... a mongrel!"

"And you, mistress, are naught but a haughty, highborn bitch!"

Stunned, Rosaleen fell silent, staring at him wide-eyed.

In silence they gazed at each other, unable to speak. After a long moment, and lowering her head so that he wouldn't see the tears in her eyes, Rosaleen walked to the door and opened it.

He said her name before she was able to get out of the chamber, said it so softly that she barely heard him, but she walked out into the hall and carefully closed the door behind her.

Three hours later Rosaleen emerged from her chamber, fully dressed and bearing herself as regally as a queen, and made her way down the stairs to the great hall. She found there, as if waiting for her, all of her ladies and several of the men, including Christian Rowsenly, who normally would have been hard at work out in the fields at this time of day.

"I'm glad you're here, Christian," she said when he rose from where he had been sitting, flirting with Jehanne, to greet her. "I must speak with Hugh Caldwell at once. Please ride out and ask him to return to the keep."

Solemnly, Christian said, "He is not in the fields, Lady Rosaleen. He is not at Briarstone at all. He rode out more than two hours past."

Every bit of color drained out of Rosaleen's face. "To where? For what purpose?"

"I do not know, my lady, but he took Amazon with him as well as money and his sword, so I cannot think he means to return anytime soon. He spoke to me for a few minutes before he left, however, and gave me very clear commands regarding yourself."

She felt faint but managed to whisper, "Regarding me?"

He nodded. "You are not to be let outside the castle for any reason whatsoever until the Lord of Gyer arrives to take you to London. And until that time every man at Briarstone is to stand guard over you, as they are now doing both inside and outside the castle, rather than work in the fields. He said if you gave me any trouble I was to lock you in your chamber until Sir Alexander arrives, and to feed you bread and water to teach you better manners. Of course," he said with a small smile, "I think that last was in jest."

Rosaleen didn't believe that for a minute. "And then he left? With no other word?"

"Oh yes, there was something more. He left a message for you. He said that he wished you a pleasant journey to London."

"That's all?"

"That's all."

Stunned, Rosaleen tried to gather her wits about her. "Christian, I know that your master gave you very strict instructions, but I fear I will have to countermand them. I must get to London, and I must leave today. My getting there is of the greatest importance, I vow that by all that is holy. I also vow that Hugh Caldwell will never be angry with you for letting me go. Indeed, if you and several of the men will only escort me there I promise he will be most grateful."

Christian's expression was unwavering. "Forgive me, my lady, but his commands were most clear, and as much as I honor you," he said, delving into his tunic pocket and pulling out a heavy chain of keys, "if you prove to be troublesome, I will do as he bade me."

The rattling keys held Rosaleen's horrified attention for several seconds, until another noise sounded over them. It was a loud banging at the front doors, and even as Rosaleen turned, the doors opened, admitting several persons who had clearly been putting all their weight behind them.

The foremost of those persons was an outraged monk, who set his hands on his hips and declared to those in the hall, "Are you all deaf? Why in God's holy name has none of you answered?"

Relief poured over Rosaleen.

"Hugo!" she cried, and lost no time in running to him and throwing herself into his open arms.

"Rosaleen! What in heaven's holy name—"

"Ah! You have gained entrance at last," came a solemn yet familiar voice. "I was beginning to wonder at

what kind of people Hugh has taken to himself. Who is
that sobbing female you've got, Hugo? It is never the lady
Rosaleen, is it?''

"I fear it is," his brother replied, hugging Rosaleen with
one arm and stroking her uncovered head with his other
hand. "Though I cannot imagine why she is so distraught. Perhaps you'd best ask some of these people
where Hugh is.''

Justin Baldwin tossed his unsheathed sword from one
hand to the other and moved farther into the great hall,
where every man had drawn his own weapon.

"Where is your lord, Hugh Baldwin?" Justin shook his
head as if to clear it. "I mean, Hugh Caldwell.''

"He is gone," Christian answered, eyeing him with dis-
trust. "Who are you and why have you come to Briarstone? And what have you done to the men out-of-
doors?''

"Gone!" Justin repeated with disgust. "He would be,
damn him! This man—" he indicated Hugo, who was at
that moment wiping the tears from Rosaleen's face with
the hem of his sleeve "—is Father Hugo Baldwin, and I am
Sir Justin Baldwin of Gyer. We are brothers to your lord.
If you believe me not, all you need do is look at Father
Hugo to see that he is Hugh Baldwin's...I mean, Hugh
Caldwell's twin. We have come to Briarstone at his invitation, and what we have done with the men out-of-doors
is subdue them, else they would have brought great harm
upon themselves." He took a few more careful steps closer.
"And now that I have answered your questions, sir, I
would ask a few of my own. What in God's name do you
mean by attacking every man who comes through your
gates in peace? Have you no better sense than that?''

"Justin, please!" Rosaleen demanded, having got herself under control. "Keep your peace and do not press

him. This is Christian Rowsenly, and Hugh left him in charge of Briarstone and bade him protect me against any stranger who passed our gates.''

Eyeing Christian consideringly, Justin said, after a moment, more politely, "My pardon, sir. I mispoke. None outside have been harmed, I vow. They have only been kept from harming themselves against the soldiers of the Lord of Gyer's army."

Nodding, Christian said, "That is well. If you are, in truth, Hugh Caldwell's brothers, then you are welcome at Briarstone, though we did not expect you. Hugh Caldwell said it was his eldest brother, the Lord of Gyer, who would come."

Justin frowned deeply.

"We left Gyer two days past, and my eldest brother made no mention of journeying to Briarstone. Why should he have sent us with half his army if he himself had planned on coming?"

It was Rosaleen who answered.

"I believe I can explain what has happened." She looked at Hugo. "If you and Sir Justin and Christian will come with me to a place more private, sir, I vow I have a plan that will make all well."

Chapter Twenty-Two

"There, now, my dear. That wasn't so difficult, was it?"

Rosaleen's hand was shaking so badly she had barely managed to make her signature legible. She stared at the document before her almost in disbelief until her uncle began to slide it off the table.

The tip of a sword came down upon the parchment, stilling its movement.

"Until the signatures have been duly acknowledged," Justin Baldwin stated, "the document remains where it is."

Sir Anselm made a sound of impatience.

"Rosaleen, have you not yet explained to this insolent whelp who I am and of my rank among the nobles? Why does he continue to behave with such foolish disregard?"

"Don't anger Sir Justin, Uncle Anselm," she advised wearily. "Please leave him be."

But he wouldn't keep quiet and kept berating the solemn younger man until Rosaleen placed both hands over her ears to shut out the sound of him.

She felt so weary. From the moment she had arrived in London the night before with Hugo and Justin and half the army of Sir Alexander Baldwin, so many events had happened, one right after the other, that Rosaleen's unhappy mind had had no chance to rest.

Some great celebration had been planned for this morn, so that the king, having been informed of her arrival and of her urgent desire to see him, had refused her an audience, claiming that he was far too busy seeing to the many details surrounding the celebration. He had sent his apologies and his assurances that he would see her the following afternoon, and then he had ordered her to be taken away to a private chamber at the farthest end of the castle without even inviting her to attend whatever the important celebration was.

She had found herself with only Hugo and Justin for company, cut off from the rest of the king's household and from all the revelers. Which had been just as well, in truth, for the last thing Rosaleen had felt like doing was celebrating, especially when she hadn't the faintest idea what the celebration was for. It was not a feast day or any kind of holy day; she could only assume that the celebrated event was a personal one, such as a marriage or knighting. Why she, the heiress of Siere and one of the highest personages in the land, had been excluded from the revelry was a mystery, for her presence would have been seen as a great honor to those involved.

And yet, the long evening had not passed unpleasantly. Justin and Hugo had left her to rest for an hour, and when they had returned to share her evening meal, they had brought with them some unexpected guests.

The first of these had been their sister, Candis, who had been at court for several months with her elder brother Willem. She was a tiny, delicately lovely creature with billowy auburn curls and enormous hazel eyes, which were so captivating they caused people to stare at her quite against their will. The lady Candis Baldwin reminded Rosaleen of a golden butterfly, for she floated on her tiny little feet as though she never touched the earth and was in constant motion, fluttering from one moment to the next and from one entertaining topic to another. Rosaleen could only imagine how many hundreds of men had been felled by her sweet charm and exquisite beauty.

The next of Rosaleen's unexpected guests was Sir Willem Baldwin, a very tall, very handsome, very shy man whose dark hair and deep brown eyes reminded her of Justin, just as Alexander Baldwin's dark hair and green eyes reminded her of Hugh and Hugo.

"Willem's going to be married very soon!" Candis announced brightly, just as Rosaleen had finished greeting him, and Willem blushed a deep red.

"What!" Hugo demanded, while Justin simply frowned thoughtfully at his elder brother.

Sir Willem dropped Rosaleen's hand, which he'd been holding quite properly during their introduction. "N-no," he stammered. "Candis is mistaken. I'm not to be wed."

"He most certainly is!" Candis insisted, though she spoke like one confiding great secrets. "Lady Gwynneth Worley went to the king and demanded Willem's hand in marriage. She claims he behaved freely with her in the gardens one eve, and now he must wed her as recompense."

"Why, Willem, you old rascal," Justin murmured with the slightest of smiles.

"There was naught . . . naught of import that happened between Lady Gwynneth and myself," Willem insisted, clearly mortified. "She had lost a piece of jewelry in the gardens and asked me to help her search for it. That was all. Nothing happened."

"That may be as it is, Willem," Candis said, "but the king has said he will consider Lady Gwynneth's request. Would it not be the most wonderful thing if you were to wed with her?" Candis turned to chatter at Rosaleen. "She is the most beautiful lady and has been chasing after our dear Willem for such a long time.''

Sir Willem looked so embarrassed that for a moment Rosaleen thought he might bolt out the chamber door, and she felt terribly sorry for him.

''Stop teasing your brother, young lady. You've more than enough difficulty of your own, picking and choosing from amongst all those peacocks who follow you about, preening for your attentions. At least Willem has the sense not to make a spectacle of himself.''

This reprimand came from one of the last of Rosaleen's surprise guests. Hugo and Justin had happily discovered that their Aunt Leta and her husband, Sir Terence Simonton, were also at court, a fact neither of them had been aware of when they'd first gone searching for Willem and Candis.

And so Rosaleen had found herself surrounded by Hugh's relatives for the better part of the evening.

The Baldwins were a lively family, and Rosaleen did more listening than talking during the meal they shared as the family members, save Terence Simonton, who seemed to be content to simply gaze at his wife as though she were an angel come from heaven. All took turns telling jokes and stories as they caught one another up on the recent events in their lives. Occasionally, Rosaleen found herself grinning at some of their humorous tales, though she could not seem to make her heavy heart lighten any further than that. When the conversation turned toward her, and when Aunt Leta and Candis began demanding the latest news of Hugh, Rosaleen nearly thought she would have to excuse herself. The memories of her last meeting with Hugh were too fresh, too painful, but she put a grip of iron on her emotions and replied to their questions as best she could.

"They love him and serve him well and willingly," she answered when Aunt Leta asked how the vassals of Briarstone served Hugh. "He is a skilled leader. It is something born in him, I think, for such ability as he possesses cannot be learned. He could easily manage an estate ten times larger than Briarstone, or several estates of much larger size, and I truly believe each and every one of the vassals and serfs who worked for him would love him just as fervently as the people of Briarstone do. He is not one of these dull, weak lordlings who live like leeches off the sweat of their servants' labors. Every day he goes and works beside his people, laboring with them from the morn until the time the sun sets. For this they give him due reverence and honor and would be glad to do anything for him, even to die."

"God's mercy!" Candis said with a laugh. "That doesn't sound like our Hugh! I cannot imagine him wishing to do such hard work. It seems he has grown to be like you, Hugo. We shall have to begin calling him 'Saint Hugh.'"

"But you said that you have overseen the household of Briarstone these past three months, Lady Rosaleen," Willem said timidly. "Surely your contributions have been just as great as Hugh's in making Briarstone successful. Perhaps even greater."

Rosaleen lowered her eyes to stare at the deep red wine waving gently in her goblet. "It is a strange thing," she said softly, "but Hugh has often said something much like that in the past months. He would claim that I am the one responsible for the improvements at Briarstone, and perhaps that is a little true, for I did fight to make him accept that loan from your brother, but it is not entirely right. I realized only a few days past how unnecessary I have become to Briarstone, how unnecessary I am to him. Any of my ladies could oversee the household quite easily, and will do so now that I have left. All they truly need is Hugh's guiding hand and they will be able to succeed. One day, I vow, Briarstone will be returned to its former greatness, as in the days of William the Conqueror, and Hugh Caldwell will be master of one of the finest estates in the land.''

"But I do not understand," Candis said. "You speak of leaving Briarstone, yet are not you and Hugh to be wed?''

Rosaleen drew in a sharp breath, but it wasn't enough to keep two unruly tears from spilling over her cheeks.

"Candis, be silent!" Justin demanded angrily.

Too miserable to care what her guests thought of her behavior, Rosaleen stood. "I pray you will excuse me....''

A loud pounding at the door interrupted her, followed by the bellowing of a well-known voice. A moment later Uncle Anselm strode into the room, shoving aside the two frightened servants who tried to keep him out. The surprise on his face when he came to a quick halt showed plainly that he hadn't expected to find anyone other than Rosaleen there.

His expression changed from one of fury to one of instant concern, and when he made to take Rosaleen in his arms as though he were relieved to finally have found her, Rosaleen backed away with as much horror and disgust as though he were some kind of demon.

All of the men in the room had stood when Uncle Anselm had so suddenly intruded, and Justin proposed tossing him right back out, a comment that had outraged Uncle Anselm thoroughly.

"Do these people not know who I am, my darling?" he asked Rosaleen in a sickly loving tone that had turned her stomach. "Tell them I am your uncle, who is so grateful to have finally found you safe and well, and ask them to leave so that we may have our reunion in private.''

This suggestion elicited a very crude word from Justin, who had drawn his sword at the sight of the five big brutes who'd followed Uncle Anselm into the chamber. Justin's word in turn made Candis cover her ears and incited both Aunt Leta and Hugo to deliver a short sermon. Willem, on the other hand, agreed with Justin and promptly told Uncle Anselm in less than gentle terms that he might take himself off to roast in hell. Terence Simonton, one of the king's most politic legates, wondered aloud whether the king had been informed of Uncle Anselm's arrival in London.

When the situation threatened to turn into a brawl, Rosaleen brought all of the angry words to a halt by announcing that she did indeed wish to speak alone with her uncle and would do so at once in her bedchamber if those assembled would please wait outside until they had finished.

Every single one of the Baldwins present, as well as Sir Terence, had refused to allow this, but Rosaleen had held firm, and when she marched into her bedchamber, Uncle Anselm obediently followed. Ten minutes later he and his men left her rooms quietly and peaceably, and Rosaleen had settled down to entertain her guests once more.

They had questioned her regarding what had passed between her uncle and her during those ten minutes, but Rosaleen had politely refused to speak of it. She never wanted to speak of the man again, and after today, she never wanted to see him again.

"I do not approve of this, Rosaleen," Justin said now, his voice forcing its way into her covered ears, "and there is still time to retract it before the priest arrives to witness the signatures."

"No," she whispered. "It's done now. Let us speak of it no more, else the knowledge will kill me! It's done, and that is all."

"Yes, it is quite done, my dear," Uncle Anselm agreed. "You must be glad and think of it no longer."

Justin wasn't satisfied. "If Hugh knew of this, my lady, he would be furious. He would force you to strike your name from that damned document."

Tears welling in her eyes, Rosaleen mutely shook her head.

"I tell you he would! Why will you not listen to reason?"

"You foolish *boy*," said Uncle Anselm. "Can you not see that your words fall on deaf ears? Leave her be, and cease speaking of this bastard brother of yours. Has he not given her enough misery? Does she not already have reason to hate him in the coming years for what he has done to her?"

"No!" Rosaleen shouted, her body trembling with rage.

Justin's reaction was more expected. He looked steadily at Sir Anselm and asked, very calmly, "You would slander my brother's name so openly?"

Laughing, Sir Anselm eyed Justin with scorn. "I would slander your bastard brother in *public*, boy."

"For these words," Justin stated, "I must kill you." Lifting his sword, he proceeded to suit action to word.

"No, Justin!" Rosaleen set a restraining hand on his shoulder and glared at her surprised uncle. "I told you not to make him angry! I told you to leave him be! Why can you never, *never* listen?"

"He wouldn't dare to kill me," Uncle Anselm replied with confidence, though he regarded Justin as though he were an unstable substance. "I'm a peer of the realm."

Justin frowned at the man. "No, I must kill you. You have insulted a member of my family beyond reason, and as a knight who has taken vows before God, I must fulfill my duty. Rosaleen, you stand over there by the wall and I'll try not to make too great a mess."

"Please, Justin," Rosaleen began, stopping when the sound of loud cheers came floating up from the streets and through the open window. Distracted, she said, "Listen to the crowds. What is happening?"

"Why don't you go find out while I finish with your uncle?" Justin suggested, trying without success to push her in the direction of the window.

She turned her attention to him once more. "Justin, I'll not let you die for such a crime as killing a beast like my uncle. The Lord of Gyer would never forgive me."

The door to the chamber opened, and Hugo and Candis walked in.

"The priest has arrived to witness the signatures!" Uncle Anselm said with relief. "May God be praised!"

"Is aught amiss?" Hugo asked Justin, seeing that his sword was drawn.

"Oh, Justin, Lady Rosaleen, it was the most beautiful ceremony I've ever seen!" Candis cried, rushing toward them with her hands clasped. "I do wish you could have been there, my lady. You would have been so proud!"

Rosaleen stared at the girl.

"Hugo, please be good enough to take Candis and Lady Rosaleen out of the room so that I can kill Sir Anselm," Justin requested. "Five minutes should be sufficient."

Hugo raised his eyebrows at his perfectly serious younger brother, and the familiar gesture made Rosaleen's heart ache.

"I perceive that you've run up against another debt of honor, Justin," Hugo noted calmly. "I'm sorry to be difficult, but I do think that one debt of honor a week is enough."

The chamber door opened again, admitting a beautifully dressed Aunt Leta and her handsomely dressed husband.

"What a marvelous ceremony!" Aunt Leta declared, beaming at Rosaleen as she moved farther into the room. "Never have the Baldwins had a prouder day, my dear."

"Yes, it was quite splendid, indeed," Sir Terence agreed.

"You will never forgive us for letting you miss it, I fear," Aunt Leta said, "but there was no help for it, as Justin and Hugo swore us all to silence."

Rosaleen tightened her grip on Justin, more for support than to hold him back. A dreadful premonition tingled down her spine.

"I fear I don't...what is it you speak of?"

"God's mercy, Rosaleen, call the boy off!" Uncle Anselm demanded when Justin began to approach him, dragging Rosaleen along.

"Justin, if you must kill the man, can you not at least wait until tomorrow morn?" Hugo asked impatiently. "We've not time for it now."

"Well, perhaps," Justin said consideringly, slowing his assault.

The chamber door opened once more, and this time it was Sir Willem who entered, along with another man dressed blindingly in white.

"Thank a merciful God that's over!" said the man as he walked through the door. "What a cursed nightmare!"

He stopped just inside the room and stared at the sight before him.

"By the rood, what's going on here?" he asked as he stripped the gauntlets from his hands.

And then he saw Rosaleen.

"Hugh," she whispered with disbelief.

Hugh's arms dropped to his sides.

"Rosaleen."

She was so stunned by the sight of him, dressed in a suit of spotlessly shining armor robed with the whitest of pure silk, that she couldn't even speak. He looked, she thought dumbly, grander than the king.

"How did you come to be here?" Hugh demanded. "Justin . . . and Hugo," he said as he saw, with growing surprise, each of those brothers present. "Where is Alex? Never tell me he sent you in his stead."

"Hugh," Hugo began in a calming tone, "Justin and I traveled to Briarstone under a misconception. I had received a missive and . . . Justin, will you please stop chasing Sir Anselm around the room and put your sword away!" He waited until his frowning younger brother did as he was told before continuing. "I received a missive from the lady Rosaleen two months past explaining that Briarstone is in desperate need of a priest and asking whether I might come and fill that need. I assumed she wrote me at your request, Hugh, but this, she has explained, is not so. When Justin and I arrived at Briarstone two days ago we took your people by surprise, I fear, and caused no small difficulty."

"I left Chris with instructions not to let Rosaleen leave Briarstone," Hugh said angrily, "yet you have brought her to London. I hope, dear brothers, that you did no harm to any of my people."

"No one was hurt, Hugh," Rosaleen assured him quickly, taking a step in his direction. "I contrived to get Christian alone with Hugo and Justin, and once he was taken captive, the other men gave in easily. I left Alice the keys to the dungeon and I'm sure they were set free just as soon as we rode out."

"I see," Hugh said, staring at her with a look of wretched defeat. "You did not wish to wait to get to London so that you could settle matters with the king. I understand, Rosaleen."

"No! You don't understand at all!" She took another step toward him, uncertainly, and glanced at their audience. She hadn't planned on making her declaration in front of so many people, but her shame was so great that she knew she deserved just such a public humiliation. With determination, she made her feet move toward him. Standing utterly still, Hugh watched her come, his eyes wide upon her.

"I did not know you would be here," she said, trying to control the trembling of her voice. "Indeed, I did not know where you would be, though I vowed I would somehow find you, no matter where I had to go or how long I had to search." She stopped before him and forced her tear-filled eyes up to meet his questioning ones. "I wished to beg your forgiveness for the things I said to you, Hugh," she whispered, "and I wanted to tell you that if you will do me the great honor of allowing me to become your wife, I shall be grateful to you for the rest of my life, and will gladly live with you at Briarstone and be so proud to be the wife of Hugh Caldwell."

"Rosaleen." His voice was filled with wonder.

"And...and so I...I..." She began to sink down upon her knees so that she could kiss the hem of his garment in an act of apology and submission.

Hugh's strong hands stopped her, grasping her shoulders, and he lifted her up. When their eyes met she was stunned to find that his were blazing with anger.

"Never do such a thing again!" he said fiercely. "My wife goes down on her knee to no man save the king. And if she does kneel before the king she'd better have a damned good reason for it!''

"But, Hugh . . ."

"And if anyone should beg forgiveness," he went on with less bluster, "it is I." He pulled her closer and held her more gently. "Rosaleen, I'm sorry for what I said to you. I wish I'd cut my tongue out before speaking to you as I did. I've been sick with hate of myself since you walked out of my chamber two days past."

With a sob, Rosaleen pressed her face against the silk and armor covering his chest.

"Don't cry, love," Hugh murmured, holding her tight. "Don't cry." Looking up, he saw seven fascinated sets of eyes watching them, and he scowled and turned Rosaleen in his arms so that her tears were hidden from them.

"I believe Hugh and Lady Rosaleen would enjoy some privacy," Aunt Leta stated loudly. "Perhaps we could return later to see whether these two young idiots have made some sense of the mess they've created."

"An excellent idea, madam," Uncle Anselm agreed, snatching the signed sheet of parchment from the table and rolling it up.

Justin's sword came out again. "You are not leaving with that. Return it at once."

"God's teeth, Justin!" Hugh swore. "Never have I seen a man more ready with his weapon! Do you make a habit of challenging everyone you meet?"

Justin's reply was stopped by the entrance of a castle page.

"I have a message from the king for Sir Baldwin."

"Here," answered both Willem and Justin.

"For Sir Hugh Baldwin," the boy clarified.

"Ah," said Hugh, "that would be me." He extended one hand toward the boy while keeping hold of a suddenly stiff Rosaleen with the other. "I must become accustomed to that, must I not?" He chuckled, looking at his family.

"Hugh," Rosaleen whispered, pulling away to look at him, "what have you done?"

Hugh's smile grew sheepish. "I've made myself an honorable man, sweeting. That will give all my old fellows something to jest about, will it not?"

"Oh, no. *No!*" she cried with distress. "You can't, Hugh! I'll not let you! You must have it taken back!"

"Taken back?" he repeated. "*Taken back?* After everything I went through these past two days? Nothing on God's earth could make me have it taken back! I haven't suffered and been made a great spectacle of for naught!"

"Spectacle?" she said. "The celebration . . . the crowds and all the cheering from this morn . . . that was for *you?*" As if just seeing him, she took in anew the polished armor he wore and the white robes. "God in heaven," she said weakly, sounding as if she would faint, "you've been knighted. Hugh . . . you let yourself be knighted . . . for me?"

"I certainly did," he said with a huff. "And I'll be damned if I'll have gone through it for naught."

"And you have taken the name of Baldwin." She shook her head in disbelief. "For me. Oh, Hugh Caldwell, I love you."

"Baldwin," he corrected. "The great and noble Sir Hugh Baldwin. I rather like the sound of that."

"You will always be Hugh Caldwell to me," she replied with a laugh, throwing her arms around him and hugging him with joy. "And I shall always love you! But, God's mercy, Hugh! It wasn't necessary. None of it. I hope you'll not come to hate me for causing you to do something that you never wished."

"Ahem!" the waiting page cleared his throat loudly to gain their attention. "His majesty is ready to see you, my lady, and you, Sir Anselm."

"Thank you," Rosaleen said, pushing out of Hugh's embrace. "Please tell him we shall be there at once. Hugh—" she took his hands "—my audience with the king will be brief, and I must see you at once afterward. Will you wait for me here?"

For the first time Hugh looked more closely at the stranger standing amongst his family.

Keeping his eyes on the big man, he asked, very slowly, "Rosaleen, is this man your uncle? The one who is your guardian?"

"Yes, this is Sir Anselm Druste, my half uncle, actually, as he was my mother's half brother."

"I see," said Hugh, and gently put her from him. "In that case, Sir Anselm," he continued pleasantly, approaching the man, "I am very glad to meet you."

The next moment found a stunned Sir Anselm lying flat on the ground, arms splayed wide.

"That was only a taste of what I'm going to give you when you get up, you filthy bastard," Hugh said angrily. "I saw the results of the beating you gave your niece, and for every lash you gave her, I will repay you tenfold. Now get up!"

"Don't, Hugh! You must leave him be!" Rosaleen tugged on Hugh's arm to make him listen. "By the rood, you've just laid a hand in violence on the future Earl of Siere! He could have you put to death for such an insult! Do you not understand? Leave him be!"

Slowly, Sir Anselm sat, rubbing his aching jaw in the spot where Hugh's fist had struck it. "Don't bear any false hopes, Rosaleen. Your lover is as good as dead now. I shall make certain of it when I speak to the king."

"No!" Rosaleen cried. "Not if you wish me to continue with our bargain!"

"What do you speak of?" Hugh demanded. "He's not going to be the Earl of Siere. Rosaleen is the inheritress of that estate."

"No longer, *Sir* Baldwin," Uncle Anselm replied haughtily, rising to his feet. "She has just this morn signed everything over to me, including all of the estates and various titles. In exchange I have agreed to let her wed with you, for as her guardian she must have my approval. We are going to the king now, and once he has approved the document it will be perfectly, absolutely legal."

Hugh turned to gape at Rosaleen. "How could you do such a thing? God's my life, all those centuries of ancestors must be turning in their graves!"

"I could think of no other way to show how sorry I am for the things I said," she told him, "or to tell you of how much I love you and wish to be your wife. It is the only way we can be together, Hugh, and I realized on that day when you left Briarstone that I cannot live without you, no matter what that means to my family name."

Hugh shook his head in amazement and wonder. Rosaleen's words made him feel a storm of emotions such as he had never experienced before.

"Oh, my darling," he murmured, pulling her trembling body into his arms. "You did this for me? You were willing to sacrifice all you hold so dear for me?" When she nodded, he kissed her. "I cannot think of words perfect enough to tell you what that means to me, or of how grateful I am. Of course, I cannot let you do it. You did promise that my eldest son would be the future Earl of Siere, and that's a promise I will hold you to!"

Wide-eyed, she stared at him. "But it's too late, Hugh! I have already put my signature to the document! Unless the king sees fit not to approve it, my word is binding!"

"Rosaleen," Hugo said, "I think I can—"

"Not now, Hugo!" Hugh sent him a warning glance. "Later, after I've killed Sir Anselm, we'll be in need of spiritual guidance."

"Lay another hand on me, bastard of Gyer, and I swear by God above that I'll not approve your marriage to Rosaleen. I will force her to honor the marriage contract drawn up between Simon of Denning and myself. It would be an easy task to accomplish, for the king has already approved that contract, and I am the only one who can say it nay."

Realizing the truth of the man's words, Hugh gritted his teeth. "Rosaleen, my darling, I love you with my whole heart, but there are times when I could readily wring your beautiful neck! What in God's name were you thinking to sign that damned document?"

"Hugh," Hugo said, "there's really no need for this."

"I'll not have it!" Hugh stated angrily, ignoring his brother. "I will *not* have it."

Angry now, Rosaleen stamped her foot. "If you will recall, my lord, it was *your* idea for me to sign everything away!"

"I don't care if it was a command from God himself!" Hugh shouted. "I will not have it, Rosaleen, do I make myself clear? God's toes! I let myself be *knighted* just so you could keep all your damned land and titles and family jewels! Do you have the slightest idea of what I had to go through? Do you? I spent *all* of last night on my *knees* in the chapel! I allowed myself to be *bathed* by strangers in front of a whole assembly of onlookers!" he shouted, outraged anew at what he'd been made to suffer. "I...I let the king *slap* me, for God's sake!"

"Don't be foolish!" Rosaleen countered just as furiously. "You know very well he was only dubbing you!"

"I am not an idiot, Rosaleen!" he raged. "You can call it a tickle under the chin for all I care and that won't change what it was! It was a damned hard slap! And he was *smiling* when he did it!"

"We've no time for this nonsense," Uncle Anselm interrupted. "The king awaits us, Rosaleen."

"You're not going anywhere until I've finished with you!" Hugh shouted at the man. "And don't speak of Simon of Denning to me again, for I'll kill him before I'll let him set a hand on my wife!"

"You can't kill him," Rosaleen said.

"Don't tell me what I can't do!" Hugh roared wrathfully. "If he puts his filthy hands on you I'm going to damned well kill him!"

"Hugh," Rosaleen said patiently, "you cannot kill him because he's already dead."

"Well!" said Aunt Leta to her husband, much impressed. "You must admit, my lord, this is quite the most interesting entertainment we've had in a long while!"

"'Struth, my dear," agreed the placid man.

"I really think I must sit down," Candis said weakly, putting a hand over her stomach as Willem moved to set a supporting arm around her.

"Simon of Denning dead!" Uncle Anselm repeated in disbelief. "It cannot be true! Where is the man who could raise a hand against him and live? Where is the man who could kill such a one as he? I do not believe such a man exists!"

"He is quite dead, Uncle, I assure you," Rosaleen told him. "And the man who killed him stands before you. Sir Justin did it."

Hugh's eyebrows went up so high they almost got lost in his hairline.

"Justin!"

"Justin Baldwin!" Aunt Leta said with disapproval. "I'm going to tell Alex to take your sword away. You cause more trouble with it than any ten men together!"

"Oh dear, I think I n-need some wine," Candis moaned sickly.

"Is this true, Justin?" Hugh demanded. "Did you kill Simon of Denning?"

"Yes," Justin replied simply. "It was a matter of honor, and as a knight of the realm who has taken sacred vows, I had no choice."

"God's my life!" said Hugh, thoroughly stunned. It was difficult for him to look at his youngest brother and realize that he was no longer a nine-year-old boy but a man full grown and capable of killing other men.

"Sir Simon was trying to kill Lady Rosaleen," Justin explained. "It happened at the inn we stopped at two nights ago. Before we left Briarstone, Rosaleen had sent word to both Sir Anselm's and Sir Simon's armies, requesting that those two men meet her in London. Simon of Denning came directly after us, and that night, when Rosaleen told him that she intended to wed with you, he said that he would see her dead first. Of course, I had to kill him after that. There were plenty of witnesses to attest that I was in the right."

He spoke of it so calmly, so factually, that Hugh felt slightly ill.

"Well then," he muttered, dragging his gaze away from his brother's calm face to look at Anselm Druste. "We've no further reason to speak of Simon of Denning, have we? There's no fear of Rosaleen's marrying him, now that he's dead.''

"I still have the document making me the Earl of Siere," Sir Anselm said, patting the place in his tunic where the parchment lay safe, "and it bears Rosaleen's unforced signature. Indeed, the whole matter was her idea, her offer, and to that she must admit if the king asks her whether it is true. I simply accepted her offer."

"Damn!" Hugh growled. "There must be a way out of this mess, somehow!"

Sir Anselm smiled. "There is no way out, Baldwin, and you'd best accept it. Now, if you will excuse us, my niece and I have an audience with the king."

"I'd not show that contract to King Henry, Sir Anselm," Hugo advised. "Not unless you wish to be made a great fool."

Everyone looked at him.

"I've been trying to explain," he said, "that there is no need for worry. Since I am a priest, it made sense for Rosaleen to ask me to write out the document." Hugo gave a slight shrug. "I was glad to do so once she explained what its purpose was. I thought she might have reason to be angered with me this morn, however, but it is clear that neither she nor Sir Anselm has taken time to read the agreement they signed. Rosaleen, I know, has been too distraught of late to care for such things," Hugo said warmly, smiling at Rosaleen. "While Sir Anselm—" he gave that man a harder look "—is too greedy. It is a sad truth that greed will blind a man to all else. As our dear Lord said, 'Beware, and be on your guard against every form of greed, for not even when one has an abundance does his life consist of his possessions.' And as the prophet Isaiah said, 'And the dogs are greedy, they are—'"

"Hugo!" Hugh broke in impatiently.

"Hmm? Oh yes, the document. Well, of course, I couldn't let Rosaleen do anything so foolish as what she proposed, so instead of making Sir Anselm the inheritor of Siere, I conferred upon him an honor and title that I was certain King Henry would find most amusing, especially after his most recent efforts."

"And?" Hugh prodded.

"And," Hugo said with a mischievous grin, "when Rosaleen signed her name to that document this morn, she made Sir Anselm the King of France."

Chapter Twenty-Three

"I never knew the king had such a sense of humor," Rosaleen said sleepily, making her head comfortable against her husband's warm shoulder, "or that you were so well-known to him."

"Why do you think he slapped me so hard when he knighted me?" Hugh replied with a laugh, curling his arm around her. "I nearly slapped him back as it was."

She smiled. "Was it so bad, being knighted?"

"Worse than bad," he replied with feeling. "Almost as bad as being wed in front of half of London without any warning whatsoever. As glad as I am to be married to you, Rosaleen, I'm done with ceremonies, and so I give you warning. No more. I've done with such public displays."

"My lord," she said, lifting her head to look at him, "you have only begun. As the Earl of Siere you will be required to attend more ceremonies than you could possibly imagine."

"God's mercy."

"'Struth, I warn you. Best set your mind to it. My father complained about it often."

"God's mercy," he repeated with renewed horror.

"It will not be so terrible, my lord. I shall ever be there to help you, and afterward I shall recompense you most thoroughly to make you forget how awful it was."

His eyebrows rose. "That sounds promising."

"I love you," she said. "I will never forget that you gave up so much for me."

He hugged her tightly. "I have gained much more than I have lost," he told her. "On the day I arrived in London I spoke with my Aunt Leta, and she confirmed all that you said about my father and told me more, so that I can believe now that he loved me as much as I always wished he did, and can accept that I have a right to name myself a Baldwin."

"Oh, Hugh! I'm so glad!"

"I'm the one who's glad," he said, "but I feel as though I have lived the last ten years of my life for naught. I kept running from the truth, when the truth only would have eased my mind. If I had never met you, Rosaleen, I never would have found peace, but would have kept running until my life found its end." He turned his head until his nose touched hers. "Now look at me. I've been transformed from a lowly soldier, a bastard, to the Earl of Siere. How will I ever thank King Henry for bestowing such an honor on me?"

She laughed, hitting one of his hard shoulders with a small fist. "Wretch! You make it sound as though he's condemned you to death. You will be a wonderful earl. If my parents could only know how well I have wed, Hugh Caldwell, they would be so glad."

"In truth?"

"In truth," she vowed.

"I do not know that you are right, love, but I'll do my best to make you, and them, proud."

"And your father and mother and family proud, too."

"Mmm," he returned, closing his eyes against the delightful feeling of her silky hair against his chest. "My mother, yes, and family, yes, but which father? You've no assurance with me, Rosaleen. I've the blood of one of the worst devils ever born in me, and the influence of the other. You must pray each night that I do not fall into either of their paths."

She closed her own eyes. "Yes, my lord," she agreed meekly. Yawning, she asked, "Do you think Christian will be happy to have Briarstone?"

He nodded against her head. "I think so," he said while his hand explored the gentle curves of her hip. "It is only right that he should have the estate, and as soon as the harvest is complete there should be plenty of funds for him to run the place properly."

"He will do well, and Hugo will be there to help him. And Justin, too, for a short while, at least."

"Justin!" Hugh said dismally. "Whatever will become of the lad? He's the most heartless fellow I've ever known."

"He isn't heartless, Hugh," Rosaleen objected. "He's simply possessed of a very serious nature. There is no middle ground for him, only right and wrong."

"Well, I say he's damned unnatural. He kept insisting that he had a debt of honor to kill Sir Anselm even after I'd beaten the man to a pulp. God's my life, there was hardly enough left to kill!"

Rosaleen grimaced. "And you call *him* heartless!"

Hugh opened one eye and glanced at her. "I had a perfectly good reason for what I did to your uncle, and he's damned lucky I didn't kill him, as I want to do whenever I think on what he did to you. Justin, however, had the least of reasons for wanting to do away with him. 'Struth, Rosaleen, the boy can't go around killing everyone who makes a slight against a member of his family. We'd have dead bodies lying all over the streets.''

"Staying at Briarstone will do him good," Rosaleen assured him. "He and Christian are of an age with one another. Perhaps they will become friends."

A shout of laughter escaped Hugh. "Oh yes, I can just imagine what an exciting time those two sober souls will have together. If there's one lad who's even more serious than Justin, it's Chris. They'll probably sit around in the evenings and bore one another to death right along with everyone else."

"Oh, Hugh, that's not fair! And the people of Briarstone will be so grateful to have two of your brothers there in place of you. Can you not imagine how distressed they'll be when they discover you'll not be returning?"

"They will miss me, won't they?" Hugh replied with pleasure. "I was such a good master to them. I daresay I shall go down in history as the great savior of a famed estate."

Rosaleen smirked. "Oh yes, certainly. Perhaps they'll honor you with a monument of some kind. It will read 'Hugh Caldwell, Master Of Briarstone, Who Bravely Rescued The Land From Ruin.'"

"Well, I did have a little help from you," Hugh admitted reluctantly. "Perhaps they shall put a small monument honoring you next to my much larger one."

She thumped his chest again. "You're a beast," she said.

"'Struth, love." He smiled, rolling to his side and pulling her naked body against his own. "But I'm your beast. And your beast is getting hungry for his wife again."

"I'm not certain you have time to sate yourself, husband. I believe we were to have been at the wedding feast over an hour ago. Your brother, the Lord of Gyer, and the king will be angered with us, mostlike."

Hugh lifted his mouth from her shoulder long enough to say, "Alex was rather angry when he arrived this afternoon, was he not? I thought he was going to turn one of us over his knee for the fright we gave him when he arrived at Briarstone to find neither of us there and the place in such a commotion. I doubt there's much more we could do to get in his black thoughts." He lowered his head and took up nuzzling her again.

"Be that as it may, Hugh," Rosaleen persisted, moving her head to give him greater access to her neck, "the feast is in our honor. Do you not think we should at least make some effort to attend?"

"No," he muttered against her skin, giving her a playful nip. "Besides, the feast is to honor Willem and his new wife, as well. I don't see why we have to be there and make such a crowd. Let Willem and Lady Gwynneth have all the attention."

"Poor Willem! I think he hates ceremonies more than you. I've never seen a more miserable man than he was during his wedding."

"And I've never seen a happier bride," countered Hugh, pushing the covers aside so that he could gaze at his wife's breasts. "If Willem was ever to be wed, that was how it was going to happen. All at once and without giving him a chance to escape. He'll be happy with his lady, though. She's quite a lively beauty, and just what he needs to light a fire beneath him. Rosaleen, my love," he said, touching one breast reverently, "how did you come to be so perfectly made?"

"Oh, Hugh." She shivered beneath his touch. "I do think we should stop this and go down to the feast. The Lord of Gyer will never forgive us."

Smiling, Hugh brought his mouth close to her own. "Rosaleen, darling, my lovely wife, I have no intention of letting you leave this bed for the next week, at the very least. You had best set your mind to it. And I don't really give a damn what my eldest brother thinks, because for the first time in my life,'' he said with a wicked grin, ''I outrank him.''

* * * * *

BRIDE'S BAY RESORT

UNLOCK THE DOOR TO GREAT ROMANCE AT BRIDE'S BAY RESORT

Join Harlequin's new across-the-lines series, set in an exclusive hotel on an island off the coast of South Carolina.

Seven of your favorite authors will bring you exciting stories about fascinating heroes and heroines discovering love at Bride's Bay Resort.

Look for these fabulous stories coming to a store near you beginning in January 1996.

Harlequin American Romance #613 in January
Matchmaking Baby by Cathy Gillen Thacker

Harlequin Presents #1794 in February
Indiscretions by Robyn Donald

Harlequin Intrigue #362 in March
Love and Lies by Dawn Stewardson

Harlequin Romance #3404 in April
Make Believe Engagement by Day Leclaire

Harlequin Temptation #588 in May
Stranger in the Night by Roseanne Williams

Harlequin Superromance #695 in June
Married to a Stranger by Connie Bennett

Harlequin Historicals #324 in July
Dulcie's Gift by Ruth Langan

Visit Bride's Bay Resort each month wherever Harlequin books are sold.

HARLEQUIN ®

BBAYG

Harlequin® Historical

Harlequin Historicals is very pleased to announce a new Western series from award-winning author Ruth Langan starting in February—The Jewels of Texas

DIAMOND February 1996
PEARL August 1996
JADE January 1997
RUBY June 1997

Don't miss this exciting new series about four sisters as wild and vibrant as the untamed land they're fighting to protect!

If you would like to order your copy of DIAMOND (HH #305), the first book in the series, please send your name, address, zip or postal code along with a check or money order (please do not send cash) for $4.50 for each book ordered ($4.99 in Canada) plus 75¢ postage and handling ($1.00 in Canada) payable to Harlequin Books, to:

In the U.S.:
3010 Walden Avenue
P.O. Box 1369
Buffalo, NY 14269-1369

In Canada:
P.O. Box 609
Fort Erie, Ontario
L2A 5X3

Please specify book title with your order.
Canadian residents add applicable federal and provincial taxes.

JEWELS

Harlequin® Historical

Coming in February from Harlequin Historicals

The next book in Suzanne Barclay's dramatic
Lion series—

LION'S LEGACY

"...fast paced, action packed historical romance...4 1/2 stars."
—*Affaire de Coeur*

"...absolutely captivating!"
The Medieval Chronicle

Whatever you do. Don't miss it!

What do women really want to know?

Only the world's largest publisher of romance
fiction could possibly attempt an answer.

HARLEQUIN ULTIMATE GUIDES™

How to Talk to a Naked Man,

Make the Most of Your Love Life, and Live Happily Ever After

The editors of Harlequin and Silhouette are
definitely experts on love, men and relationships.
And now they're ready to share that expertise with
women everywhere.

Jam-packed with vital, indispensable, lighthearted
tips to improve every area of your romantic life—even
how to get one! So don't just sit around and wonder
why, how or where—run to your nearest bookstore
for your copy now!

Available this February, at your favorite retail outlet.

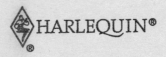